AWAKE

BOOK OF AVENZYRE I

GB MACRAE

AWAKE

Follow the silver-dappled unicorn

GB MacRae

Fannar Press

New York

AWAKE by GB MacRae

This is a work of fiction. Names, characters, places and incidents
are either a product of the author's imagination or used
fictitiously. Any resemblance to actual persons living or dead,
businesses
, events, locales, or other works is entirely coincidental.

ISBN-13: 978-1508501992

ISBN-10: 1508501998

Acknowledgements:

Many thanks to friends and family who have supported and believed in me for so long.

To Joel, for understanding everything
To my wonderful and patient betas (in no particular order) Terri, Jason, Joe, and Christine
To my amazing mentor, KT Pinto
To Dr. Warren Olin-Ammentorp for making me realize this was something special.
To Mike for helping me see.
To Reb for being in my life.

Stories also available:

Fiona

The Perfect Girl for the Price of Horsehair

Ethel's Bane

Precipice

Cassius Book of Avenzyre II

Available soon:

Arise Book of Avenzyre III

Pronunciation Key

Amarynth—AM-a-rinth

Azqebryne—AZ-kay-brin-eh

Cassius—KA-shus

Connylia—KON-e-lee-ah

Currain—Kur-AIN

Dournzariame—Dorn-zar-ee-a-ME

Fuarmaania—Fwar-MAH-nee-ah

Gallylya—Gal-li-LEE-ah

Gellia—Ge-LEE-ah

Quenelzythe—Ken-EL-zith

Saquime—Sa-KEE-meh

Sen Dunea—Sen Dun-NEE-ah

Xianze—Zhan-zeh

Xzepheniixenze—Zef-en-ee-ZEN-zee

Zephronia—Zeh-fron-NEE-ah

Zyendel—Zy-EN-del

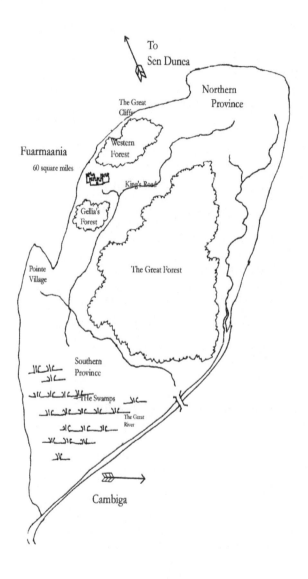

To
Sen Dunea

Northern
Province

The Great
Cliffs

Western
Forest

Fuarmaania

60 square miles

King's Road

Gellia's
Forest

The Great Forest

Pointe
Village

Southern
Province

The Swamps

The Great
River

Cambiga

Prologue

I stared down from the battlements with the rest of my family, overwhelmed by what I saw. My mother wept; my father, the new king, was frozen with fear. I can still remember the pool of blood as my grandfather lay dead on the grass in front of the castle. There were men on white horses on the hill; their armor gleamed in the sun as they rode away. My grandfather always told us that one day people would come for him, but we thought we were safe in our kingdom...

The rain is near its end, spring is close, and I sit here to watch from the battlements once more. This time my grandson is waiting with me. I've told him, as well as all the children, the story of my grandfather. So here we wait. I watch the road that will take us from here if we dare travel it. We are too afraid to do it alone. They are out there, the people who killed my grandfather. ...It is misty and bleak; everything smells of dampness and mud.

"There's no one out there, grandmother," my grandson

tells me.

"Perhaps soon," I reply. He is a good boy to listen to an old woman like me. His older brothers spend most of their days playing dice and arguing over women.

…The day my grandfather died was a mixture of blur and acute clarity. I remember being shuffled about by adults; I heard grandfather was to face the enemy alone. I remember how he looked as he rode from the gates. He was always our shining hero. His blonde wavy hair, his blue grey eyes. We knew he was old, but age hadn't touched him since he was thirty. He was a kind king who looked after his people with great care, he taught us how to do the same, and told us about our true empire. It is far from our present home, and some day we will inherit it. He said his friend would come back and bring us there, that we would be protected should anything happen to him.

The battle was short. Magic arced, swords flashed. I never understood magic, but I knew it seemed to cause grandfather pain and sorrow. Any time he used it he tired and withdrew. My elder brother said the army that came was only for grandfather, would only attack us if grandfather didn't go out to face their leader alone. Those great shining warriors were larger than anything I ever saw, and I couldn't tell one from the next…

"Tell me again, the story about great, great grandfather," my grandson says.

The boy is young, shows no potential for magic that I can see, but again, I know little about it. "You wish to know who we're waiting for, don't you?" I ask him. Servants bring us tea. Yes, my actions are a mystery to my existing family even though I've told them the tale. It's been so long I doubt any of them believe my stories anymore.

My thoughts return to those days, those strange days. My grandfather's friend. He only visited once a year, came from far away. I never spoke to him, none of us dared. Few were brave enough to speak his name for fear of mispronouncing it, and over the years I've forgotten it.

If my grandfather was the sun, his friend was the moon. Straight black hair, eyes like icy amethyst. He always looked at us with a leer that never failed to send us running. When I was a child I didn't understand how such opposites could be friends, but as an adult I realize they were more alike than anyone else I ever knew, like brothers. They spoke in languages none of us understood, reminisced about situations that seemed extraordinary and epic. I think I remember grandfather mentioned his friend saved his life more than once.

The friend seemed almost void of cheer, but for when grandfather was near. When our grandfather wasn't in the room he glared down at us from under his ebony hair. Never did that man give us a kind word, and if he spoke it was in tones of malevolence. My brother said the friend didn't like us, and he was a great leader in another realm.

When grandfather was dead, he arrived. None of us on the battlements knew what to do but continue to watch in horror. Grandfather's dark friend galloped up and promptly threw down his sword before the enemy leader, they exchanged curt words and disgusted looks. It wasn't long before the enemy left. I don't know what they said to each other. My family scattered, my maid tried to take me to my room, but I wouldn't go. I watched as my family ran to where their former king lie. His friend knelt beside him, it was the first and last time I ever saw him show emotion, and it was fleeting at that. He refused my family access to the body. Rumors later told me he called my family filth and blamed us for my grandfather's ruin.

My father explained to me that the friend took grandfather's armor, his sword, and several other belongings, cleaned them and locked them away. He said we weren't worthy of such treasure. To this day I've never known where they were hidden.

We were fortunate to be invited to the funeral. I wondered why my father, the king, didn't send grandfather's friend away. Now that I'm old and wise I understand he was beyond our power. I watched him at the funeral as the flames rose from the elaborate pyre he built. He always reminded me of dark clouds, of a coming storm in the middle of the night. He said nothing as grandfather burned.

I stood with my parents for hours in the great hall, listened to tales about strange lights outside the castle. My parents believed it was safer inside. Someone said it was magic, others thought it was the divine. They spoke loudly enough so our visitor could hear in hopes he would respond. He told us nothing. After the ashes cooled he collected them and forced us away with looks of loathing and the threat of magic. My father asked him what he was doing and a reply came: "I'm taking him back to where he belongs."

It was after his departure that our father, our king, reminded us what grandfather said, that the dark friend would return to take us back to our rightful empire. Grandfather wouldn't lie to us. Over the years many lost faith in such a story. Grandfather's friend hadn't returned; many didn't expect him to. My father instilled into me and my brothers the firm belief that it would come true, and the need to pass the story on. Grandfather always said his friend would return, spring would be on his heels. So here I wait, spring is near. Or perhaps my relatives are right, that I am mad. I'm the only one of my siblings left, and am trying to hold on to traditions that seem more like myth to the younger generation.

"Do you come out here every year, grandmother?"

"Yes." I sip tea as best as I'm able, the ache in my shaking hands is sometimes unbearable. "And you must too, after I'm gone. It is of the utmost importance that you never forget the story."

"What will happen if he comes?"

"He'll take us to the empire that is ours."

"But this is our kingdom."

"I know, but there is a greater land far from here, a land of magic that is ours."

"What if he doesn't take us with him?"

I set my teacup down and look at my grandson. "My grandfather told us he would." In my twilight years, I know I wish for my grandson to go. Our kingdom is small and isolated, and it is deteriorating quickly. I try not to lose faith. I tell myself that the great empire exists, that it isn't a fairytale.

The rain stops. After a moment the sun peeks through the clouds. My grandson jumps to his feet. "He's here! He's here!" He skitters back into the castle, leaving me to see for myself. There is a dark rider on the road.

It takes me a long time to make my way to the stable yard these days, even with my servant's help. By the time I arrive everyone else is assembled. My grandfather's friend dismounts and looks at all of us. I feel joy as well as anxiety through my old bones. He looks the same way he did all those years ago. I know childhood memories are skewed, sometimes things are not as great as we thought them in our younger years, but he is every bit as I remember, regal and spiteful. I dare not speak. He looks at me for a moment and his eyes narrow; I assume he recognizes me even after all the decades.

"You've kept your promise to us," my grandson says.

He still has the look of ice. "I never promised you anything," our visitor tells us.

My eldest son speaks up, "You said you would protect us." He has a look of surprise, for he had lost faith in the tale.

"Who thinks I haven't? When was the last time you saw someone like me, someone like your founding king? When was the last time you were attacked?" He gazes at me, and I feel myself shrivel, and I am royalty.

We were silent.

"Is this all of you," he asks.

I do a quick scan of the crowd. "Yes."

His eyebrows press together and he remounts, turns his horse towards the gate.

"Wait!" I shout as best I'm able. He seems to ignore me.

"You said you would take us with you. Please at least take my grandson."

He raises his hand but doesn't turn. "Later, it seems."

It dawns on me; how would my mundane family rule an empire of magic? None of my present family shows any signs of that talent. My legs fail me. My family gathers around me and watches him ride away. I hear my grandson. "Don't worry, I'll wait for his return every spring. You'll see grandmother. I'm sure when the time is right he'll take us."

I close my eyes. It is the end of my time. It will be up to my grandson. I only hope I did enough to instill faith of our destiny.

1

With all the commotion in the castle, it was sometimes easy to forget the dreary weather beyond the stone walls. It was only once a year such a thorough cleaning was given throughout the halls and chambers. Rushes were moved, floors scrubbed, wax drippings were removed from candlesticks. Everyone had a bath. Sometimes it seemed to be in vain considering the muck that was just outside the gates.

The rainy season was still upon them, and low-lying villages and farmsteads had been swept away by swollen creeks. Disease spread, people starved, but as was tradition, the kingdom of Fuarmaania prepared for the annual Welcoming Festival. The roads would mire coaches and maybe even horses, but nobles from near and far would come to the king's castle despite the conditions.

Naturally this event was very exciting to the young women of the castle. There was much primping and powdering and chatter, so much so the men in the castle chose to brave the weather rather than stay inside. The men, and one woman: Princess Gellia. She often ventured to the stable without regard to her hem or hair to visit the horse she inherited from her mother. True, the grey stallion hadn't been born when her mother left, but it had been her mother's favorite mare who bore him, and he was hers.

As more nobles arrived at the castle and crowded the stable, she retreated to the quiet of her library to avoid the commotion. Only Cresslyn, the king's bastard, kept company with her majesty.

ଛଚ6ଓଷ

All the guests had finally arrived. The castle was teeming with people. Noble guests filled the rooms while homeless peasants huddled in-out-of-the-way corners of the stable yard. It seemed the library was the only place of solace for their princess. She was examining a foreign book while Cresslyn looked out the window at the rain and the stable yard below. Cresslyn smiled and sighed.

"You don't have to stay here with me," the princess said with a smile.

"I don't mind," Cresslyn replied. "I like your company."

They could hear the occasional servant go by the door. The servants' quarters were only an antechamber away, and on the other side was a tiny gallery and the chapel, which was also a lonely space. The library was a rather dark and unappreciated room filled with old tomes along one wall, tattered tapestries covering the stone of the other walls. Gellia had always wished it was closer to her room, but alas, her room was surrounded by the many rooms of courtiers. She had to venture through galleries, sometimes the kitchen or kitchen's foyer, the chapel and another gallery before reaching her treasured space. It was the place where she and her Aunt Charlotte spent much of their time, when Charlotte wasn't with the king. Gellia tried not to let the loss of Charlotte put a damper on her love of the room.

With Cresslyn at the window Gellia let her thoughts slip away to other places, which was often a costly pastime. She could feel at ease here or on a horseback ride, and those moments were what she lived for, when the world felt right and she could be at peace.

Cresslyn watched the guards at the gate stiffen. "Someone's coming," she said. "I thought everyone was here already."

"I wouldn't know," her majesty said. She tucked a black curl behind her ear. It was one of the rare days she didn't wear a wimple. Even though she wasn't married, the king insisted she do so in public. He said it would improve her humility. It was her eyes, he said—they were defiant—and her exotic black curls didn't help. However, here she was alone.

Gellia felt her breath catch, and had to breathe deep as a strange wave of anxiety swept over her. It was different from anything she'd felt before, deeper, unsettling, like something inside her broke loose. How she longed for Aunt Charlotte, for she was the only one who seemed to understand. The pain of losing Charlotte came back in a wave and she wondered if she'd have to flee the room. A few deep breaths later and Gellia was under control once more. Cresslyn, thankfully, hadn't taken notice.

The rain was ending as a drenched rider on a dark horse came through the arched gate into the stable yard. At Cresslyn's insistence, Gellia went to the window to have a look. The rider paused in front of the large stable door, took off his wide-brimmed hat.

He looked unlike any person either of them had ever seen. One of the stable boys took the reins of the horse, but before the rider dismounted his gaze moved across the castle. His eyes rested on the library window and Cresslyn couldn't look away. Gellia, looking over Cresslyn's mousey brown braids, spoke, her voice breaking the spell. "You silly girl, Cress," she teased. "I suppose you've fancied yourself in love with him already." Cresslyn was a sweet girl, naïve as Gellia had once been long ago. The truth was, Gellia had a terrible feeling about this new stranger.

She smiled broadly. "How could I not?"

"And how do you know he's not a scoundrel?"

"How could anyone looking like such a dream be evil? He's far too beautiful."

"Cress, you are a fool, falling for every man who rides through that gate." Her majesty picked up her book and sat on the rickety chair, losing herself in the cryptic pages once more. The festival hadn't brought her joy in many years, not since she was a child and too innocent to realize the nasty looks and whispers were directed at her.

"How do you know anything?" Cresslyn said as she skipped across the room, and didn't wait for a response. "Well, I don't care what you think; I'm going to get dressed. I have to look my best! I'm going to be fourteen; I have to find a husband before—"

"You're an old maid like me?" the princess, who was twenty four, said. "Go pretty yourself." She shook her head and continued to study as the younger girl rushed from the room. For a woman of value Gellia was terribly old, but it wasn't for lack of trying that she wasn't married. So far, any betrothal had ended in ruin. She looked out the window and the newcomer was gone. She was certain Cresslyn would one day find a husband; she was a sweet and agreeable girl.

***

The great hall was filled with rosy faces as drink was poured and people danced. King Hugh was in their midst, singing with the minstrels and raising his full cup. It was as bawdy a celebration as would be in any tavern, but with three times the food and drink.

The princess veiled herself in the shadows and watched the dancers through the smoke. A brawl between soldiers started across the room; eventually one went down and the victor stumbled away for more drink. There were always soldiers about. In fact, the king's nobles were his soldiers from his warring days. One would never believe it to look at him now, but the country still remembered his prowess during his deadly campaigns. She doubted he could even wield a weapon now, for his bulk made him tired from the least bit of exertion.

She leaned against the stone and let herself drift into her own thoughts. A gathering like this would thrust her into the light, something she hated above all else. She was the only heir to the original king, and the only path to the throne. It was the only rule the kingdom had always followed. Her noble father had married her mother to gain a kingdom, but she was not his kin. No one spoke openly of her mother nor true father. It was also everyone's favorite lie: that she was Hugh's daughter. But the people liked family trees to be full, even if they were full of falseness. In King Hugh's quest to add a son to his family tree he'd married her aunt, and it subsequently ended in Charlotte's demise. There were no other family members but for Gellia, and she thankfully had been spared marriage to Hugh when she came of age. However, now the only thing Hugh could do was find a husband for Gellia to continue the line, or be seen as a failure. This didn't create fond feelings towards Gellia.

There had been previous betrothals. The one she was promised to at birth was killed in his bed when he was fifteen. Then there was Percy, who was closer to her age; young for a princess' betrothed. She liked his smile, and they got along well enough. For an arranged match she'd felt fortunate. He loved to ride and didn't care to dance, but he'd dance with her. He also enjoyed the hunt and taught her how to use a bow. Percy was found dead on the road, an arrow in his back. All of his belongings were intact, and his horse nearby. Who had murdered him was never discovered.

Gellia smiled as she watched Cresslyn dancing with a young knight.

Gellia's third betrothed was an aged duke who she'd never met. He was on his way to inspect her and he and his entourage had disappeared. No sign of them had been seen since. From then, rumors from the superstitious ran rampant. Some said she was cursed, and because she'd always been odd it was easy for many to believe. Men were attracted by her beauty and title, but the tale of her curse kept many away. She gave up on worrying about a marriage, and felt she really didn't care to be married. Since Percy she'd paid little attention to suitors. Even though she was the proper heir, she would never rule for she was a woman, and her husband would be of the king's choosing... likely someone he could control or someone who was of the same mind.

Cresslyn came to her, doing her best to be lady-like in her excited state. "Come with me to fetch some wine, your majesty," she said. Cresslyn was too sweet to deny, even when Gellia wanted to stay out of sight. Cresslyn believed that wine and dancing could cure just about anything.

The princess reluctantly followed so Cresslyn could find a servant with wine. Their movement attracted the king's attention. Even in a crowd with many women in wimples, Gellia still stood out. It didn't help she was taller than most women. He shouted at her from across the room. "Show yourself, woman! There are buyers here." He guffawed and turned to his newest mistress, a woman who was equally in her cups as he. Then there were the stares and whispers of the other attendants. A group of young ladies giggled at sneered as she walked by. Gellia kept herself standing erect even though she wished to crawl under a table. It was too often in the past she heard murmurs of 'curse', 'hag' and 'witch'.

A pair of noblemen passed her looking her up and down, not that there was much to see in her modest brown frock. However, they barely dared look her in the eye, which was typical. A young soldier drew Cresslyn away to dance. Gellia was alone once more.

When the time was right she started edging towards the door. It had been many years since she'd done more to please the king, and the truth was he would never be pleased with her no matter how modest and obedient she was. As an adult she realized if she suffered his wrath to do something to please herself, it was often worth it. He would toss her out if he could, but the heir tradition was so strong everyone believed some terrible fate would befall the kingdom if they broke it. He couldn't even remarry, for none of his heirs would be seen as legitimate since they weren't from the original line of royalty. Although, there were rumors that the king was unable to beget children any longer.

Gellia wondered if he knew all the complexities of the kingdom when he decided to take Grandfather King's offer to marry his daughter. Hugh had become too powerful, and a threat to Grandfather's rule. The only way to keep the kingdom from a civil war was to hand the throne to Hugh via marriage so Grandfather could still hold influence without war. In Grandfather's old age he'd retired to his hunting lodge and thankfully left everyone alone.

In the darkness and safety of the eastern gallery she paused to see if she had been followed. The room was empty; she had chosen the correct one. Upon glancing back she saw the world she never fit into. Most of them thought she was mad for behaving the way she did. She often heard the servants speaking of it outside her library door, talking of her insanity, her strange moods. She was often distant, solitary. As a child she was raised by her nurse, and when Charlotte was married to Hugh she found a new friend. Charlotte had been the weaker of the two sisters, and lived in the country for her health. She too felt out of place in the castle. Charlotte and Gellia had a connection no one else understood. It was one more thing Hugh held against Gellia.

The princess hiked up her brown skirts like a peasant to make a faster escape, and took one last look behind her before she made her way through the comforting dark. Something was amiss; she could feel it deep within herself, tightness in her chest, a flutter. That rush she'd felt before, the fleeting terror.

"Running away—to what end?"

She dropped her skirts and froze. Someone approached from shadows and she wanted to bolt, but pride held her steady.

He spoke again. "Not that I would say anything of your disappearance."

No one she had ever known spoke with such elegant cadence, even while omitting formality. The old ladies of court often spoke of vapors coming from the voices of demons that ensnared young women. The princess didn't believe any of that, but this could make her reconsider the possibility. "I was merely stepping out for a moment," she said. She squinted to try to see him through the darkness.

"My mistake." His tone was deep, calm. "I imagine the king will miss you before long."

"That's a complicated statement. His highness is far too joyous to miss the likes of me."

"How anyone could be indifferent to your presence is quite beyond me. You are the princess, aren't you? Perhaps even more so than you realize." He glided past her towards the great hall, bringing the smell of cleanliness, balsam forest, and cloves with him through the stagnant air. She recognized him as the rider she saw at the gate. He was tall, muscular, but there was something about him, something strange she could feel in her core, the air around him was different. It made the hairs on the back of her neck stand up. Or maybe it was nothing, and she was as mad as they said.

He continued with a smirk. "Only a person of your heritage would be so bold as to leave such a party with such a glorious king in such a magnificent kingdom." He started towards the great hall, and she found herself following him. She could barely believe what he said, and although some would disagree, she was certain he was being insulting. When he stepped into the light of the hall she went no farther.

Up until now, it hadn't occurred to her that her people had rough features and dull, brownish hair for she had known no different. The women with eager, painted faces and elaborate headdresses crowded around him. The men, considered superior in her kingdom, all wished to speak with him; the tallest of them stood only as high as his shoulder. The stranger was dressed head to toe in black and forest green fabric so fine it looked luminescent, and his hair was unbound and fell in a black cascade to his narrow waist. His features were refined, likely perfected from centuries of noble bloodlines, and his natural expression seemed to be of detachment. From the way he moved around the room, the princess felt he spent his life at court—one finer than this. What was this kingdom he was from, how far was it from her land? She'd met so many nobles from near and far, yet this one was unlike any she'd ever seen…

He looked back at her and gave her a sort of impish smirk as if they shared a secret. Why are you here? She wondered. She knew nothing about him, but he had awoken something in within her. Not attraction, not like that. She'd felt that before in her younger years. It was something else, a sort of longing. But her existence was chained here, to this life. A thought that didn't feel like her own rose in her mind. Take me with you. She crushed the thought as quickly as it came. He was just another man, but from a faraway place, and in her heart she still felt a growing anxiety. For a reason she couldn't explain, she knew he was cunning and malevolent at a level this kingdom had yet to see. Illogical, perhaps, but her instincts were often right.

She was alone in the darkness of the gallery for a few moments longer before returning to the throng. It was likely the wrong choice, for returning would only open her to more scorn, but she could barely help herself.

The king raised his big hand to beckon her, so she straightened her frock and made her way through the flailing dancers like a proper lady. Her father became impatient and pushed his way around the room to meet her with his new exalted guest in tow. Hugh wasn't a short man, and was very stout, broad of shoulder and of hips. His brown hair was cropped short and showed some grey, his bushy beard had streaks of age through it. He was glaring at her from under his heavy brow.

"Lord Father," she said with a curtsy.

He grabbed her arm and barked: "Why have you not acquainted yourself with our new friend yet?" The king waved his cup as he usually did when trying to impress a newcomer with his hospitality. He was too inebriated to impress much of anyone, though, for he tilted to and fro.

She knew better than to struggle in the king's grip. "Sire," she stammered. His fingers dug into her arm, his foul breath was upon her. It was a familiar experience. She could easily survive bruises. What wasn't familiar, however, was a champion, for no one dreamt of opposing the king.

Their new friend tilted his head to look at his host. "We have already spoken, gentle highness. Princess Gellia is admirable, I must admit. I can barely remember when I last I saw such excellent character."

A miracle happened. The king dropped her arm and wiped his dark sleeve over his sweaty forehead. "Oh yes, she's clever like her mother, that's why we have to keep a good watch on her. Unpleasant, I must say."

"I beg your majesty's pardon, but I have to disagree; she is quite a charming young lady." His voice was soft and pleasant as it was in the corridor, but at the same time resonant and could be heard over the noise of the party. "I was just about to ask her to dance." He held his hand out to her.

"You foreigners must marry old crones to think she's a young lady," the king replied.

"We have differing views, yes, good highness," he said.

Taking the outstretched hand, Princess Gellia followed him through the sneers. She was as uncomfortable as she could be and was certain that this man, like so many others, was up to no good. "I thank you, sir," she said. "But I'm more resilient than it seems and smarter than most will admit." It was easy enough to dissuade men by being an outspoken woman.

"Oh, I would never doubt your abilities." They started to move across the floor. "We haven't been properly introduced. My given name is Cassius."

"Just Cassius?" Not a long, pompous title?

"For you, princess, Cassius will do," he laughed a little. "For a Fuarmaanian, you're able to pronounce it properly."

Did he know he was being insulting? She probably still wore dust from the stable, and next to him she looked exceptionally wretched, but she still retained her air of regal indifference. "I'm known for addling my mind with books; I'm sure it was pure luck."

He chuckled. "I already know you're exceptional. It's why I'm staying." He was quiet for a few moments as they danced across the floor. She'd had many dance partners over her life, and he was by far the most graceful and strong. "Tell me," he said, breaking her musings. "How did you come to have such a lovely and unusual name?"

Why did she feel so much that this was a trap? Her breath quickened and her mind was a whirl. "My mother named me, and I don't wish to speak of it." She couldn't meet his gaze, but he had no problem looking at her.

"I apologize. Do tell me, what am I allowed to converse about?"

Still feeling it was a trap somehow, her anxiety grew. What was this feeling? Her heart told her it was a game, a terrible game that would not end well for her if she lost. It was easier to speak to local nobles than this man. Something told her he would bring a new level of mockery upon her. All she wanted to do was flee. She hoped he would not be her new betrothed. He spoke again. "Perhaps then we should discuss horses. You like horses, yes?"

"Horses are useful tools."

He smirked but said nothing.

"I apologize. It's late, I must retire," she said and pulled away.

"If you truly must."

She pushed her way through the crowd and tried not to trip over the dogs lazing about the great hall. She ignored the sneers and laughter of the other guests. Gellia made it into the long gallery, the quickest route to her chamber. She sighed. The festivities tomorrow would undoubtedly be exhausting. Once alone in her room she sat down and cried for the first time since she was a child.

Her nurse, Corrah, silently came in and dressed her for bed, brushed her black hair. When Gellia finally dried her tears Corrah spoke. "What makes you so sad, milady?"

Gellia shook her head. "I wish I knew."

***

"I'm so excited I hardly know how to contain myself," Cresslyn whispered.

She watched the other riders and almost vibrated in the saddle. Every few moments she adjusted her headdress or fidgeted with the reins of her strawberry roan mare.

"It's a nice enough day, I suppose." Gellia said. The sun was out, but the hills were hardly dry. If the day ended with only a few breaking their necks it would be a good day. Just milling around in the field as they were was enough for the horses to lose their footing and slip about. To make matters worse, most of the riders were still inebriated from the party the night before. At least the horses knew what they were doing.

Cassius, who she'd learned was a baron, then joined the riding party. His was indeed a beautiful ebony mount. The horse had strong joints and heavy bones but was still sleek and athletic. Like his rider, he was taller than his peers, who seemed to step back instinctively as he passed. Gellia admired the steed's arched neck and noble head, pert ears, gleaming black coat, and wise eyes. It was easy for her to lose her horse-loving heart to him.

Cresslyn spoke. "From what the other ladies are saying, it seems that he's quite taken by you. I can see why. You're the most beautiful woman in Fuarmaania," she said. "You even have the same color hair but yours is curls—you are the only two I've ever seen with black hair. What a striking couple you would make."

Gellia sighed, resisted the urge to return to the castle. A ride was the one thing that could truly tempt her from the protection of her library. Tempest, her horse, still brought her joy despite his age. She would ride no other. Over time his coat had turned from steel grey to faded dapples, and his dark mane and

෨16ल

tail were filled with white, but his spirit was still strong and his legs sound.

A few moments later when they were all assembled, the hunt began. Gellia stayed towards the rear where she would be forgotten. Gellia's keeper, one of the valets who was a strong rider, was distracted by flirtation. Eventually the old ladies on the ponies overtook Gellia, and Tempest tossed his head and pushed against his bit in protest.

As soon as the group turned a corner into another field she veered Tempest away from them. She allowed him to thunder towards the forest where they dropped onto the path over a steep bank, and slowed to a canter.

It was a pretty morning; the fingers of the sun tickled the mossy forest floor. Her companion snorted and swished his tail. She laughed as they jumped over a fallen branch and Tempest hopped and squealed playfully. Gellia giggled. Here in nature she could breathe. Nothing seemed more natural than she riding her horse over the land, and she often traveled as far as she could to see all that she could, which was sadly not very much. She'd never thought of running away as her mother did, but she wasn't sure what she was searching for in the wilds. Out in the countryside there were few rules and no nasty looks, no rumors, no confusion or doubt, no conflict in her heart. Tempest meant freedom. Her only regret was he couldn't speak.

Parts of their path were mucky, watery and hazardous, but that had never stopped her before. Gellia ducked under branches while Tempest jumped over logs and swerved back and forth to make all the tight corners through the trees. She'd always been a strong rider, and no one would admit it, but she was even stronger than many of the men. The sun no longer shone through the canopy as they hurdled almost blindly through the woods. She wished he could gallop forever.

***

The king grumbled about the weather and surveyed his company. Thunder rolled across the fields, horses fussed under their riders. The king's mare heaved beneath him after carrying the royal heft for so long. The king took a swig from his drinking horn. "Where is the princess?" he bellowed.

The baron reined in beside him. "Fear not, majesty, I will find her. Lend me proper retainers and I'll be off. Your majesty should not be caught in a storm."

The king was easy enough to convince, especially with the promise of drink and his mistress back at the castle. Two of the men in the king's crimson livery stayed behind to accompany the baron on his task.

Cassius smiled at the retainers. "Shall we, gentlemen?" he asked. He turned his horse towards the forest. A crack of lightning startled the horses but for his.

"I don't like the look of this storm," one of the retainers said. "Thunder is a bad omen."

"We shall see, shan't we?" Cassius said.

***

Tempest snorted. It rained again, but there was something different this time. She couldn't put her finger on it, but something felt strange. Gellia scanned the surroundings for shelter. Her hair was matted against her head, her clothing heavy. Tempest struggled through the deepening muck; steam rose from his hide. Finally she spotted what seemed to be a cave big enough for them both to fit into. She dismounted and led the grey through the underbrush. Thorns ripped her clothes and cut her skin, the mud seeped up the hem of her dress. She ruined her already threadbare gloves as she cleared the bushes that blocked the cave entrance. Dutiful Tempest stayed near and only jumped a little when she slipped and fell in the mud. Gellia pulled herself to her feet and felt the chill through the forest that announced the coming of night. "Come here," she grumbled. "Can't stay out here all night. Really cursed myself this time."

It took all of Gellia's patience to coax the grey into the dark cave that was sure to hold all sorts of horse-eating monsters, or so she was sure Tempest thought. Of course, once inside Tempest was perfectly calm. The princess unsaddled him but left the blanket on him. It was so very dark and cold, and night would soon arrive. She slid to the floor and shivered in her wet clothes. The crash of lightning kept her awake for some time; she watched the water droplets fall from the foliage. Normally storms intrigued her, but this one… She stood up and paced through the cave, sat back down then was up again and back down again. Eventually sleep won the battle as she curled up with her saddle as a pillow.

***

"The footing's a bit tricky," the baron said. "I hope your horses are agile." As riding went it couldn't be much worse conditions. Darkness, deep mud, paths were washed out, and standing water could hide any number of dangers. "Well," he said mostly to himself, "this land could use a good cleanse."

"We'll be lucky to find her in one piece this time, my lord," the taller of the retainers said. "Then we'll all be finished. His highness won't be pleased if she's broken her neck by the time we reach her."

"Have that little faith in her?" the baron asked.

They looked at each other. "It's dangerous conditions, my lord," the shorter said. "Women are good at getting themselves hurt."

The baron smirked. "We better be moving faster, then." Nighthawk trotted through the dark as easily a cat would. "The ground is unstable here," the baron said. "Best keep moving." But it was too late. As the ground broke away from the hillside it took a retainer and horse with it. The baron barely paused. "He's lost," he said. "It's not safe here."

Although clearly shaken by the loss of his compatriot, the remaining retainer kept going. In the dark and rain, they could still hear the sound of running water. "That's the creek!" the retainer said.

"Truly?" the baron said. "I couldn't tell. Thank you for pointing it out. We'd better cross. Shall we?" Nighthawk started to ford the raging creek and came out the other side unscathed. The retainer's horse balked, and after some kicking to no avail, the man dismounted and started to lead the animal into the water. Before the baron could warn him against it, the retainer was swept away. The baron continued on his journey.

***

In her dreams she saw Cassius. There were unicorns and dragons, winged people and strange light—he was there amidst it all and she was not herself. It was not her body she was in, but another's, someone young and clever. She could see blurry colors of fabulous gardens, and heard music with rhythm she could feel in her very soul. There were waves crashing on rocks. He seemed to wait for her there, amidst the beckoning landscape. It was the clearest these strange dreams had ever been, and she hated that he invaded this one. Why? No one else from this life had ever been in her dreams.

A noise from outside of her dream-realm caught her attention, and there was an orange glow in the cave that found its way through her eyelids. Gellia pushed herself upright, aching the entire time. There was a fire in the cave. Cassius sat on the other side of it. She suddenly was aware of the heaviness of his cloak on her shoulders. She bolted to her feet. He was standing on the other side of the fire, near the cave entrance.

"How did you find me?" she asked.

"You were remarkably easy to find once I was aware of your existence." He turned to look at her, a dark wave of hair fell over his face.

She felt he was being mysterious, and was very uncomfortable being alone with him so far from the castle. The cave seemed much smaller now. Men were not known for their honor in such situations, not in her kingdom at least. What a mess she'd found herself in. Damn foolish. "Don't think I won't fight you off," she blurted. "I can defend myself."

"I can't imagine why you'd need to."

"I won't allow you to compromise me."

He raised an eyebrow and snorted. "I assure you I have no intentions of doing anything of the sort."

"Why else would you have come to find me on your own? This is very unusual."

He smiled. "You misjudge me, princess. Your father's retainers are not as good riders as I thought, and found their deaths on the way here, and the ride was certainly too treacherous for a proper chaperone."

She started to speak but couldn't really argue with his explanation.

He looked as though he was suppressing his laugher, which only flustered her further.

"How did you make that fire when everything is so damp?" Gellia asked, trying her best at small talk in the uncomfortable cave.

"Magic," he said, "and I know you aren't defenseless even more than you do."

What on earth did he mean? He was being cryptic again, and it felt very much like ridicule.

"Is everyone in your country as disagreeable as you are?"

"Certainly. Some even more so." He threw another stick on the fire. "So you don't believe in magic. Yet Cresslyn does and you are far better read than she."

"Cresslyn will believe anything a potential husband tells her." She drew the cloak more closely around her. Tempest sneezed and she looked for him. He and the black stallion stood at the back of the cave, Tempest seemed to doze while his new herd mate watched the rain.

"Then Cresslyn shouldn't believe a word I say. Just as you don't."

Gellia felt the same dread, but it was lessening. She didn't want to speak to him, for she felt she would betray herself somehow. Part of her wanted to curl up in a ball, cover her ears and fall into a fit of crying. Gellia tried to make herself comfortable on the stone floor, pretended to sleep, and planned to keep an eye on him, but in a blink he wasn't where she last saw him. He was nearby brushing Tempest's ruffled coat. The fire was warm. She snuggled into the cloak and settled for the night.

***

Tempest whuffed into the wet leaves, snorted away the dew that clung to his nostrils. Gellia's new companion offered to saddle her mount for her but she refused and did it herself. With ease and grace she swung upon Tempest's back, her damp, musty clothes didn't impede her. She looked down at his mane and rubbed the buckle where the two reins joined. Always awakening to the confusion that was her life. Home was never a wonderful place to return to. If only she could be as normal as the courtiers were. How she envied their seemingly content lives.

"Shall we?" her escort asked, pulling her out of her reverie.

She nudged her horse forward but made no reply.

Despite the downpour the night before, the forest wasn't as dreary as she thought it would be. Beams of light fell through the canopy and the birds seemed happy to fill the trees with song.

"How do you know the way back?" Gellia asked. She didn't know if she did, and she'd been to the forest many times before.

"There are enough landmarks if one is paying attention," he said, glancing back at her. They then rode in silence for a time.

"Where did you say you were from?" she asked, while she finger combed the nearest bit of Tempest's mane. Although he'd been introduced at court, the formality of announcing his country had been omitted.

"I didn't. I come from Xzepheniixenze."

"Zef-en-ee-ZEN-zee." she said, smoothly, "Xzepheniixenze." The sound of it brought out an ache from within her heart. It was a place she'd never heard of. It must be far, far away.

"Nicely done," he said. "It's from a language older than time."

"What is this Xzepheniixenze like?"

"Its complexities can only be experienced." Even though it was subtle, he seemed to change. She wasn't even certain if it was a physical change or something she felt. "Although the empire's potential has not been reached in recent years...."

Was there an evil king that ruled his land? She knew what that was like. As a baron he probably had little power when there were so many other titles above him. They entered the fields.

Cassius slowed his horse to wait for her to come along side and said: "But that's not a subject to discuss right now and is rather boring to tell you the truth, especially to a princess who hasn't involved herself with politics. What is it that young ladies like to talk about these days? So mysticism doesn't interest you? It seems very popular in this country. I heard once that there was a dragon in the east." He smiled down at her.

She hadn't heard of such tales, and scolded herself for being interested in what he had to say. However, she couldn't let him know that. "I don't believe in them. There are many superstitions in this country, and I don't give much merit to them." She wanted nothing more than to be home and in the solitude of her library, or anywhere other than this conversation. Truth be told, she and Charlotte often wondered about the great wide world beyond Fuarmaania, and what fantastic creatures there might be.

He chuckled.

Gellia's thoughts returned to her trip home and she became even more somber. Cassius rode in front of her again as they walked over the narrow path through a hedge. He pushed the wave of ebony hair from his face. It caught her attention; she'd seen hair often enough, but this was certainly hair that looked freshly washed and well-tended, beautiful in fact.

"Why did you come here?" she asked. Asking such a forceful question was a bold move for a woman, but it came out of her just the same.

With a glance behind him he answered: "It is a kingdom rich with history."

"I don't see why anyone would ever want to come here for a visit." She knew she was speaking nearly like a traitor, but for the moment she didn't care. There was little written history about Fuarmaania, at least not that she ever found, and certainly there was no one who spoke of it. Charlotte said there was a king many years ago who burned most of the original library, wishing to hide truth from others. "Our nobles are drunkards while our peasants starve. We go on hunts and throw parties while those who tend the land try to rebuild their homes from floods and fire. Our people are overtaxed and abused." She said nothing to her father, ever, about her concerns. She was surprised she told this man. He could easily betray her.

Cassius raised an eyebrow. "And of course I'm here for an alliance."

She wanted to tell him it would be no use for an alliance. The king's soldiers were mostly just bullies now, and his generals were nobles who had grown fat and lazy living off the peasants' hard work. How they would be useful in an alliance she didn't know.

The castle came into sight. Its weathered grey stones stood starkly against the sky; she was certain the moss clinging to the walls held it together. As the years passed it seemed in greater disrepair, or perhaps it was her despair. She wondered what it looked like when it was new, and what kind of rulers her ancestors were, hundreds of years ago.

Cassius spoke again. "I do find it amusing that this is the 'Welcoming Festival'. Do you ever wonder where it originated?"

"Welcoming spring," she said. "Everyone knows that." But she had never heard an actual story of how the festival came about.

He chuckled. "Silly me."

***

"What troubles you, love?" Corrah asked as she combed through Gellia's knotted hair. Corrah was Gellia's only servant. Not only did Gellia not trust others, but it was deemed a good idea to keep any knowledge of Gellia's behavior to a minimum. Her fitful sleeps, and bouts of slipping into trances didn't sit well with the courtiers. Gellia learned long ago not to confide in anyone about what occurred in her strange dreams, or feelings that apparently no one else ever had.

"Nothing but the usual." Gellia looked at her striking yet somehow wretched features in the mirror. Her tired brow, the sadness behind her eyes. Her mind wandered and she pictured herself in a fantastic palace surrounded by unworldly splendor. How wonderful it would be. A castle of surpassing beauty and perhaps peace and a real purpose for her. She would never have to dream of better things again. "It's that man."

"The baron?"

She nodded.

"Come now. He has a way about him that calms your father, which in itself should grant your favor. I know you prefer your books and horse to people, but you're the heir, and you need a king. Perhaps he would be better than the local nobles, hmmm?"

Gellia had been distrustful as soon as she was old enough to know better, the adults and their gossip had taught her that, but Cassius brought her suspicion to new heights. When he was near she felt even less like herself, more confused, more conflicted. It wasn't something anyone she knew would understand. No, it would give them more reason to think she was accursed.

"Well, milady, you better find a husband before you're old and grey like me. You need to have babies and give an heir to the kingdom. We all could be doomed without one. This baron could give you a good life. It's obvious he's rich. He could bring prosperity back to our country. If his majesty gives an approval…"

Gellia sighed. That wasn't why he was there.

"My dearest, you have so much against you. So many have turned away because of the curse. If this baron will have you, accept it. What better fate is there? Someone of your father's choosing?"

She couldn't argue with the logic, so she didn't. "I wish to be alone."

"Yes milady." Corrah shuffled away.

Gellia stared at the old tapestries that lined her dark room. Somehow she knew if she stayed in Fuarmaania she would continue to die inside. No, something in her seemed to shout, this is not your world. If only she believed the voice in her head, or only if she could accept her life as it was. Perhaps it was her aunt's fault for letting her indulge in fantasy.

***

Dinner was its usual nonsense of greasy food, drunken nobles, dogs fighting for scraps, and an untalented dancer for their entertainment. Gellia did her best to be invisible until it was late enough for her to flee without punishment. She'd become somewhat talented at making these escapes after so many years. It was fortunate for her the king didn't allow her to sit at his table, and once everyone was happily enjoying the hospitality she could slip away between courtiers and servants.

Grey walls welcomed her and surrounded her with their familiar coldness. She went to the chapel, where only servants seemed to go as they passed from one room to the next. There were a few old chairs, a tall statue of a beautiful woman, old draperies and a single painting of the queen. In the painting, the queen sat atop a black horse. Gellia was the only one who dusted it, and it was the only painting left of her mother. Gellia stopped and stared for a moment. It was her secret wish that her mother would come to her rescue, that she wasn't truly dead. Bernadette wasn't talked about in the castle, especially in front of the king. The king thought he'd been cuckolded when she left, and Bernadette's name would send him into a rage. Who was my father? She wondered. She resisted asking the painting aloud. Was he a nobleman? A soldier? A peasant? How did he and her mother meet? Did anyone know who he was?

"Your mother."

Gellia jumped and wondered how long Cassius watched her before he spoke. He always moved noiselessly like a shadow. She felt ambushed. None but the servants, she, and occasionally Cresslyn ever came through these rooms.

"I see the resemblance," the Xzepheniixenze said. "You have her eyes."

She moved away. All others were afraid to look her in the eye, and she was used to it, but not him. It unnerved her, like he could see into her soul and judge her even more than the others could. "Excuse me, I have places I need to be."

"I know you do," he said. "But not where you think." He watched her walk away until she was out of sight. He gave a nod to the old statue before he left.

***

"Milord, I would like you to meet my daughter, Eliza— isn't she a pretty picture?" Lady Viella pushed the sallow girl towards the baron, who smiled and kissed Eliza's pale hand. The perfumes swept around the baron like a lethal cloud of poison as Viella took his arm and insisted on accompanying him through the hall. "Eliza is an accomplished musician, you should listen to her play—" she continued.

They turned down another passage and came to a loggia that opened into a bright courtyard filled with a tangle of wild flowers. "Oh, there's our princess," the lady murmured. Gellia was practicing her archery in the sunlight. Lady Viella felt Gellia seemed to lack humility and any regard for etiquette. Although she said nothing, her feelings were easily read off her expression and gestures.

"She's an impressive archer," he chuckled. "A natural, I'm sure."

"My lord, perhaps my daughter could play for you. She's quite skilled at the lute as well. I would be honored if you would join us for a concert." Viella couldn't help but scowl as she looked into the courtyard.

Gellia tried to focus on her archery even while receiving the glares. This was the very courtyard Percy had taught her how to use a bow. Even though he was dead, she still thanked him for it. It was a pastime she enjoyed when she could. She wouldn't show how much their treatment hurt her. She started to hum a little tune, perhaps one she heard at a party, and placed the wooden missile on the bow.

The melody she sang changed at bit, matched one she sensed in her heart. Where she had heard it before she had no idea. Soon she was out of arrows and had to fetch the ones embedded in the target. Her mind started to fill with a soft music, in her mind's eye it almost seemed like swirls of emerald. Someone called her, but who it was she couldn't hear. She paused as she fought the madness, unable to move while her senses betrayed her.

Gellia could bear it no longer and left the courtyard. She hurried as much as her skirts would allow, walked past ladies who stopped their conversations as she passed. Then she heard a gruff voice echo through the great hall. The king approached. She knew his mood just from the volume he used. Without another thought she hiked her skirts and scampered through the dreary galleries to the stable, which was much closer than the library.

She rounded the corner and made a final dash for Tempest's box stall where she could bury herself in the stone manger like she had since she was young. The lone stable boy she passed would be the only one who could say where she was, and she hoped that he would remain silent. After she hopped into the manger she pulled up a blanket of hay over her head and settled down to wait. This is lunacy, she thought.

How long she stayed there she didn't know; she fell asleep and didn't wake up until someone other than Tempest stared down at her. She glared at him. "Who are you? That's right, the stable boy." She pulled herself from the hay and attempted to be poised.

"I guess you could call me that. I'm Currain," he said. He had a strange accent. Gellia eyed him suspiciously. He was as tall as she, thin like a rail with a mop of dark hair and dimples in his cheeks. He looked very much like a dullard, Gellia thought. The facial expressions he used were exaggerated as if he just learned them, and he never removed his quirky smile. "I came to tell you they're gone. Your father is too busy with drink to care about much now."

She brushed the hay from her dress and tried not to look embarrassed. "You should address him as his majesty, the king, and shouldn't discuss…"

He burst out with a hearty laugh. "I've met some people worth respecting and believe me, there's no one here who deserves mine."

She frowned and made her way back to the castle. Even the servants treated her poorly, but there was no use complaining about it.

***

Cresslyn burst into Gellia's chamber and received a scolding from Corrah. "Milady, you shouldn't burst into the room, especially the room of a princess."

This didn't hinder Cresslyn's excitement. "Gellia, you have to come tonight!"

ຮ>28ଔ

Gellia sighed. "I know, Cress."

"Not just for his majesty, you have to come because it's such wonderful entertainment!" Cresslyn carried her cat mask in her hand, but was otherwise fully dressed in a mottled yellow and brown dress resembling the colors of a tabby. She loved all parties, but especially loved a masquerade. They only ever had one during the festival.

"I'm not so sure about that," Gellia said.

"Oh come now, sister! When you wear a mask no one knows who you are! It's such fun!"

Gellia shook her head but smiled all the same. It was easy to tell Gellia from the others, she was taller than the other women and it was obvious she wasn't a man because she'd be wearing a dress. In fact, the dress she had was designed to stand out, and she'd be fortunate if someone else had one more elaborate. Cresslyn looked at Gellia with her brown eyes and eager face and realized she would have to wear the costume. When Gellia took a deep breath Cresslyn bounced up and down before helping Corrah prepare their princess.

The dress was white and shimmery with beading and gossamer layers. It was truly a thing of beauty. It had been a gift from an anonymous benefactor, but Gellia had her suspicions. While many of the masks for such costumes tended to have an artistic flare towards the grotesque, this one was beautiful and graceful. She was a unicorn. While Gellia was in love with the beauty of it, the reality of it brought her grief.

Cresslyn vowed to stay by Gellia's side, but Gellia knew better and wasn't surprised when Cresslyn joined the jolly throng dancing in the great hall. Then began the stares, and being that everyone was faceless, they weren't afraid to continue to stare. Gellia did her best to become part of a wall, a regal decoration of white and sparkle. A statue that hopefully everyone would forget. What was she thinking? Was she so controlled by a beautiful garment and a friend's pleas? Did Gellia think that a beautiful costume would somehow improve how people saw her? She grew more uncomfortable by the moment, and was too obvious to sneak away.

Cresslyn and her dancing partner parted while the minstrels finished their set. The room was stuffy and she needed refreshment. When Cresslyn came to her senses and saw her beloved friend she realized people were gossiping. Where had the costume come from? A mysterious and wealthy lover? From faeries she'd enchanted? Gellia thought she was better than everyone, but everyone knew she was only valuable because of her family line. Gellia was further tarnished by Charlotte's ill health and Bernadette's lunacy. Cresslyn was saddened that in her excitement she'd talked Gellia into wearing the costume and now faced increased disrespect. Why did the others behave so cruelly? Gellia was not as bad as they said, if they'd take the time to know her. A shadow moved past but she didn't look up until it spoke to her. "What concerns you so?" the baron inquired.

The Cresslyn the kitty looked up at the shining emerald scales of the dragon. She didn't know what to say to him besides: "Save her."

"I will if she allows me," the dragon said and smiled. He glided away.

The unicorn-princess looked out from where she tried to hide but never even noticed that she was being approached until a dragon parted the sea of young ladies and stood before her. "I won't let you be a wallflower for another moment," he told her. His size blocked out the others. She didn't want to trust the feeling, but Gellia felt safe, as if she has stepped into another world far from here.

"I'm not a flower, I'm a unicorn," she said, not understanding.

He smiled. "Yes, I know. Certainly more than you do."

"This is merely a game for you," she said. Why was he there? Why did he come to her? Her mind was screaming at her to reject him in any way possible.

He gave her a smile, but she felt there was darkness in it. "The games I play are not for the likes of this superb kingdom. Come dance with me."

"Do I have a choice?"

"It's either me or your father," he said and smirked and looked over his shoulder at the glowering king. She gave him her hand and allowed him to draw her out despite her fear.

The whole night she wished he would trip and fall on his handsome face, but he never did. They did however, manage to bump the king and spill the drink he held all over the demon costume he wore. There were many apologies from their honored guest, who explained his inexperience with the dance steps. Gellia, who knew Cassius lied, tried to control her laughter. For a moment she forgot herself and laughed as they swung away from the spill. "That was mildly amusing," Cassius said. "We should plot together again someday."

She nodded, still giggling a little. He smiled down at her, and once she realized she let down her guard, was embarrassed. "If you'll excuse me..." she mumbled; he allowed her to retreat. Once in the narrow gallery she pulled at the ribbons that held on her mask and yanked it from her face as she hurried to her chamber. What was this power of his she so desperately tried to fight? Why wouldn't she let herself trust him?

2   —

This had been her and Queen Charlotte's haven. The old books waited for her in the dim library. No one else would turn their dry pages and admire them as she did. Gellia took her time as she walked along the single wall of faded books. She'd read all the books in her native tongue. She found the spine of the ancient book she wished to explore and pulled it from the shelf in a cloud of dust. No servant ever bothered with the room, Gellia was the only one who really used it since Charlotte died, and the servants were better being busy elsewhere than cleaning the library. Even the ones she couldn't read she still revisited like old friends, and this was one of them. In the past she had compared other foreign tomes to her favorite one, and deduced that they all were in the same language. She often admired the graceful characters, the ornate decorations on the pages, the quality of the pages. What mysteries did they hold? She and her dear aunt often mused at what it might be. Often they read to each other and discussed the stories held within their native books. When they'd found only one book that had been part of a set Charlotte told her of the king who burned the books. It made them both sad for the loss.

Most of the readable volumes in the tiny library were observations of the kingdom from times when such things were recorded. Other books were stories with fantastical situations and amazing magics, but they weren't particularly happy stories. The dim light from the single window was enough to not need to light any candles, and as she gingerly leafed through the pages, she wished that she would find something more about herself. Perhaps she had a great ancestor, one even better than her true father or her grandfather. No one spoke of their history, perhaps no one really knew or cared to know.

Gellia turned the pages, hoping there were be pictures she'd somehow missed before, but there was only the single map of a place she didn't know. The rest was beautiful penmanship; all scrolls and loops and swirls that all intermingled, not the scratchy, abrupt written word of Fuarmaania. She pushed the ancient text onto the shelf and continued her quest for whatever it was her soul was looking for. She rested her head on the spines of the books and let her thoughts return to her aunt.

Charlotte understood Gellia's strange feelings; senses that there was more than what they understood, and something greater out there that they had yet to see but belonged to them. Charlotte said she felt the same way, but had the fortune to be the sickly princess and able to live most of her life in quiet and solitude. However, Charlotte was happy to befriend her niece, and before childbirth stole her from Gellia, Gellia had the only true confidant she'd ever had. Cresslyn was sweet and she was company, but her gregarious nature often made her tongue wag.

Gellia remembered Charlotte talking of so many things. They spent so many hours in the tiny library. "I barely knew your mother," she said. "I was sent away very young, and never expected to amount to much, perhaps not even to survive…. But one's duty is to the crown, so here I am…. I heard nothing of your mother's lover for it was kept quite secret, but it pleased our father that she proved fertile and marriageable, for there was little hope for me, and Hugh had grown too powerful." And of the feelings Gellia had, Charlotte said, "My dear, I don't have them as deeply as you do, but I do have them. I tell you it is a gift, and one that isn't understood. I don't know what it is or what the purpose is, but it is a gift, of this I'm sure. Perhaps someday if I live long enough, or you do, you can find out what it is and for what purpose."

Gellia sat in the old chair and leaned on the windowsill. Something called to her, but she didn't know where to search for it, or if she should.

***

Corrah arranged the curtains to allow the sunlight in. It was a beautiful day; everything seemed green and new. Gellia entered her room when Corrah was shaking out a blanket. "Good morning milady," Corrah greeted.

Gellia sat on her bed for a moment and thought about her books, her horse, and how she could avoid as many people as possible that day. She wished above all else to be alone with her thoughts.

Someone tapped at the door and Corrah called to enter. A manservant poked his head in and cleared his throat. "A message for her highness," he said, handing it to Corrah. Gellia took the letter from her maid and eyed the young man. He looked tired, but carried himself with great pride, unlike the rest of the servants in the castle.

The princess opened the crisp and exotic black paper and read the lovely writing in silver ink. It was the first time she'd seen *his* handwriting, and seeing it made her breath catch in her throat. The meaning of the message was lost on her for a few moments while she stared at how he formed his letters. It was written in Fuarmaanian, but was beautiful in its flourishes; elegant loops and swirls seemed to dance across the page. When she realized Corrah was staring at her, Gellia pulled herself to her senses.

Cassius asked her to go out on the horses with him. "Tell the baron that I will meet him in the stable," she told the manservant, who nodded and left. "Help me with my riding habit," Gellia told Corrah. "Father won't be angry with me if I'm off with his favorite baron." She had so many questions, but did she dare ask them? He was here for an alliance, but not with King Hugh. As Corrah helped her with her riding habit she slipped into a daze of wonder. Was her imagination running away with her? Why was she so conflicted when it was black and white for everyone else? Why couldn't she be as everyone else?

***

"Hello, you," she said to greet Tempest. He was already tacked and ready to go. Tempest watched her with his gentle brown eyes as she offered him a carrot she had taken from the kitchen. She loved the sound of a horse munching. After a final pat she led him out into the aisle—she didn't need a stable boy to do it for her. She heard hoof beats at the other end of the stable, no doubt it was Nighthawk and his baron. Riding with him would be difficult, the constant unease she felt around him was still tormenting her.

They walked into the sun of the courtyard and one of the stable boys dutifully held the stallion for Gellia to mount, although Tempest was never one to walk off. She waited and adjusted her seat. There were no other horses saddled so it was evident they would go without a formal escort. She kept her eyes forward as they rode out, she didn't look back to see if he was there. Unfortunately he trotted up alongside her and smiled as if she amused him.

In time the decrepit castle was out of sight. A gallop was calling her. That freedom of the ride bid her to press into Tempest's flanks, but she refrained. No doubt the black horse could keep up with the old dapple-grey. She had herself so upset about decorum that Tempest responded to her stiff posture with shortened strides.

Cassius broke the silence. "Is that really how they teach women to ride here?"

Gellia frowned. "Good manners include…"

His tone never changed from pleasant. "I'm not as oblivious as you hope."

Her anxiety rose. Had she offended him? She felt regret, but tried to push it away. "As if you have any feelings to hurt," she muttered under her breath.

"I don't remember making mention of being hurt." Gellia looked at him, ashamed at her behavior, watched him eye the tangles in his horse's mane and mutter something inaudible. She didn't know if he was aware of her gaze or not, but for some reason his quiet complaint about poor grooming made her smile. Tempest's ears flopped in rhythm with his march as she relaxed and let him have a long rein. From what she'd see so far, this wasn't much better than a ride with Cresslyn or any of the other timid ladies in the castle, but she was out in the sunshine.

"Restless?" Cassius asked as he looked down at her from his great stallion.

She said nothing for a moment, measuring her words. "It is little consequence, the feelings of a cursed princess."

He still seemed amused. "There is the vast field before us, one that needs to feel the thunder of galloping hooves." He gave her a sly look. "Do as you wish, I won't stop you," he said, adjusting his gloves. After a moment he chuckled a little; it was a deep, rumbling sound. "See if you can escape me as easily as you escape others. Must be a talent passed through the generations— one of the few." Then he muttered something that sounded like, "you'll never escape me."

Even though it tempted her, she forced herself to forget what he said. She hoped he would grow tired of her company, but she felt she would be in his presence for a very long time. Tempest flicked his ears to and fro as Gellia tapped her feet in the stirrups.

They neared a grove, one she knew well. It was a place she and Percy loved to visit. This was her favorite wood, not only because of her memories but also because of its beauty. Trees stood thick and tall as pillars to hold up the sky. The canopy swayed in the breeze. Mosses grew on the old trees while bramble carpeted the forest floor. The path was a small leafy road that meandered through the old trees to another brownish field. Gellia breathed in the forest air as they rode. No, Percy didn't appreciate some things like she did, but he loved the ride. His horse seemed half mad, half wild, but Percy loved that mare nonetheless. Perhaps that's why he got along so well with Gellia. She could never confide in him as she did Charlotte, about the strangeness, but he didn't mind her odd demeanor.

A falcon called. It soared above her; she reined Tempest to a stop. What would it be like to look down at the world from the sky? To have such freedom? The falcon flew out of her sight and into the trees but then drifted downward into the columns of the trunks to perch on Cassius' gloved hand. In her distraction he had overtaken her on the path.

He stroked the breast of the magnificent animal and spoke to it softly. "I think she envies you," he said to the bird. The falcon eyed the princess and her steed. The black stallion moved towards them, his hooves almost silent as they approached. When Nighthawk was alongside Tempest, Cassius carefully moved the falcon towards her so she could enjoy its company. Although he had moved, she found herself comfortable with his distance, for he stayed farther from her than the rest of her people would have to one another.

"Yours?" she asked. She hadn't heard about anyone with raptors and she hadn't looked to see if he had one when they left. The castle had never kept a mews. It seemed odd to her that this bird was not with them before, yet acted as if it belonged to him. She had to admit she knew little about the subject.

Cassius watched her with his otherworldly violet eyes. It unsettled her—not that he looked at her with anything but his usual aloofness. But there was something beyond those eyes, something that seemed far more complicated than she could imagine. For the first time she looked back at him and let his eyes speak to her. As she searched for some hint of who he was she found that she became more aware of herself. Cassius was there—she knew him—and there was something that surrounded her that had always been there but she had never known. Something that awoke within her, but it wasn't emotional. All too quickly she felt out of control. She looked away.

"No, I don't own it, but I do have an affinity for nature." He launched the falcon and it flew to a nearby branch. "I don't think anyone can truly own such a wonder, although many think they do. Nature always finds a way to prove them wrong." Gellia had so many more questions, but was afraid once more that it was a trap. Tempest moved forward. She was sure she heard Cassius laugh to himself. Gellia rubbed goose bumps on her arm but didn't drop the reins.

They arrived at the clearing of the next brownish field. "What do you wish to do? Where do you wish to go?" Cassius asked from behind her. "Would be terrible to waste such a pleasant day by just staying around here."

"I don't think it would be a prudent choice," she said.

"Oh?"

"A wild gallop with a cursed princess seems unwise," she said.

He chuckled, the rumbling sound of it pleasing to her ears. "Are you referring to your previous engagements?"

She nodded.

"I'm not afraid of your supposed curse, for I am not a suitor, and four dead betrothed sounds more like a conspiracy than a curse."

She looked up at him, her surprise likely obvious on her face.

His usual smirk was on his.

"Three," she said.

"His majestic-ness told me four."

"He would know," she said. She stared at Tempest's mane while her mind rushed. Why had this idea not occurred to her? And there had been four?

"Fuarmaania is full of its superstitions," Cassius said. "But at present that is neither here nor there. Where would you like to go?"

Gellia's brow furrowed and she gripped her reins tighter. She would have to steel herself and talk to the king, but indeed, they were riding for the time being. *Wherever the wind takes me,* she thought. "What pleases you," came from her mouth.

"You must think I'm absurd by asking what it is that you want to do and not telling you what you want to do." He chuckled. "Don't worry, princess, I don't report to your illustrious king."

She frowned, stared at her horse's neck and shifted the reins in her hand. Tempest pranced a little and she felt she couldn't refrain. She needed to be free, even for just a moment. Gellia pressed her calves into his dappled flanks and they thundered across the field in no particular direction; her shadow was still with her as they went. The wind swirled around them as they galloped through field after field, hedges barely obstacles to keep them from their ever changing destination. Tempest's breaths matched the rhythm of his hooves as they enjoyed a very rare open field gallop. They kept going until it seemed they'd reached the end of the earth, which proved her world to be very small. They had reached the border of the kingdom.

The stallion leapt and bounced to a standstill at the edge of the Great Cliffs, his hooves sent gravel flying over the edge. Beneath them was endless fog and treetops. Nighthawk and his baron stood next to the princess; his stallion wasn't winded as Tempest was. "Sen Dunea," Cassius said.

The wind pushed against her, nearly took off her wimple. Cassius didn't seem concerned as the wind teased them. Soon it changed direction and pushed them towards the edge, encouraged them to jump into the swirled mist below. The baron looked into distance and smiled, his ebony hair blew past his face in a graceful wave. Fog beneath them started to move away. He sighed. "We should be going," he said, "unless you enjoy riding through the dark as much as I do."

By the time they reached the castle the sun had disappeared. This time she left her horse to be tended by the boys; she didn't say another word to Cassius. She hurried the king's chambers while she still had her nerve.

It had been several years since Gellia had attempted approaching the king in such a way. The last time had ended in her being hit so hard it knocked her down. But if she could convince him that she was not cursed, and there was a conspiracy to be blamed, perhaps her life would be just a bit easier. When she was admitted by the manservant she heard the king say, "What does she want, is she with child?"

"Sire," Gellia said with a curtsy. "I have something important to discuss...."

He snorted and took another swig from his cup. He'd been lounging in his favorite chair, where he conducted most of his royal duties. "Unlikely, unless you've managed to snare a man on your own."

"Sire, no. Sire, I believe my betrotheds' deaths are conspiracy, not a curse, if your highness takes a moment and…"

Hugh's face turned crimson and he roared, "What foolishness is this? What ridiculous ideas. This is what happens when you fill your head with books."

"Sire, I…" she said, which was a mistake.

The king pulled himself to his feet and Gellia took a step back. She started to speak rapidly. "Sire, the baron suggested…." Hugh was alarmingly swift as he came to slap her. She'd learned not to cry, but a noise of pain escaped her. She did manage to keep her feet, but she was now hunched over.

"Look at you," he said. "Standing so slovenly there. Blaming others for your stupidity. Do you take me for an idiot? Conspiracy instead of the obvious reason."

Gellia straightened herself only to be hit again. This time he hit her with a metal candle stick wielded like a club. He hit her squarely in her side, and she did indeed fall. She couldn't breathe, and the familiar pain was there. However, the pain was then covered by a strange rush, fire in her soul. Something she felt she could lash out with, but her mind told her it was foolishness.

"May that knock some sense into you," he king growled. His servants took her by the arms and dragged her to the antechamber where they dropped her in a heap. Corrah rushed to her side and helped her up.

Gellia only needed a moment to collect herself. She was fairly good at hiding her pain. Corrah adjusted Gellia's wimple while Gellia took a few deep and painful breaths. It was time to return to her room. Why did she think this would work?

***

It was long after that Gellia returned to her secret place in the woods. Her bruised side made it too painful to ride, so she stayed in her room or the library until it was healed. Early that morning she'd slipped into the stable to tack Tempest and sneak away unescorted.

This was her kingdom—the grass carpeted clearing in her forest. Gellia could still see Percy's smiling face. They often spent time together, playing like children while the chaperones were nearby. She would read to Percy, and he'd lie in the grass and watch the clouds. She didn't know if he was just being patient or if he enjoyed her reading to him, but it was the thought of it that made the memory pleasant... Who would want to kill a young man like him? Or smother a babe in the cradle? Who would have the ability to cause a duke and his entourage to disappear? Maybe it really was a curse. She'd condemned herself for thinking the king would listen.

...She once again thought about just riding out of her situation, to run away as her mother did. The warm breeze blew through the evergreens that surrounded her miniature realm of wildflowers and horse-cropped grass. Every time Gellia visited her private kingdom she turned Tempest loose to graze; he never ran away. As long as she had her horse and her books—she assured herself—everything would be fine. So the princess was content for a while, but still missed having someone to talk with…

Gellia stroked Tempest's ear as he grazed next to her; he pushed the faded grey fabric of her dress out of his way as he went. His soft muzzle sniffed for her pocket and found nothing so he shoved her with his nose and sent her head over heels into the grass. "Tempest!" She laughed and untangled herself from her dress. He trotted away in search of what he thought was better grazing and Gellia stayed on her back and looked into the sky. Lazy clouds drifted through the sea of blue like great flying beasts. She tried to think of what the world would look like if she were on one of them. A falcon passed overhead and Cassius returned to her mind.

"Hello, there you are."

She leapt to her feet and stared at a lanky youth. It was the stable boy who had in the past spoken insolently to her. "What are you doing here?" Gellia snapped.

"I went for a walk," he said and shrugged. "There's no laws against that is there?" He grinned at her in an almost child-like way. Tempest greeted him with an arched neck and flared nostrils and gave him an elaborate sniffing.

"You must be daft." She said and adjusted her dress. Maybe he was seventeen—it looked to be the case when he was smiling so foolishly. What was Tempest up to? How odd.

"I'm smarter than a horse," he said and tilted his head, still he smiled. He didn't seem bothered by Tempest.

"I suppose you are." She prepared herself to leave and took up her horse's reins.

"You don't have to leave on my account," he said.

"I'm going." She mounted and started away. A day ruined by an intruder. She was sure the servants would be spreading rumors again. Was it so terrible that she wanted to be alone? When she was alone she wasn't bothering anyone else.

"Suit yourself." He watched her go; his dark eyes glimmered from under his thick forelock.

***

Nighthawk hung his head out of the tiny window of the stall as he watched his master cross the stable yard. "Greetings, yer lordship," the stable overseer called from the door. "Yer going let that horse loose again, aren't yeh, milord?"

The baron answered him as they entered the stable together. "Yes I am."

"I'll never understand why he comes back every time yer lordship let's him loose."

"He knows where his duty is." A whinny hailed them from down the aisle; Nighthawk arched his sleek neck over the stall door. The baron unlatched the door and silently watched as his horse trot to freedom.

"I still don't understand it." The old man's calloused hand passed through his wispy hair. "None of our horses would ever do that, ever. How d'ye say yeh train these things were yer lordship lives?"

Feminine laughter echoed through the corridor and the hostler and baron exchanged glances. "I'll be leavin' yeh, milord, yeh've got company comin'." His wrinkly face twisted into a smile and the old man left the prey to the predators. A group of the ladies of the castle approached, their eyes locked on their objective.

The massive form of Lady Madeline came to him first. She carried her dog with her; a spiteful, shivering little creature. "I heard that you are quite taken with that horrible princess," she hissed. She squinted her raccoon-like eyes at him, a truly horrifying sight.

"Good day, ladies," he answered, ignoring the comment. Some of the finest had graced him with their presence: Lady Madeline, Lady Viella, and Lady Avington. None of them had much better to do than terrorize him with their chatter, especially after he'd been a guest at the castle for so long. He found out recently that amusingly, Viella was the widow of King Hugh's murderous brother, and Madeline was Hugh's spinster sister. All of them wished their children qualified for the throne, but the superstitions were far too strong.

Cassius smiled. "How lovely it is to see you," he said, trying not to inhale; they must have recently bathed in perfume.

"There is a situation we need to discuss," Lady Viella said. "We aren't here about our own gain. We're here about your health. Surely you know about the princess."

"Yes, a devil she is," Madeline added, the rolls of her chin quivered. Her dog growled under its breath.

The third spoke. "If you don't end up dead first, she'll be a terrible wife and she won't bear any sons, that's for sure. She'll make your hair turn white." Tightly stretched skin over the narrow bones of Lady Avington's face moved around in some sort of smile that was probably meant to captivate but fell horribly short of what she hoped.

The baron waved. "I don't fear for my life," he said with a smile. He had little use for children, especially sons… "I doubt she has the power to turn my hair white," he added. "I doubt even the goddesses have that power. I certainly don't remember discussing a betrothal with his highness."

"She seduced you, didn't she? You're obviously madly in love with her." Viella's thin lips disappeared into her mouth with her anger.

"I'm afraid I don't understand," the baron told them. The slanderous talk continued and they included him enough to talk at him but he was never able to fit in another word. He had to remind himself to be patient.

***

The world beyond the tattered drapes was showing only a little promise of sun. Corrah frowned and opened them—it was too dark in the room the sun needed to be let in, even if it was only a little. Gellia was still in bed, not quite ready to rise for the day. She'd caught a chill as she often did and had been confined to her room. Gellia sighed. "I miss the stable."

Corrah worked in the fireplace, her ample buttocks jiggling as she swept the ashes. "You'd marry that horse if you could, I'd wager, milady." She rose and adjusted her wimple.

The princess smirked. "He has a better temperament than any human I know."

"There are plenty of good mannered men here. Great men don't have to follow the same rules as regular folk. You can't marry a horse, a horse won't give you a family… Besides, what kind of companion is an animal?" She wiped her hands on a rag.

"Better than most everyone here."

Corrah grinned shrewdly. "Something tells me that the baron would make a good companion."

"Why is it everyone thinks so highly of him?"

As Corrah hobbled to her bedside she replied. "Not everyone, I found."

Gellia's eyebrows pressed together. "I don't believe it."

"Your grandfather doesn't like him."

This was an interesting development. "Why?" Aunt Charlotte had spoken often enough about grandfather king. Grandfather was not of the royal line, it was grandmother who was of that line, and he'd handed over Bernadette and Charlotte to keep the peace.

Corrah shrugged. "I don't know, it's just what I've heard your father's servants saying."

Grandfather was as much a tyrant as King Hugh, but didn't have enough clout with the armies as Hugh did. Gellia was fortunate he seldom left his hunting lodge and she certainly hoped he would never visit. Something wicked indeed came if they had word from grandfather.

Gellia dismissed Corrah and stared at the window… Could everyone be so wrong about Cassius and only she knew the reality? It seemed highly doubtful. Not all of them could be that foolish. She listened to her wind chimes and stared into nothingness…

***

It was another dream. Grey stone surrounded her, light poured from huge windows, millions of facets freckled the floor with rainbows. This was a beauty she knew couldn't exist but in her dreams. The cavernous room stretched out corridor limbs. Platinum and inlaid jewels glittered everywhere; the unicorns and winged people were carved from stone that glowed with life and seemed to watch her as she wandered through the massive chamber. There were paintings. There were flowers…flowers everywhere. They were a part of her. Gardens, acres of gardens, and fountains. A cobalt sea. Windows adorned with velvet drapes and billowed silk like clouds. The stone had soft curves that sparkled in the sun. A ballroom, several tiers around its edge. The floor tiled in gems, a black unicorn. Roses. A unicorn in the rose gardens. She felt her soul weep and smile at the same time. The air was warm. The ocean pounded the rocks below. There were people everywhere. There was something familiar. They were gone. Warmth, like a friend, a companion, a love. The castle spoke to her. There was sadness. "What's wrong?" She asked. Something familiar. There was a unicorn, grey like her Tempest, no, dappled with silver. He watched her. She knew he smiled. She felt contented. "You are Mystic," she said. She stepped onto a stone balcony and up to the gilded balustrade. Towers glittered amethyst. Roses crept up the walls. The land was covered in a blanket of color. A land of surpassing beauty. A wind chime sang with the castle. There was a key. A key everyone searched for. The castle held her, welcomed her, whispered to her. The pale faces of two moons watched her through the daylight. Flowers from trees decorated her with petals as she stood near a small lake. Swans glided over the smooth water. Tiny lights floated all around her. The silver dappled unicorn watched her. This was a dream but he was there. Rose blooms floated on the water; colors of this nature could almost blind a Fuarmaanian. The castle glowed behind her. It beckoned her. I want to stay here, she thought. I want to stay here forever. Her thoughts echoed through the gardens and orchards. Emerald music. She looked at the bloom in her hand. A purple rose. Dew still clung to its petals. There is no winter here. Why? The silver-dappled unicorn watched her.

"You are winter's love, are you spring?" She asked.

"No, I am sorrow," he answered. "You shall be spring." The castle sang to her. The ocean beneath the tower soothed her. The night welcomed her. Something was in the air. She felt it before. Awakening beckoned her. Someone called. No. Her cheeks felt damp. I will die. She heard her wind chime.

"Gellia, Gellia, are you awake?" Came Cresslyn's voice. Murky colored stone walls, tattered tapestries and curtains, a partially crumbled fireplace, blankets filled with holes. Gellia didn't move for a moment, then crawled from bed to watch the night creep over the dull landscape from her window. The wind chime sang softly. "Gellia, Corrah said it would be all right if you came to the gathering tonight as long as you don't exert yourself." Cresslyn stood in the doorway and watched her sister. "Are you still unwell? If you are I can fetch Corrah."

Gellia seemed to drift further apart from everyday life every moment. Cresslyn knew how the others spoke; since she was of lesser standing talk flowed easily around her. Some thought of her as barely better than peasant. They said Gellia was quite mad as well as was cursed. They spoke of dark forces around her, a demon within her. Cresslyn wouldn't believe it. Gellia was tormented, but by what Cresslyn couldn't tell.

"No, I'm fine." Gellia lied. Her eyes were on the window where the sun melted into the horizon in a pool of gold. "I'll come down presently."

Cresslyn made no reply as she left the dark room. Gellia tried to recall how she felt in the dream moments before. It felt more real than this life, but there was no one who could understand such a thing. She listened to the wind chime in the window and felt her heart start to crumble.

That night, wrapped in a shawl like an old woman (and she felt old) their proud princess stood under an archway where she could watch the nightly festivities.

The usual circle of admirers surrounded the baron, boldly asked him to dance, and talked at him endlessly. He responded in smiles and kind words. One of the lady's daughters spoke to him but his eyes left her and found Gellia, who for once accepted his attention, she was too tired to resist. He could communicate with her so well with just a look. No one else seemed to be able to tell how bored he was, but she could. Once more he turned his attention to his admirers.

As she stood there she overheard the latest news. The most interesting was a young noblewoman from Cambiga had come to stay with a relative at the castle. It seemed she and Cresslyn had become fast friends. The new girl, Alexandria, was easy pick out, for she was quite timid and stood alone as Gellia did most of the time. Gellia watched Alexandria blush furiously when amiable Cassius approached her. Being that the two of them weren't far away, Gellia was able to listen to their conversation. Perhaps she would gain some sort of insight.

"You should be dancing," Cassius said as he took Alexandria's hand and kissed it. He smiled with an almost sardonic twist; Gellia noticed but the girl obviously didn't.

"I don't know anyone," she answered.

"I'm the Baron of Caddyan, Lord of Tintagel. Now you know me and you don't have an excuse not to dance." Alexandria lowered her eyes and Cassius led her out. "I know what it is like to be a stranger... now that you know my name; may I have the pleasure of yours?"

"Alexandria."

"From?"

"A very small country... Cambiga?" She glanced around and wouldn't keep eye contact, Gellia noticed.

He smiled down at her. "Ah yes, Cambiga. Wonderful grazing country there and I do remember seeing quite an exquisite ruin in their great forest, am I correct?"

"Why, yes! How did you know? I thought only a few people in my country knew about the ruin..."

Gellia tried unsuccessfully to catch the rest of the conversation, but she was certain that he won Alexandria for her face changed from nervousness to a wonderful glow. So she watched the others enjoy themselves in their foolish games and continued to let her mind to wander to distant, mysterious places. For a long time she stayed in the depths of her mind even when the dark shape steadily approached her through the sea of browns and greys. Cassius stood next to her. "Come with me," he said, not dissuaded by her heavy sigh.

Gellia only nodded. When Cassius exited Gellia slowly followed. Several times she lost him in the shadows, but oddly knew where he was and knew which way to go. They walked out to stand in the dark courtyard and Gellia irrationally fantasized how she would slap his smug face. She stood more than an arm's length away and stared at him. At least they were out of the smoky air.

She adjusted her shawl. "Yes?"

"A strange tone to take with a potential ally." He seemed to be part of the enigmatic dark, silver and shadow embraced him. "I wish to inquire if you are well, away from the chatter of the hall. And I have something for you."

"I'm well," she looked into the night.

"Are you really?" Even though he kept his distance he seemed too close for her comfort.

"Yes, I'm fine."

A smirk crossed his face and Gellia shifted her weight. From out of the iridescent fabric of his doublet he produced a large, pale rosebud and held it out to her. Its delicate fragrance made her feel longing for something she didn't understand. There were no roses in Fuarmaania. There never was. She only ever saw them in the pictures in her books and in her dreams.

"Where did you get it?"

"My home."

"I'm sure you give others riches, yet you give me a flower." But she was in fear that he could read her mind, knew her dreams and fantasies. Was he a suitor? Was that what he meant by an alliance? Then a strange thought came to her. Indeed, if he could give her mind peace, she would leave with him in an instant. But she had no way of knowing what he really wanted, or if it would be to any benefit to her, or if it would be her ruin.

"What I offer is far more significant than trinkets."

"Maybe what you're trying to give me is something I don't desire."

"You don't know what I present and you already refuse it. You mistake what I'm trying to provide. I suppose this makes some strange sense." He gave his hair a toss. "I suppose I'm expecting too much from a Fuarmaanian." He stuck the stem into her hand and started away.

In her fluster she blurted foolishness. "Of course I know what you propose. Everyone does."

He spoke to her from the doorway, his back still turned to her. "No, no one knows what I offer, but for your soul—and your backwards Fuarmaanian upbringing will not allow you to believe it." As he departed she strained to hear what he muttered, but it sounded like, "I've been away for far too long."

**

Gellia stared at the canopy with little intention to join the ride that day. Maybe she would go to the library after everyone left the castle. With a sigh she rolled over and stared at the pale, long-lived blossom that resided in a cup on her table. Since the interlude with Cassius in the courtyard he showered Gellia—and her horse—with gifts. A saddle and new bridle crafted with great care, but with simplistic and graceful design for Tempest; jewelry, sashes, hair ornaments that she'd never seen before, and dresses for Gellia. She felt sorry for being so rude to him in the courtyard, but her pride wouldn't let her admit it. She appreciated that most of the gifts were of beautiful quality but modest at a glance, so not to bring attention to her, all but for a lavender gown that made her sigh with love. She could never wear it in public for it would make a spectacle of her, but its shimmery, nearly glowing silk was a sight for her to behold. A fuller skirt than what was the fashion, beautiful long, narrow sleeves, silk ribbon roses encircling the waist. She even found it in herself to write him a thank you note.

He continued to rescue her from the king more often than not. It was strange to have a champion, especially from the king, but no one had a way with the king as Cassius. With the king no longer in constant search for his favorite person to hate, the courtiers slowly started to cool their own bitterness, and Gellia started to feel just a touch better about her life. She was still alone, and blissfully unaware if there was another suitor in the wings, but she had her horse and her books and all seemed well enough for the time being.

She forced herself out of her bed and sat in front of the old mirror. Corrah was away on other errands so she braided her black curls, a rare hairstyle for her. Luckily it was so long ago that her father beat her bloody, the scar at her hairline could no longer be seen. It had been even luckier he hadn't ruined her face making her even less desirable than she already was. She tossed her braid over her shoulder and sighed. Most ladies didn't know how to dress themselves or tend to their hair, but having only one servant meant sometimes you had to do things for yourself. Gellia went to the trunk that held all her dresses to find something to wear. She dug through the mass of woolen cloth and her hand passed over the silk gown. Gellia wished for a moment that she could wear it. Why couldn't she? Most everyone but servants were gone.

Quickly she shucked the nightgown off and pulled on the lavender gown. She looked at herself in the mirror and ran her hands over the smooth fabric. For a moment she wondered if it were possible for her to become a lady in waiting in Xzepheniixenze so she wouldn't have to marry and could avoid squalor. It couldn't be any worse than Fuarmaania. She touched her hair and turned back and forth in the mirror. How strange it was to see herself in such a gown instead of the dull frocks she was so used to. She twirled around and almost laughed at the ridiculous amount of time she already spent in front of the mirror, as if she was one of the other girls... her smile disappeared as she was reminded of her loneliness. Cresslyn had spent little time with her of late, and although the younger girl's foolishness was often trying, Gellia really did miss her.

* * *

The solitude of the library welcomed her, and she locked the door. From the dusty shelves Gellia pulled several books— the foreign ones—and sat by the window for a morning's worth of indulgence. After a while she started to scribble some notes on a slip of paper, drew the characters she saw the most, and copied the ones she liked over and over. She looked at the pages for so long that it started to make some sort of sense.

Her neck cramped from being bent over for so long. The mid-day sun was warm on her shoulder. She looked out the window for a moment to see a stable boy talk with none other than Cassius; his back was turned to her as he spoke to the boy. Content to spy for a while, she closed the book and leaned on the sill. Another stable boy hurried out with a big chestnut horse, saddled and ready. The baron swung aboard the chestnut and trotted from the castle. Nighthawk must have been lame, she wondered if her father loaned Cassius one of the royal horses. He didn't belong on that horse—it was by far a lesser mount.

The whistling wind swept through the room and heralded another storm; it blew away some of her papers and she had to chase them before they flew out the window. She returned to her chair and sighed as the wind gave a few more strong gusts then began to die. The lone tapestry with its faded hunt scene billowed against the wall; she heard it tear a bit as it fought the wind. Its rods shook in its fixtures and once again she was chasing papers through the room. Once the last paper was captured, she straightened herself and found her gaze resting on a new hole in the tapestry. It was not stone on the other side. Her heart leapt and she couldn't move for a few moments. Why hadn't she seen this before? She rose for a closer look, carefully pulled back deteriorating fabric.

Under a layer of dust she found a door grey with age, split through from lack of moisture, its hinges and lock completely rusted away into dust. Surprisingly, a pull was still present. If she pulled the door, would it break? When she touched it, it seemed to tremble, and she felt something give, but could see no evidence of any change. She worked at the old timbers, picked it up and slid it gently against the wall so it wouldn't fall over but would give her enough room to go through. She gathered her skirts and carefully entered, following a tiny shaft of light from within. She held her hand out so not to run into a wall and hopefully to avoid spider webs in her face. She felt a curtain she could draw back to let the light enter.

The heavy curtain was slow to move, but revealed three narrow windows, but that was enough to illuminate the small room. She held her breath and turned around to gaze on a space that was only several paces deep. A glorious mail armor shone back at her from the opposite wall. It was unlike any armor she'd seen before. She'd only ever seen chain mail, but this had small plates like scales. It was polished to a surreal shine, bore no dust. Gauntlets still held the hilt of the most beautiful sword she had ever seen. The pommel, a flawless globe of Alexandrite mounted on a leather-wrapped handle; the hilt, two silver unicorns that leapt from the center jewel—a beautiful amethyst that caught rays of light. The surcoat was bright purple velvet, edged with silver thread, a unicorn emblazoned on the front. Not even the king had something this grand. Gellia sank to the floor in a puff of silk to do nothing but stare for some time.

When her senses returned she rose and started to examine rest of the room. A story of the ancients lie before her in this room, a scrap of an unknown world. Bookshelves, a massive wooden trunk, and numerous other wooden boxes, all decorated with the same rampant unicorn motif, all covered with a thick layer of dust. She barely knew where to begin. Was this what she sought? This treasure?

The first box she opened was shallow and long and in it she found a dagger to match the sword. As she closed the lid she thought to keep it with her—she could hide it under her skirt and no one would know... In other boxes she found men's clothing, a purple pendant with a crack in it, a fine black cloak lined with plum satin; tall, black riding boots. Everything was folded and placed within the box with great care, was well preserved and there was a faint scent of what she then realized was dried roses and evergreen.

The largest box Gellia left for last, and upon lifting the huge lid she found a magnificent black bow and matching quiver equipped with dozens of arrows (her heart leapt for joy at the idea of a new bow) and a great deal of unidentifiable black cloth. In a very tiny pouch on top of the pile she found a ring made from silver and some sort of purple jewel that had been cut into the shape of a rose. It had writing on it she couldn't read. She slipped it on her finger and watched the light dance through the rose's facets for a few moments.

She turned to the books on the wall and chose one at random. Gellia was careful to handle them, afraid they would fall apart but they seemed perfectly preserved. They were in another language, but they did have beautifully drawn pictures inside. Castles, maps of different lands and the stars, and a vast array of dragons were drawn on the old pages, many with labels. She started to feel overwhelmed.

"Who were you?" she asked.

She looked through every book she touched. Every so often she found a pressed flower between pages, many varieties she'd never seen before. The light slowly dimmed in the room. Gellia replaced the last book she handled and left for the night. Her mind was busy with plans to return, and even wondered if she could sneak there during the night. Servants always talked, though.

She crept through the narrow space and rearranged the tapestry to hide the door once again. Not that anyone else frequented the library, but one could never be too careful.

"There you are."

Gellia was sure she'd jumped out of her skin, but luckily it was merely the stable boy, Currain. "Oh, it's you," she said. "What are you doing here?" She was certain she'd locked the library door.

"I should have known you'd be here."

"Where else would I be?" She arranged books on the shelves and tried to look bored. She was still a little rattled. "You'll probably be whipped for skipping your duties."

He chuckled. "I doubt that—I'm not an old cart horse." He walked to the window and stared out at the stable yard. "You must like the view."

As she tried to focus on him to avoid thinking about her discovery, she found she rather liked his appearance. He wasn't exactly handsome, but his brown eyes were kind and his dark hair looked recently washed yet seemed a bit wild. He was long and lean and appeared to be athletic; his hands were clean but his nails were dirty. Furthermore, his plain clothing was a neat as a pin, far too spotless for someone who worked in the stable. "You must be the son of someone special to avoid being whipped when you certainly shirk your duties." Gellia tried to gauge his reaction to her words, but his face was expressionless.

"Oh, no one would dare whip me," Currain answered. He turned around to face her, his eyes were soft and lively. "You know, the two of us should go for a ride one day. I could be your escort, and we could gallivant over these fields without a care in the world."

She laughed, but her heart shouted, yes! In fact, she'd love to go for a ride with him. Where the desire came from she had no idea. "You ride?" she asked.

"I suppose you could call it that," he said with a smile.

She giggled. "Sometimes I can escape, sometimes I can't, so we'll have to see. I don't think the king would approve of me fraternizing with a stable hand."

"I could go in disguise. I'm very good at being in disguise," he said with a wink.

Gellia smirked. "I'm sure."

He smiled. "You'd be surprised. And I'd be wonderful company for an exceptional princess."

"A complement! Imagine. And from someone who isn't a suitor." She received enough sarcasm from the others and had to hold her tongue, but to this one she could return the favor.

"I was being truthful." His smile remained in his eyes. "You should get back to your room, the others will be back shortly. You're supposed to be sick, aren't you?"

"My, how the servants gossip." But in agreement with him, she started for the door. Her mood was still light. "You should be going to if you don't want to be beaten," she said with a smile.

"Beaten, no, but I will be missed."

Gellia hurried towards her room, but then decided to peek at her stallion before the others returned. The guards would announce the hunting party's return and give her time to escape. Yes, the servants might talk, but they generally didn't to nobles, just to each other, and her sneaking about wasn't anything new.

The stalls were clean, buckets and mangers filled for the returning party. It was still light enough to see with the big door on the end of the aisle open. Gellia snuck to Tempest's stall where he napped with his head in the far corner. She didn't disturb him, but leaned on the door and watched for a little while and laughed silently at his drooping lip as he slept as many horses did. Another stablemate a few stalls away snorted and Tempest swiveled an ear slightly to listen.

She went to look at Nighthawk and see why he had been brought back. He seemed fit from a distance as he poked his head out towards her and nickered. She grinned at him. "Hello you," she said from down the row of stalls. Nighthawk suddenly pinned his hears flat against his head and his eyes were rimmed with white, he jerked his head and made a roaring sound she'd never heard come from a healthy horse. Against her better judgment concerning dangerous animals, Gellia continued towards him. "What's wrong?" He started to pound at his door. She froze.

Someone grabbed her arm. When she turned, she saw a stranger, not the stable hand she was expecting. In fact, he looked foreign.

"Unhand me," Gellia demanded. She felt her blood rush, and something else, something deep within her started to burn and feel that it would burst within her.

He blathered at her and looked frustrated as he tugged her down the aisle. Who was he? Where did he come from? He was unusual, had blonde curls and azure eyes like a prince in a ballad, but for the fact he might be trying to kidnap her. It seemed ridiculous, but she doubted he was leading her to a pageant in her honor.

"Let go of me," the princess shouted. She tried to throw her weight into her attempt at freedom. He spoke to her in a hushed, anxious voice and glanced around.

Down the corridor Nighthawk pounded at his stall door, pieces of wood skidded across the floor. It was a terrible racket. His coarse, loud whinny echoed through the stone aisles of the stable. The brigand dragged her as far as the tack room where Gellia grabbed onto the door with her free hand and held on for dear life. He turned and seemed to scold her, and for that she spat in his face and surprised herself that she did. He continued to babble at her.

"Let me go!" Gellia said. Where were the guards? The stable attendants? He turned to drag her with both hands as she braced herself against the timbers of the tack room. Both of them were equally startled when a dagger sank into the wood of the door as if to break their gaze. It was just a hair's breadth from the man's nose. Her captor's face grew pale and the two of them stared at the dagger between them for a split second before he dropped Gellia's arm and fled. The princess spun to look down the aisle and glimpsed a shadow.

Nighthawk crashed through the remains of the door, snorted and clattered out of the stable; seconds later the chestnut horse trotted up the aisle, his eyes rolling and his nostrils flared, his coat drenched. Gellia quickly caught up the chestnut's reins and led him to his stall. Once he was safely secured she scrambled back down to the tack room and pulled at the dagger. It was her only option if she wanted a weapon. Of course, it would help if she could actually free it. Cassius strode through the door by the tack room in a swirl of black cloak and asked in a calm, business-like manner, "Are you all right?"

She nodded. Gellia let go of the dagger and allowed Cassius to dislodge it. She kept still as the baron strode into the main corridor and looked around. Nighthawk trotted back through the end of the stable, over the shattered door and into his stall.

"Is he trained to do that?" she asked quietly.

"His training still lacks," he muttered. "Are you injured?"

"It's just a bruise, I think."

Cassius had saved her. No one else came to her aid, even with all the noise. Why did he choose to do so? What would he acquire by doing so? He glanced here and there, and if she didn't know better, she would have thought he was communicating with the shadows. It was the look in his eyes, like he saw something familiar. All the excitement must have addled her mind.

The guards appeared, finally. Cassius dismissed them and muttered something about their incompetence. "Where is everyone else?" she asked.

"Still out in the field. It seems that this horse," he motioned to the chestnut horse he'd been given to ride, "isn't as fit as they said he was."

Luckily for her fate was on her side. Long moments passed as they regarded each other. Then it dawned on Gellia that her gown was the one he gave her and was embarrassed, and she was sure he saw the ring. She rubbed her arm again and was certain he smirked as she looked down the corridor. "Whoever that was, I want him dead," the princess said. Her words surprised her.

"Dead or would you information tortured from his hide?" he asked.

"Dead. I don't like loose ends. I would take care of it myself if I knew how to make sure it was done." A strange sensation was still within her and some undiscovered energy coursed through her. She did her best to push it away. It was not the same as a near fall off a horse or the burst of nerves when the king approached. No, it was far stronger.

He cocked his head ever so slightly. "Shall I teach you?"

She couldn't respond—her voice wouldn't come to say yes or to say something ridiculous. She sensed the question was for him, not for her.

"You weren't frightened?" he asked.

"No, I wanted to defend myself. Why am I telling you this? I must go." With a rustle of lavender silk she fled the stable, despite trying to make it seem she was storming away. He was on her heels.

"Consider it done." Cassius stopped in the stable yard and watched her. She turned to him and something made her shiver. The night was nearly upon them, the sun was gone. Her mouth refused to open so Gellia stared silently. Corrah came up behind her with a shawl and spoke, but Gellia ignored her. There was something about Cassius, that something he hid from the others, that something they couldn't see, but for the moment she could see it plain as day, but didn't know what it was.

"You need to disappear before he finds you," Cassius said.

She felt another chill, and her mind asked him a resounding: who? The obvious answer was the king, or perhaps her assailant, but she felt that's not to whom he referred. Corrah led her into the dim castle. The riders trotted through the gate, their excited shouts almost drowned out the hoof beats on the cobblestone.

"Baron, I heard there was an intruder," the king called as the party entered.

"Yes," the baron said.

"I'll send—"

"Allow me to take care of this, your majesty," the Xzepheniixenze said. "I have people who can make quick work of a would-be kidnapper."

"Very well.... all guards on duty at the time will be punished for not doing their obligation," he blustered. He heaved himself from his exhausted horse. "I'll not have people thinking they can run off with that girl for free, although it might be easier for me than marrying her off." Several people chuckled.

Cassius listened to the king ramble on about the state of the nation and his claims of the intruder being someone from Sen

Dunea. The baron didn't correct him. King Hugh was sure that Gellia would have run away with this person if it hadn't been for Cassius. As they started for the door Cassius looked at the narrow windows by the library and noticed the curtains had indeed been opened. It seemed fate had finally picked up the pace. Night took the castle.

***

The king had asked again for Cassius' council, and being a courteous guest Cassius complied. In fact, Cassius had become one of Hugh's favorite advisors. It was his charisma, really, that the king couldn't resist. They sat in the king's chambers while Hugh complained. Cassius poured his highness another cup of wine. "What do you suggest I do about Sen Dunea?" the king asked. "They're planning something, I just know it." He drained the cup.

"If they are, you will undoubtedly outsmart them and destroy them as you have so many other enemies," Cassius said as he filled the king's cup once more.

"Ah, you're right," Hugh said with a laugh. "Those fools wouldn't dare cross the border of the mighty King Hugh."

"It would be pure madness, I suspect," Cassius said. "But there is something to be said for being prepared."

Hugh waved his hand. "Bah. They're always ready for a fight. Just like that princess. So much fight in her." He gulped down a few mouthfuls. "I really should have her beaten more often. You can see the fire, can't you? That fire she has even when she's trying to be meek? She's a hellion, I tell you, and everyone knows it."

"Some women you can only beat for so long before they strike back," Cassius said.

"She's more likely to run off like her mother than strike back, my friend."

Cassius filled Hugh's cup again. "That would only happen if she's properly motivated, which obviously hasn't happened yet."

"I need to find someone to marry her," Hugh said, becoming distant for a few moments. "Don't know who, though. Don't know who."

"Someone foolish, I would think."

Hugh nodded. "He would have to be to marry her! Even with the promise of a throne!" He bellowed with laughter.

Cassius smirked. "Fools are easier to control," he said. "As I'm sure your highness knows first-hand. You could have your kingdom exactly as you want to keep it."

The king nodded again, still chuckling to himself. "And you should marry into the family, as well. It would be an alliance of our lands."

Cassius might have twitched a little, but it was difficult to tell. "Like a knight to the quest, I'm married to my land and nothing else."

"Too bad. A man like you, you deserve a good wife." He emptied his cup again, and it was immediately refilled.

Cassius shook his head. "No, I don't think it's what I need. I have plans that need to be moved to their next stage, and that's the most important."

"Don't we all? Hahaha!"

He didn't answer, just gave a tight-lipped smile and cock of his head.

"Oh-ho, friend, what of this knave who tried to have his way with Gellia? Will he be found? Do I need to put a bounty out? I'm certain he's from Sen Dunea."

"Not from Sen Dunea, no. And no bounty will be needed. I will tend to this. You needn't worry about it at all."

"That's good, that's good." Even as much as he could withstand alcohol, the king was starting to succumb to its power. He watched blurrily as Cassius poured a very full cup for him. He started to drink once more and spilled some down his chin. The baron rose gracefully from his chair like a dark pillar of death. The king shivered and spilled more.

"Goodnight, your highness," Cassius said. He turned and left.

***

On the next morn, a group of unusual riders arrived.
Gellia, who was in the stable at the time, let her curiosity get the
best of her and walked to the door to investigate.

There were four of them, all on sleek ebony horses and
dressed in smoky greys and black. All metal they carried—bits,
buckles, stirrups—were black. All of them looked similar to
Cassius with longish raven hair, but were of slighter build, and
looked authoritative despite their youthful good looks. Some of
the stable boys nervously tried to hold the horses for them but the
horses kept their heads from the boys' reach. The strange men
ignored the few braver Fuarmaanians who tried to approach, but
they did seem to take notice of Gellia despite her efforts to stay
in the shadows. She watched their eyes as they so calmly waited.
Indeed, they scanned their surroundings and paused often to look
at her.

Only when Cassius arrived did they prove they had
voices. Gellia watched him talk with them in melodious tones of
what had to be his native tongue. She wished she could listen to
that sound forever. She noticed then their grace, much like their
lord, but Cassius was still much more refined. As servants and
guards and even some of the nobles passed by she realized just
how awkward they all moved compared to these
Xzepheniixenze. The riders said little—they responded mostly
with nods and looks—within moments they rode out the gate.

"You will have your revenge," Cassius said to Gellia as
he watched the group ride away.

She felt there was a dark absoluteness in his voice, and it
left her feeling unsettled. It was then she realized the unease she
felt in the past wasn't directly caused by him, for the fear of his
statement was much more the normal type of fear. He was not
one to be trifled with. Soon enough he was lost amongst his
admirers, all flooding him with questions about the mysterious
riders.

Gellia had taken some of the books from the secret room
to study and planned to ride to her clearing in the forest. If she
moved quickly enough she could escape in the commotion.
Being on her own with her new treasures was worth the risk.
It was just as Gellia was out the gate that the king made his
appearance. He'd missed the excitement he was intending to see,

but he didn't miss Gellia's escape. "Where is she going by herself? Damn her. She's just like her mother. Not even a day after we were invaded." The king's face turned two shades brighter red and the folds of abundant flesh quivered with rage. "Likely going to run off with…"

"I beg your pardon, your highness, but I was going with her," the baron said. The girls around him didn't hide their disappointment. Nighthawk came from the stable, saddled and ready.

The king nodded. "Tell her that she'd better learn some manners soon. I've written to someone who can likely break her of her disobedience." He guzzled wine from the cup in his hand. "Perhaps when she's no longer my problem you can have your alliance."

Without offering further recognition to the king, Cassius mounted up and was gone.

***

Tempest munched grass along the trees while Gellia looked through one of the musty volumes in the sunlight. Partially hidden in a patch long grass, she lie on her stomach and twirled a lock of hair round her finger. On the pages before her was what seemed to be plans for their castle—it had many similarities—although now the castle was rather pitiful and this one was grand even if it wasn't large. She once more thought that the castle truly must have been glorious when it was first built, but that was a very long time ago.

Tempest nickered and raised his head a little, but quickly buried it in the long, autumn-aged grasses again. Whatever it was that he thought he noticed wasn't that important to them if he paid it so little attention. She smiled and continued to study the book.

She'd often thought of inviting Cresslyn with her to the clearing, but even Cresslyn thought she needed a man ever-present. Not that Cresslyn would leave Alexandria's side. But who needed them and their silly chatter?

"...I always knew I wouldn't sit on my father's throne..."

Gellia jumped at the voice. She stumbled to her feet and backed away from the intruder to her clearing kingdom. Once she saw it was Cassius she sighed with relief as well as annoyance.

"...the Azqebryne have taken the throne and will likely do a better job than I ever could." Cassius picked up the book and turned the page, shaking his head. "He'll never understand why I chose to leave my homeland behind, but it's a safer place, safe from my uncle and far away from that life…" He smiled a little, but his eyes did not.

"What are you talking about?" she snapped.

"It's what you were reading," he replied.

"That's what's written?"

"Yes," He looked at the book's cover then leafed through some of the pages.

"You're able to read it?"

"Of course." He didn't take his nose out of the book to speak to her. "It's ancient Xzepheniixenze, the eastern dialect. Although there are certainly some Zephronian words mixed in."

"Truly?" Why were Xzepheniixenze books in her library?

"What reason would I have to lie?" He chuckled.

Gellia noticed the black stallion stood patiently by the tree line, swished flies with his thick tail as the autumn leaves fell around him. His approach must have been what Tempest reacted to. If he could teach her the language she could read so many wonderful things. How was it that he came by knowledge of the ancient languages? She couldn't imagine such a scholar could be so young. "How old are you?" she blurted. Had he studied his whole life? What a wonderful past it must have been. She couldn't imagine even learning one other language, especially not in this ignorant kingdom.

He laughed.

"Tell me."

"What do you think?"

"Five and thirty."

He laughed again.

"I wouldn't have taken you to be a scholar," she said. He was only ten or so years her senior. Oh to be a man! What knowledge she could have! All the studying in faraway places she could do. So much of her life was already wasted while he was reading everything he could find.

Cassius raised an eyebrow and smirked at her, she felt there was some joke that she didn't understand. He could keep it to himself for all she cared. She didn't want his humor, she wanted his knowledge. "Sometimes knowledge just comes to you."

"Will you teach me Xzepheniixenze?" Gellia said, feeling rather bold.

He didn't seem surprised. "If you wish."

"Yes, I do. You shall teach me so I can read this book on my own."

"I will teach you *anything* you want to know." He continued to smile.

"Good..." She thought of her secret room and all its contents. "Well then, will you teach me how to use weapons?" For this she didn't expect a yes. It was ludicrous to try and teach a female how to fight (not to mention her father would never consent to it) but what did she have to lose? He did say he would teach her anything she wanted to know.

"What weapons do you wish to learn?" Cassius asked. "I know you are quite skilled in archery."

"Sword?"

"Then I will teach you. Bring your sword next we meet and we'll begin."

Gellia wondered why he was so agreeable. He looked thoroughly amused but as usual, but there was something else behind his eyes that made her uneasy. "Well. Well, what do you wish in return for my schooling?"

He thought for a moment. "A favorable thought now and then would be nice." He cocked his head only slightly. "Perhaps a smile, too. You do know how; you smile enough at your horse..."

He was teasing her! "You aren't a big oaf like he is."

"Is that a complement?" He started to walk towards his own horse.

"You miserable lout." Only part of her was joking.

"She is fickle. Your first lesson will begin when I return," said he.

"When you return?" Gellia tucked the book under her arm and hurried towards Tempest. "Where are you going?"

"I have business to attend to elsewhere." He swung onto Nighthawk and took up the reins.

She found she was more excited than angry, but had to give him a hard time all the same. "Don't you leave without teaching me you pirate. Oh, I understand. You have to go find little baubles for all the girls in your harem." She mounted up as well, although not as gracefully as he.

"Harem?" Cassius gave her a look. "Revolting," he muttered, but she didn't hear him.

Gellia guided Tempest to Nighthawk, who eyed her and twitched his ears. "Yes. Women would do just about anything to capture a husband. Except for me of course." Without thinking, she was smiling.

"Oh, of course. That only makes sense." He nodded. She noticed delicate silver chains shimmer through his hair when his head moved. She spent so much time to avoid his gaze that she never noticed before. Some of them had tiny jewels attached, in the sun they sparkled.

"When will you return?" The two horses walked through the path in the trees.

"Soon."

"I'm tired of you teasing me."

He eyed the buckle on his reins and frowned at what she was sure was the dirt the stable boys missed when they 'cleaned' it. "You certainly need an outlet for your energy," he said, "it comes from doing what is in our nature to do… I shouldn't be long." He chuckled. "Not long at all, in fact. I need to be back before this kingdom is taken from under your king's nose."

"What do you mean?" She urged Tempest to keep up with Nighthawk's longer stride.

"I see the princess pays little attention, but that is not her fault, and who in this kingdom would listen to her when she is so strange and a female besides?"

Gellia glared at him.

"The king has lost his competence. But it is not time for Fuarmaania to be conquered. Not yet."

"What on earth does that mean?"

"War, dear princess. War. But a small one, and likely settled quickly."

"Won't you tell me more?"

"At this juncture? No, but you'll be there to see it unfold." He was wearing his usual smirk, clearly amused by something.

Gellia made herself be patient, for there would be no other choice. It would be a difficult wait.

Nearly as soon as the kingdom's favorite baron rode from the gates the king's malice returned to its usual level. Gellia's only salvation was a new courtesan who was a wonderful distraction for the king. The princess had a feeling from where the woman came and why, but it seemed too foolish a thought to say aloud. So Gellia did her best to stay out of the way as much as possible, and often wondered if she could or should try to write to Cassius. Part of her said he was never coming back. But that couldn't be true, could it?

Many of the days she spent in the library and the secret room. I might finally have answers, Aunt Charlotte, she thought. I don't know how, or to what end, but I feel some answers are near. I just have to be brave enough to seek them out.

3

It had been far too long since Cassius left, and Gellia's life had deteriorated. However, it didn't bother Gellia that the rain kept her from her ride. The bruises from that morning's beating didn't disturb her as she gazed at the shimmer of polished steel. Gellia traced her fingers down the leather scabbard of the sword and let her mind tell her that this blade was alive somehow with some ancient spirit. Maybe it was only her imagination, but it seemed come to life under her fingertips. Then there was the armor—how many battles had it seen? How many charging horses, waving banners, flailing weapons? It had very few scratches on it; maybe it hadn't seen a single battle, but she knew next to nothing about battles.

The secret room was a good place to stay when avoiding everyone after her regular humiliations. She'd almost forgotten how difficult it was with the king. After Cassius' departure she was again trapped in an ever-shrinking world. The king was less distracted, more often deep in the drink, and angrier about her marital status. There had been another suitor, but he took one look at Gellia and decided the curse was real, that the barely-contained spirit in the princess would be his undoing. Not that she wanted to marry him, but it was still embarrassing she was so undesirable.

A horse whinnied down below and brought her from her thoughts. Horses always whinnied to each other—it called again. Was it Tempest? It sounded like him.

Gellia went to the window. No one was in the stable yard. No one came through the gate or rode through the entrance. Everything was wet from the rains. She tucked a stray wisp of black hair behind her ear. A drop of water fell on the lavender sleeve, changed it darker; she watched the color change. It was a day like this that Cassius first arrived, she thought. It was that time of year again. After a moment of spinning the rose ring on her finger she turned back towards the room. She took another book, sat on the floor and leafed through it. There were so many she still needed to look at. So many had beautiful art and interesting drawings. She wanted to read them so badly it nearly broke her heart.

There was a small book tucked in under some others, this she pulled out next. From the moment she put her hands on it she felt it was a treasure. It was small enough to fit in a pocket, its cover was velvet fitted with silver and tiny jewels. Upon opening it she found it was very carefully written in silver ink and even though she had no idea what it said she felt it speak to her. In the final pages was pressed flower that could barely be fit between the pages. It was a beautiful shade of purple, its color still true. Under it was writing, and for once she understood what it said: *Young one, when the time is right, someone will come to give you the knowledge to take your rightful place.* Gellia closed it and put it in her pocket.

It was a trick to return to her chambers without event; she had to avoid as many people as she could, she didn't even trust the servants. She felt like a thief the way she had to skulk through the castle. The king had been especially vexed by relations with Sen Dunea, and once again she was his favorite outlet for his anger. She thought it would be reasonable for her to be married to one of the Sen Dunean princes as an alliance, but apparently the king would rather die than allow someone from Sen Dunea sit on "his" throne. Gellia didn't think it would be any worse than any other option.

With an unladylike rush she traveled from the library to the gallery, the chapel (with a pause at her mother's portrait), cut through the kitchens to the final stretch of narrow gallery to her room. As usual, Corrah worked by the fireplace. "Corrah," she said.

"There you are, milady," the woman greeted, but didn't take her head out of the fireplace.

"Corrah, you must tell me about my mother, please."

Corrah shuffled stiffly to a chair and sat for a moment. Gellia sat in the chair opposite her lifelong nurse, hoping she would finally speak. "Milady, you know your father has forbidden anyone to talk about her."

"I know, but I must know who she was. Please, Corrah."

"Very well. But I don't know who'll be listening through these walls." Corrah paused. "I came to your mother before she birthed. She was very sad. She read a lot like yourself—always reading and dreaming of other things and keeping to herself. Some of the ladies here no doubt still remember her as well, although most left the castle years ago… Your mother had you, and soon after bade me to take care of you." Corrah was uneasy, took a deep breath. "You're a woman now, so I suppose it's time. Now I'll tell you something you cannot tell anyone else, promise? It could be the death of me. She told me she would ride off and never come back. She said someone would come for her and the child and had to escape. I didn't believe her, I thought she was just in a fit of nerves from too much reading. But sure enough she was on her horse and gone."

"But Tempest's dam was left here."

"Not her. She had this other horse she rode, that's the one she took. He was wild as they came and most feared him. They say she ran off with the Gypsies or was killed by that horse. No one really knows. But I took care of you like my own and raised you the best I could and you've turned out to be more of a beauty than your mother and twice as wild."

Her mother left Gellia to face some strange and likely imagined horror, left her with Hugh. She realized that she always wished her mother would come back for her, that Queen Bernadette stayed with friends someplace and waited for the right moment to return. That perhaps when she ran away she couldn't take a baby with her and had to linger until Gellia grew up. But if something would supposedly happen to Gellia, why was she left behind? She started to wonder if madness really did run in the family. Perhaps her mother's insanity aided in how others felt about Gellia. "What of my father—my blood father?" Corrah shook her head. "I know nothing of him. Nor would I say anything if I did. His majesty is your father."

Gellia sighed.

"I don't know what I did wrong to make you such an unruly child, but that's how it turned out. I still care for you like my own, but I wish you'd just settle down with the baron—I think he'd take care of you and he seems to tolerate your behavior—if he'll still have you. Once you have children you'll find you'll feel better." Corrah sighed and hefted herself from the chair to waddle from the room.

***

Gellia looked out the window at the stormy sky. It worried her that she would have to attend dinner that evening; it was unwise to face the king while her mind whirled. A vision took her. She felt as though she traveled through the rain, then the rain stopped. It was dark and she was running through a garden, then a forest. She was chasing something. Her feet were bare and she was in her bedclothes. A light ahead of her moved between the giant twisted trees, and dozens of tiny lights floated around her. What was it she saw? It was silver and light, a barely recognizable shape that seemed to lead her. But to where? Why was she following it? Where was she?

When Gellia came to her senses it was indeed dark, and Corrah had just entered to tell her she was late for dinner. Gellia nodded and thankfully Corrah left, for Gellia couldn't hold back her tears. "I'm mad, I'm mad," she sobbed. "No one else is plagued by these visions. They seems so real. Why? Why?" She gave herself a moment more to cry before calming again and wiping her face. It was the first time she thought about falling from her window. Perhaps that would be a better option than all the others.

***

Gellia watched the rain. It had been days since she'd left her room, nor had anyone come in. It was her father's orders. Every so often the king decided to try starvation to improve her somehow. Guards stood at her door and no one was allowed in or out, even Corrah. Dark and cold, no fire in the fireplace, no firewood to build a fire. The only thing in the room was the single rose Cassius gave her. It still hadn't bloomed, and looked as fresh as the day he gave it to her. "You're as stubborn as I am," she said to it.

In her weakened state she allowed herself to imagine fanciful scenarios. It kept her amused for the time, anyway. With all her new treasures she would tame a dragon and it would lay waste to the countryside. A dragon with a heart black as night to spew forth an inferno to burn everything in its path and she would rule the world. But she would not rule without mercy. Once conquered, she would nurture her people and the land would flourish. Her people. Heaven help those who opposed her. She dreamt all this, and her fabulous castle by the ocean: how beautiful it was. "Soon" wasn't soon enough. She cursed herself and cursed Fuarmaania.

***

"You're lucky your father's nice enough to forgive you for such disobedience," Corrah said as Gellia chewed her bread. They were in the kitchen and Gellia sat at one of the big work tables that was covered with breads, tarts, and pies.

"He lets me live because of superstition." She ignored the other servants who worked around her in the hot kitchen. What specific disobedience she'd been punished for she had no idea. It was likely just because she was Gellia.

"You shouldn't say that, milady."

"I don't care if he's the king, I'll say what I want. I'm going." The princess finished her water and left the room.
She went to the secret room straightaway. If she appeared in public she would have to face the stares and whispers, and she'd done her best to avoid everyone as she made her way through the castle. She'd found the biggest saddle bags she could and planned to stuff them. Good thing she was sturdier than many other women.

Everything was as Gellia left it, it wasn't even damp from the rain outside. She dropped the saddlebags next to door. Perhaps she couldn't pull this feat off in this weather, but there would be a sunnier day soon, she was sure of it. No, it was miserable and rainy, but some of the girls still talked and giggled outside.

She rested her hands on the hilt of the fabulous sword for a moment before she lifted it from the gauntlets for the first time and placed it aside. Next she hefted the scale mail suit off its stand and wrestled it into the saddlebags; gauntlets, boots and cloak followed. It was not an easy fit. By the time everything but the weapons were packed, the rain ceased and she heard the foolish girls very clearly. The sun warmed and brightened the dark library as it snuck in through the window. Why were they being so loud? She wiped her forehead and sighed.

From below came a voice that reached straight to her soul, goose bumps spread over her in a wave. She pressed her face to the narrow window but saw nothing but glimpses of dull wool dresses and stone. The narrow doorway was uncooperative when Gellia tried to force her way through, but she hesitated as she neared the large window in the library.

He was there. Cassius was there with his admirers; he handed out trinkets from his home. Cresslyn held the bridle of a beautiful horse the color of a new gold coin and a mane of snowy white. Nighthawk stood patently nearby while everyone babbled to his master and the king shouted above everyone else. "...wonderful! I miss riding with you... that's what we'll do tomorrow: a grand ride! Your horse must be tired," he said over whatever it was that the baron tried to say. "You can take that horse of Gellia's, and she can stay home. He's old but still fit. Come on you lot, get back inside! Get the drink started!"

Their baron watched them go as the stable boys took care of Cresslyn's new horse. Nighthawk snorted. "I agree," Cassius replied. "No, that's all right, I'll take care of him," the baron told the stable boys.

When the baron led Nighthawk into the stable he found the boys had bedded down his usual stall with their finest straw. The boys filled the water bucket and the manger as the baron removed all his tack and began to brush the sleek raven coat. "What do you think, o' horse of mine?" Cassius asked as he finger-combed the thick tail. "Shall we give her a little longer? Here she is..." Cassius turned towards the stall door and smiled at Gellia. Her hair was wild, dress dirty and shoes covered with mud from coming across the stable yard. She immediately started to smooth her dress and adjust her hair when she saw him.

"I was starting to think you weren't coming back," she said.

"Good to see you as well, princess. What did they do to you?"

"What? What do you mean?"

"You look gaunt as an old beggar. Have they locked you away to starve?" Cassius' words almost sounded like a jest but his face showed that he was very serious. When she was hesitant to answer he spoke again. "No matter. I've brought you something."

"Oh?" she said.

Cassius dropped the brush into its bag then sorted through a different saddlebag. When he straightened himself, whatever it was he had concealed in his hand. He walked out into the aisle behind her; she saw a necklace lowered over her head and heard the clasp click behind her neck. It was cold and heavy. Not once in the process did he touch her. She did her best to ignore his presence as she lifted the pendent in her hand. Large diamonds and onyx surrounded seven ovals of amethyst, stones so pure they caught the dim light of the stable and sparkled wonderfully. "You always give me purple." She would have to hide it from the king. No doubt he would take it to keep for himself or give to one of his mistresses. She'd seen nothing finer.

"It suits you. It's your favorite color, is it not?"

Just like that, he was back into her life as if he'd never left. Part of her was angry he didn't take her with him, but that was a foolish idea. "You are insufferable, Cassius," she said, but not harshly. How could she ever wear this? She couldn't. Not anywhere anyone could see her. She turned a jewel back and forth.

"Pardon?"

"I said you're insufferable."

"I'm glad I didn't disappoint you by being pleasant. They haven't been treating you too badly, have they?"

"I'm well enough."

"Improve your art if you plan to make a career of lying."

"If you already know I'm unwell, why do you ask?"

"To see what you'll say," he said. "Someday you'll stop pretending that everything is as normal as it can be, and admit to yourself how it truly should be." He picked up his saddlebags to take them to the tack room. When he came back out she was gone.

***

Gellia crawled out of bed when she was sure the riding party was long gone. It was only then she rose and put on her satin gown—the only one full enough to do what she planned.

Once in the secret room Gellia tightly bound the beautiful sword to her leg under the dress and pulled the heavy saddlebags through the door, which was no easy feat. No one was around to see her drag the bulky leather sacks down to the stable. Servants always disappeared when the courtiers were on a ride. The sword was a bit too long and created a tent at the top of her skirt like her hip joint was broken. She would have to keep that side of her to the wall.

"Hallo, Nighthawk," the princess greeted cheerily. The stallion arched his graceful neck over the stall door and nuzzled her with his velvety muzzle. "Since your master took my horse I'm going to take you. I will be going out today. I'll be right back." She fetched Nighthawk's black leather tack and started to piece it together over his dark hide. She couldn't believe how finely crafted it was. Great care was taken with its maintenance as well—not a stitch rotted out, no dust under the flaps, no cracks in the well-conditioned leather. That would change now that he returned—the castle stable boys weren't that thorough and it was unlikely Cassius would clean his own tack.

How she found the strength to heft the saddle onto him she had no idea, but the bridle was easy. Nighthawk saw her approach with it and put his head down so she could pull the bridle over his ears. "What a wonderful horse you are," she said, "but now I have to put these miserable heavy things on you."

As she struggled with the saddlebags she continued to talk to him. "I suppose you might have carried something like this before but maybe not. I think Cassius is too much of a dandy to have ever seen a battle, but I suppose by the looks of him he's not a weakling either—perhaps even stronger than our knights." Nighthawk curled his lip. "We're ready," she told him. Somehow, perhaps with pure determination, she'd done what she set out to do.

She led him through the corridor and into the yard. It would be the first time she needed the mounting block to climb on a horse. Her bound leg wasn't cooperative. Once she struggled into the saddle she realized with dismay that the stirrups were far too long. "Details, details," she muttered and struggled with the stirrup leathers until they were short enough to tolerate. Nighthawk waited patiently as she slid and leaned all over his back. She ignored the few passing servants. "Let's go shall we?"

Gellia picked up the reins in trembling hands and squeezed him with her calves. It was a long fall if he dumped her. When he started to walk she wondered if this was such a good idea. In a few smooth strides they were out the gate into the open. His black ears pricked forward.

"Please, please don't run away with me," she whispered. He was so tall, so powerful. Gellia contemplated if she could handle such a mount. With one hand wrapped in black mane they began to trot. It was like they floated on air, it wasn't the trot of old Tempest. Nighthawk jigged a little, and with a squeak of fear Gellia grabbed up more of his mane. For his size and strength he was a well-trained mount, and she was starting to trust him, and trust her ability to ride him. She asked him to canter. Oh what bliss. His strides were as long and graceful as she could have imagined. His rocking gate made her smile. With a deep breath she put her legs against him and they were off like the wind.

His hooves thundered beneath Gellia as they galloped through the fields. She leaned across his neck and didn't pay much attention to where they went as long as they went. The landscape was a blur, and he easily leapt any hedge or fence in their path. Carry me away, Nighthawk, she thought. What an appropriate name. She felt him change direction, veer this way or that several times—she only watched the ground speed by below them, trusted him to carry her safely across the land. She trusted him more than she did old Tempest.

The stallion pranced to a graceful stop but she wasn't sure why at first. The princess lifted her head and looked around to find they were in her forest clearing. She slid from the saddle and let herself tumble onto the ground in a pile of lavender fabric. "Nighthawk, you are the most fabulous horse alive." She was breathless but not just from the ride. There was something that made her heart race that fluttered inside her.

Nighthawk looked back at her and sneezed. Gellia gathered herself and struggled to her feet. She untied the sword from her leg and placed it on the saddle blanket on the ground. He stayed near, waiting for her command. He was so beautiful. "He would never give you to me, would he? I would like you better than jewelry."

After she was satisfied he wouldn't run, she shed the gown and started to pull the equipment out of the bags. Gellia had to untangle it before she could even think of figuring out how to put it all on. That was another adventure all together. Her trusty steed rested nearby, watched her some of the time, as she wrestled with and somehow put on the armor. She could understand why her father's men didn't wear it. The scales seemed more for show than protection, and the chain underneath would be far more effective. Not that she knew much about such things.

For once she was happy she was taller than average, for the mail tunic fit her fairly well and she was quite proud of herself for putting it all on successfully. She strapped the sword to her hip and put the dagger in her belt and she was ready. There wasn't much else for her to do but swagger around the clearing and work on drawing and sheathing her sword. Wearing the armor and her often clumsy sword "wielding" was enough to tire her. The day went by quickly as she wore herself out, and it was time to return.

Nighthawk and Gellia cantered back through the castle gates and she looked at the people in the stable yard. The hunting party had returned early. Blood rushed to her face and her heart pounded with fear. It was unbearably quiet as everyone stared at her. If she were to run they could never catch her, not while riding Nighthawk. Under her the stallion gathered himself in anticipation, his weight shifted to his haunches, ready to pivot

and bolt. All she had to do was squeeze. She almost heard
another voice in her head. We can go. We can go now if you
wish. Her father stared at her, his face crimson.

"Did he give you any trouble?" Cassius called through
the silence.

"N-no," Gellia almost whispered.

"You gave her permission to ride your horse?" the king
asked while he glared at Gellia.

"Yes, in fact, I insisted she have him out today for a trot.
Thank you very much, princess, I do appreciate your help."

The princess cringed but her father's anger subsided like
magic, and he stumbled into the castle with his courtiers. She
remained atop Nighthawk until the yard was cleared and only she
and Cassius remained.

Cassius glanced at her and smiled. "They're gone." He
went into the stable.

She tried to maintain her dignity as she dismounted.
Luckily Nighthawk's right side faced his master so she could
hide behind his mass.

Cassius helped her untack and laughed when he lifted the
saddlebags. "What do you have in here? Scale mail? I suppose
you've got a sword hidden in your dress. Quality scale mail
unless I miss my guess—probably made centuries ago by a
master I think." He weighed the saddlebags in his hands.
"Gambeson, boots and fittings too, I would imagine."

Gellia was mortified and feared her treasures would be
revealed. She wasn't ready to share her secrets with anyone. Yet
she felt if she did, he would be the one. As she glanced at him a
voice in her head spoke. *You are the one.* The strange thought
made her blush but she managed to speak. "I, uh, well…"

He chuckled. "She's speechless, but I'm sure her mind is
a tangle of conflicts."

It wasn't helping that he could read her so easily. She
couldn't look at him, but he was still holding her saddle bags.
"That means you don't want to learn the language? Very well,"
he said.

Gellia shook her head and took a deep breath. "I have to
show you something—it's something I found and I want you to
tell me what it is or you can just teach me and I'll find out for

myself." She felt the book that was still in her pocket. "I have a place where we can meet, will you come with me and..."

"Teach you?"

"Yes."

"Certainly. If it would be easier for you, I will bring all your things for you."

"No. No, I'll bring them." She wasn't going to show him her secret room. There was only one reason why she needed him and that was because no one else would educate her in the way she needed. She repeated the mantra in her head. Only information, that was all.

"As you please... When shall we begin?" the baron asked.

"As soon as possible."

"Think it will get rid of me sooner?"

"Of course," Gellia said and he smiled at her as he always did. "What?"

He pushed his hair out of his face. "Nothing, nothing whatsoever."

"You know something and you won't tell me, will you?" she asked.

"All will be revealed in time."

***

Gellia found herself once more careening to the grass, and with new found humility knew it had been her mistake. She spit the grass out and raised herself up on her hands, then her knees and finally her feet. She ached all over, but was filled with a pride she'd never known before. Every time she'd fallen in her armor she found it easier and easier to rise again. She picked up her sword and faced Cassius again. Her mentor stood before her and waited patiently as she came back to him. "I know," she said with a nod, "my mistake."

Cassius raised an eyebrow and in Xzepheniixenze asked, "Did you say something?"

The princess sighed and repeated herself in Xzepheniixenze. "I said it was my fault. I was off balance." Gellia saw young men train before so she had some idea what to expect, but that was not how these sessions turned out. Cassius

ଛଠ77ଔଷ

taught her in a much different style than their arms master, and was every bit as strong as he looked. Despite his leisurely demeanor he was swift and agile.

"I've seen these foolish mistakes a thousand times before. It's enough to get you killed."

"You think I would actually see combat?" she asked with a laugh.

"Without a doubt."

That flutter in her stomach came once again, but this time the fear was also accompanied by excitement. It drowned out her aches and pains and made her feel warm all over.

Every morning they came together to her clearing in the forest and this was the place where she was continually amazed by his talents. Gellia's ways were as clumsy as a child, but she was determined to master this skill—no matter how many times she fell, or how much her hands hurt from the blows.

This was not a side of him she'd seen before. She thought she knew him from all the time he spent in Fuarmaania, but this was a different person, and she was too. Although she still felt he had a plot, she was part of it now. She'd never felt more alive. Over time her body became accustomed to the weight of the armor she wore. She reveled in her new strength, her new ability to at least lift and swing her sword even if she wasn't very adept yet.

Cassius had a sword very similar to her own. It had an alexandrite pommel like hers, but a green stone at its center, the hilt wings of a dragon, its body seemed to travel down the blade. Its tail wrapped around an iridescent handle and from its mouth spouted stylized flame down the blade that served as narrow, straight blood groove that widened at the end of the sword. Like hers, its artistic flourishes were dainty and elegant rather than bulky and overdone as her father's sword was.

She remembered when Percy taught her the bow, how he was so careful, and joked with her and stood by her, near her, and showed her the way. This was not the same with this man. Percy often took her hand to demonstrate how to hold the weapon and what not. Cassius never, ever put a hand on her. His distance comforted her.

Once again she initiated and the sound of metal hitting metal echoed through the trees. "That's better," Cassius said to her as he deflected her blows....

Once she dealt with her nervousness about him in the library, they read through many of the wonderful books—mostly on rainy days. Cassius seemed very interested in all the volumes in the dark old room. When it came to a companion in the library, he was far better than the impatient Cresslyn was. Many times when Gellia read to him from the journal-like manuscripts he smiled and laughed to himself. Never did he answer her when she asked what the joke was. Many were stories about Fuarmaania, the royal family and its history. It seemed that her mother's family was cursed with many misfortunes in its past which included the loss of their founding king who apparently was murdered by a powerful enemy.

Even though she read through many of these books, often Gellia was confused. The older the books, the ones from King Quenelzythe's time, were complicated and full of detail to the point it was difficult for her to understand. When she asked her teacher about it he told her she didn't have to learn them all so quickly. He also said there were indeed many, many books missing, and confirmed King Cedric had burned most of them, fearful of the information they contained. He said it was a miracle these books remained.

As the books grew younger and more numerous the language changed into the more familiar, and less about a tragic and brutal past. Gellia started to see the collapse of her family tree. The newest books were all foolish compared to the old, as the kingdom slowly deteriorated. Now she wondered of the significance of her feelings, how she'd always thought her kingdom had been better in the beginning. Nowadays information was conveyed by word of mouth, not on paper. It was a strange regression, that was for certain.

While she struggled to read through the old texts Cassius wandered through the library cleaned and rearranged the books to the point she didn't know where anything was. She tolerated it, and within a few months he had the entire library dusted and reorganized to his, and surprisingly her liking. He didn't find the secret door but did admire the tattered tapestry...

…Again she felt herself tumble and fall. The ground was still dewy. "Are you this brutal to all your students?" Gellia asked after she regained her breath.

"You need to remember to protect your legs. Take out your opponent's limbs and they'll be helpless. You are my only student," he said.

"Right now or ever?" she panted.

"Ever. I have never taken a student before you. At least, not one so formally and on my own. Nor do I expect to take on another."

"That explains it... My father wished that you would help him train the young men in the castle with the impending war."

"I know. I told him I am a peaceful person and that I would have no involvement in such a conflict."

"And they say I'm odd."

"Shall we rest?" Cassius asked as he looked down at her.

"I suppose—but I'm fine."

"Are you?"

She looked up into the eternity of blue sky. "You always ask me that. What is it? Don't you believe me?"

"You have never given me a reason why I should believe you. You do live here after all. It is a backwards place."

There wasn't anything she could say to that. She closed her eyes for a moment of much appreciated rest.

Xzepheniixenze had been easy for her to learn. It always seemed to entertain him when she forgot to speak Fuarmaanian again as they returned home... Her name was old, a very old word for 'unicorn', so from that revelation on she took the symbol as her own. After all, it was the symbol of the previous owner of her equipment. She opened her eyes again and saw her companion loom nearby. "Why don't you sit?" she asked.

"Sit?" He gave her an odd look; a wave of hair fell into his eyes and he gave it a toss.

"Yes. Sit."

"On the ground?" He looked at the ground then again at her.

"Yes you silly prig. On the ground." She smiled up him. "Well?"

After he looked around for a moment he finally arranged himself neatly beside her in the grass. Nighthawk snorted nearby. She lifted her sword and smiled. "Xianze," said she, for that was its name; written on the blade among etches of the unicorn. A breeze blew through the clearing and rustled the trees and Gellia felt at peace. As long as Cassius was there and continued to be an escort, life just might be bearable. "Are you going to leave again?"

"You mean go home? Certainly. I don't think I'll stay here much longer," he replied.

Her smile disappeared. "Soon?"

"Fairly soon, yes... I don't suppose your lord will want me around teaching you how not to be a Fuarmaanian lady, hmmm?"

"What? You actually believe those rumors?" Gellia started to feel ill. Where were the rumors coming from? Was it her father who told Cassius?

He replied, "Do you?"

"Of course not." Why was Cassius here? The idea of an alliance with Fuarmaania always seemed foolish to her, and rumor had it there would be none. She didn't understand.

"I wouldn't doubt the king's lust for power. All he needs is someone who is brutish or stupid enough not to be intimidated by your legend, someone who admires or fears him enough to bend to his will. I suppose there are many of such people in these wonderfully elegant parts. And the Sen Dunean armies are closer than anyone realizes, the king is going to need allies even if they're from Cambiga."

Gellia's stomach turned a few more times.

"Shall we?" he asked. As he rose he brushed the bits of grass off his doublet.

Gellia struggled to her feet—her muscles already started to cramp. "I'm ready to be abused again," she said.

Cassius didn't respond; he seemed pensive. The princess watched him as the wind rushed by them; his cloak billowed in a green and black cloud. Cassius' brows pressed together.

"What is it?" she asked and moved closer to him. Nighthawk whickered and Tempest answered but continued to graze. The black stallion's head was high and his ears flicked back and forth anxiously.

"Mount up."

"Why?"

"We best be off." Cassius and Nighthawk quickly closed the ground between them and he mounted as Gellia skittered to her own horse.

"What's wrong?" she called and cantered over.

"The castle is under attack."

"What?" They galloped through the forest. "What do we do? I can't show up like this—I'll be killed! Can't we stay here?"

"No one will recognize you. Fight them."

"Fight them? Are you crazy?"

"You have it in you."

"You know what's going to happen? Tempest's a coward!"

"So fight them on foot, you don't know much about mounted combat anyway. Certainly is an advantageous position, however."

"I can't believe this!" Was this truly happening?

They reached the main path and picked up speed; Tempest strained to keep up. "If you had your bow you could stay out of hand to hand," Cassius suggested.

"It's in the castle!" How could he be so calm?

"A lot of good it will do there," he laughed. "We will have to see if you've learned anything."

Her heart pounded in her chest and she could feel her body tremble, she wondered if Tempest was effected as he swerved and seemed to resist her urges to continue. "I don't know about this," Gellia called.

Cassius chuckled. "It will come to you. Don't worry princess, I won't be far away. We'll have this cleared up quickly."

They galloped towards the peak of the last hill before they reached the flats where the castle was built; she held onto her sword in its scabbard for reassurance. On the top they stopped and watched. Gellia was almost more unnerved by Cassius' calm than the battle. This was not an evening stroll—it was war. Sounds of metal and screams and horse whinnies and the coppery smell of blood and bile filled the air. Flashes of sunlight on the weapons, bodies everywhere, chaos. Tempest rolled his eyes and pranced about and threatened to bolt. The black stallion wasn't exactly calm, but he seemed almost larger, like he would rise into the air.

"What a quaint little skirmish," Cassius muttered then shook his head. "Foolish…I realize your king hasn't seen the Sen Duneans crossing your borders for the last year but I thought your people at least had seen some sort of battle in the last half century."

"The king was a strong general in the past. He has a long list of victories," she replied.

He laughed. "I don't know how. Although luck might play a large role in his victories... why aren't they pouring hot oil on the attackers? It's rather primitive but it is effective."

"With what?"

"Those cauldrons the washer women so rarely use, with the sludge left over in the kitchen after the meal is prepared. They knew the Sen Duneans were planning something, why are there no pikes? There are trees around here aren't there?" He waved his hand and ignored Gellia's trembling. "Fuarmaanians are worthless fighters these days so why are they leaving the protection of the castle? They are no match for Sen Duneans who spend their lives practicing war. Let this be a lesson to you… are you ready?" He looked at her and smiled.

After a deep breath she nodded and suppressed her nausea. "There are so many people," she said, "there must be three hundred of them."

Cassius gave her a sidelong glance. "Trust me princess, this is merely an oversized tavern brawl."

They galloped down the grassy slope and she drew her sword. In moments lost sight of him. This was real. Gellia was frightened for her life, people died all around her, she started to panic and Cassius had abandoned her. Tempest felt it, reared, bolted and left her in the mud. The princess quickly jumped to her feet, felt someone's weapon slide off her armor. She turned with her sword raised and struck her attacker down. Her sword was sharper than she expected. Gellia's choked as he crumpled to the ground. She killed someone. That strange feeling was back, the one that was still so new, it frightened her. But after a moment it warmed her, flooded her. She was dizzy but she reveled in it, as another soldier ran towards her. She saw the opportunity and thrust her blade out to meet him. Honestly she didn't know if he was friend or foe. All she could do was watch the expression on his face as his eyes lost their light. She knew she would be forever changed.

She felt a sharp pain in her back. Curse her distraction! How Cassius would scold her if he found out about this, if she lived. She could hear the talk now, 'the princess was found slain on the battlefield.' She couldn't breathe. As she fell to her knees she swung herself face up and landed in the mud, sword held to defend herself. A large, dark horse stood above her, her assailant under its hooves. It was riderless and not Fuarmaanian. It watched her. Gellia saw her ticket to escape and scrambled up onto its back. It seemed sound and rideable. They pushed their way towards the castle, but away from the battle. Gellia swung her sword as she could from horseback and injured, and this fine horse maneuvered through the melee, using hoof and mass to thwart their enemies. For once Gellia felt fate was with her.

Finally Cassius appeared out of nowhere and took her arm. She almost struck him as well, but he caught her hand. "This way," he said calmly, "they're scattering. We need to get you changed."

"Uh- ah- yes. Yes. Let's go," Gellia stammered. It felt like her mind had gone elsewhere during the battle and only now returned.

They galloped to the back of the castle and he guided them through the bushes. It was a small door, barely able to fit the horses, but it was useful in such cases being that it was built in a way that few could see it. In fact, even Gellia didn't know it was there. "How did you know about this?" she asked.

He smirked. "This castle is full of little secrets." Cassius yanked off his cloak and placed it over Gellia's messy armor before they entered. The passage was dark and filled with cobwebs but the horses followed willingly. They came out near the stable yard through a door that may have scraped off some of the horses' coats it was so narrow. They abandoned both mounts in the aisle of the stable and Cassius shoved Gellia into a tiny storage room. "Take off the armor," he said.

"Oh! Dammit! My clothes…" they were in Tempest's saddle bags and Tempest was nowhere to be found.

"Give me that." He took the cloak. "Take it off." He shut the door, stood guard, pulled out a dagger and swiftly cut holes in the fine fabric.

Gellia's voice called through the door. "Now what do I do?"

"Here."

She cracked open the door and handed her the mass of green and black fabric. The door slammed shut. "Oh, this is hideous," Gellia said through the wood, "and it's damp with gore."

"You don't like it? It's the latest fashion in Xzepheniixenze," Cassius said. "Minus the gore, of course. How uncouth."

She stumbled through the door, a rope tied around her waist, her head and arms poked through holes of the cloak. "I can't believe you did this," Gellia wasn't sure if she should be thankful for his quick idea or angry, for it made her look idiotic.

"I have others. You better straighten yourself."

She tried to adjust her hair for several moments but was unsuccessful. "I can't see what I'm doing." She was surprised by his look of outrage at what she suggested. "Is there—blood—in my hair?" She didn't think he would be that opposed…

"Certainly, but your hair is black, it hides the blood." He hesitated but then wiped her face with his sleeve, and hesitated again before straightening her hair. "Let's go." He ushered her through the door, across the courtyard and into the castle where everyone was too busy to pay much attention to her strange dress.

Once they entered a quiet room Gellia fidgeted with her ring. "I can't believe you! I could have been found out or killed!" And she was in pain but tried not to show it. Corrah would notice, though.

Cassius listened calmly to her rant as they hurried through the castle and tried to keep out of sight. "Enough of that now, we need to compose our story." He started to lead her through servants' quarters and nearly forgotten rooms as if he were born to them.

"What?" She still felt the rush of excitement, it was difficult to concentrate.

"Where we were during the fighting of course," said he.

"You're right. You say that you were scared and can't talk about it and I'll say that I figured out a way around the troops and go on from there."

"I think it might be more believable to them if the roles are exchanged."

"You're right. I'll keep quiet and say I was too frightened to look and don't know what really happened. Make a good show of it?"

"I always do."

"Wonderful. I can go on my own from here." She turned and gave him a little smile. "You're lucky I wasn't killed." She felt something strange, it was somehow coming from him, but she didn't know what it was. Certain she was insane, she didn't mention it.

"Luck had nothing to do with it. Besides, you enjoyed every moment," Cassius said. "…and don't worry, I'll take care of the horses and your equipment."

Gellia looked at him and wasn't sure what she wanted to admit so she just snorted at him. He smiled at her as she rushed to her empty chamber.

The only person the princess came across was another maid who ran down the gallery with her arms full of blankets. Gellia wondered what happened out there and almost wished she could be in the middle of it all. She would tell the other women that she was afraid of blood and that was why she didn't help with wounded. Yes, that was it—it went along with the other story as well.

Her chamber seemed exceptionally dull when she entered its gloom. Gellia shucked off the cloak-dress and grabbed up a frock then sat in front of her mirror and brushed through her black curls to re-braid it. There were still a few smudges of blood on her face—she poured water into the basin to wash up. She would wait until Corrah came to fetch her. It would be a long wait. She paced the room until she started to feel tired. Perhaps she could nap. If she could sleep. As Gellia lie on her bed she wondered what her partner was up to—did they believe his story? She jumped up and paced through her room again. Since they hated her so much and loved him they probably wouldn't question his word. Back on the bed. That's doubtless why he made the story the way he did: he would be a hero. Miserable no good...

"Princess, are you in there?"

"Yes, come in, Corrah,"

"Oh dear, I heard what happened to you. Are you all right?" The old maid hurried to Gellia's side. "You've had quite a fright."

"Oh." Gellia said. "But it was so dreadful—I didn't know what I was going to do!"

"Oh dear!" Corrah put her hand on Gellia's shoulder. "My poor lamb!"

Gellia managed to hesitate for only a moment as she realized Corrah's touch didn't hurt. Her back didn't hurt at all. "I couldn't watch I was so afraid and his lordship brought me here—safe and sound! Ohhh!" She was thankful that true to form no one asked her for details. She heard later that the battle had indeed rattled her father, and he had send word to his allies across the country. Deep down she hoped Sen Dunea would crush Fuarmaania. What a funny thing to happen to Hugh, the famed warlord. For some reason Gellia wasn't concerned about future battles. She was probably the least worried of her countrymen.

***

Cassius did as he promised. Before the sun came up he made sure that her equipment was clean and stored safely away in the library and tended to her new horse. As he started work through the knotted mane a stable boy peeked in with the morning feed. "Milord, you're in here," he said.

"Thank you, I wasn't sure where I was," Cassius replied.

"Ah, milord, your horse is missing."

"I turned him loose early this morning."

The boy smiled, "All right, good day, milord," and dumped the grain into the bin and went on about his business.

"You have quite the mess here, sir," Cassius said to the horse in Xzepheniixenze. Another head poked into the stall and the baron looked up to see Currain as he leaned on the door.

"Ohhh." The boy said.

"Yes."

"I guess that settles it," Currain said and grinned broadly. Currain watched as Cassius returned to the knotted mane. "If you don't need me I'll be going,"

There was no answer from Cassius so the boy left.

It was a long time before Cassius had the mane and tail untangled and when he finished grooming, the stallion shone like obsidian. "Gellia has her black mount," he said to no one. "And what a grand creature, what a fortunate girl. Even I could not desire one finer. I don't know if she'll ever appreciate you, truly. But it is your life to tell as you like."

***

Gellia woke and felt especially rested as she stretched and yawned in her bed—it was late afternoon. She decided that as long as she was to stay there she might as well sleep. When she awoke there was no one to tell her to remain in the room so she promptly rose and dressed to make her rounds.

First she visited the library to make sure all her things were there. She found them spotless and neatly placed inside the door. She had a feeling Cassius cleaned the armor himself for it was as perfect as the day she found it. It must have taken a lot of time, and the idea that he would do something like that for her might have warmed her heart a little.

While she put her treasures in the secret room she noticed riders coming and going from the stable yard. Likely heralds and messengers. She left for the stable before night came, when it quieted down; the rooms were dark for no one had lit the torches yet. There was something in the air that was not entirely unfamiliar, but it unsettled her. She twisted the ring on her finger and stopped. Someone watched her. She wished she had her dagger. She turned and looked down the gallery. "Is someone there?" she called.

Footsteps echoed and she waited. Into the dim light stepped an angelic figure dressed in white and gold, not completely unlike the person who had tried to kidnap her. Gellia stood her ground, watched him.

"Don't be frightened." He had a heavy accent but he spoke Fuarmaanian. "I won't hurt you, although there are some who would."

Gellia eyed him, looked for weapons. "Don't come any closer," she commanded. "I am not defenseless."

"I won't touch you," said he and stopped before her and stared. "I am here to protect you."

He was close enough that she could see that he was dressed very similar to the other intruder, but his hair was a corn silk color and his eyes were ice blue. Were these men related somehow? She glared at him. "Protect me from whom, that other blonde who nearly killed me?"

He smiled. "I'm sure he had best intentions." He never took his eyes off her, he barely even blinked.

"I don't think his best intentions were in my best interest." He might have a hidden dagger, but she didn't see a sword, axe, or bow. "Who are you?"

"I am Prince Zyendel from Dournzariame." He bowed. "I am at your service."

"Yes, and I'm the lost empress of the magic castle. Pleased to meet your acquaintance," she replied. Was he possibly the betrothed in the rumors? Or was he a kidnapper? He gazed at her with such a look of worship that she felt foolish.

"You don't know how true that may be... I wasn't expecting you to look so much like..."

"You better go before I call the guard." She started to turn away, but listened for his movement. She'd traveled these rooms long enough to know proximities of others.

"What I have to tell you is important," he said. "You must be careful—we don't know who's coming, but there's someone coming for you that you have to avoid, it will mean your death if you follow. Please choose your friends wisely." His voice became faint. "I hope to see you again soon. Never fear. I'll keep an eye on you and make arrangements..."

The princess turned but found that he was already gone. Only a lone servant was there, at the far end, lighting the torches. There would be no time to visit the stables, she was forced to go straight to dinner.

It seemed there were many more people in the great hall than usual, many soldiers were in attendance that night. There was no sign of the blond man, and no talk of him. This meant he hadn't been introduced to court. Gellia took her usual spot and waited for the rest to be seated and served.

The king was angry, brooding, while his subjects tried to make merry. They thought of their victory, but Gellia knew better. If Sen Dunea really wanted the castle they would have laid siege, not what actually happened. They attacked for some other reason.

Residents pushed and shoved around her; so many unbathed strangers, but a cool breeze blew the stench away. She knew who'd sat next to her before she looked. "It's you," she said.

"Unfortunately yes," Cassius said in his language.

"So you've been in battles before I take it," she said in Xzepheniixenze.

"I've waged a few."

"I thought barons didn't do much waging, just kings," she said with a smile.

"Hm," he smirked into his glass of sour wine. He didn't actually drink it though, she noticed, just made it look like he did. "Don't mistake my title for the summary of my career."

"I ran into one of those people again," she whispered, not that anyone else could understand what she said.

"Did you cut off his head?"

"No, he spoke to me and said that he had to warn me about the other person who will come. He spoke to me in Fuarmaanian with a heavy accent and said his name was Prince Zindel from Dourn-Dournzarie—I think it was—or something like that. It was very foreign."

"Prince Zyendel," he spoke the name with much thought. "Pity you didn't cut off his head, however it would bring his father here and that wouldn't do."

"I told him the other man was quite unpleasant and he seemed to know him and apologized although not in those words."

"Anyone from the Duvray family never apologizes for anything. The king is looking for me." He started to rise.

"He probably wants your advice on saving the country from Sen Dunea, peaceful as you are or not."

He smiled. "Fuarmaania is no longer my responsibility." Gellia wasn't sure what he meant, but it was unsettling.

***

Gellia led the horse into the sunlight and looked at him in all his glory. He was so black he was darker than night, taller than Tempest but shorter than Nighthawk and of larger, but not draft build. There were thick feathers on his fetlocks and had large, round, unshod hooves. His neck arched up in a graceful curve and was covered by a thick mane, topped with smart ears; his head refined and his eyes were wise and calm as he watched at her. "You are wonderful," she breathed, "What shall I call you?" Every step he took was brilliant; he raised his feet elegantly high and barely needed a command from her, but when she wanted to lead him around in a circle to stare at him he refused and she didn't feel she could force him.

While stable boys brought out tack and fitted it to the ebony stallion, Gellia thought about what to name him, and had a visit with Tempest who had found his way home. Cassius wasn't going with her that day—the king had him busy—she was on her own again. Once the stallion was tacked she climbed aboard and trotted out the gate before anyone could stop her. Today she would only bring a few books with her and leave the sword at home.

Gellia decided not to go directly to the forest but to go for a gallop. He was so grand—she liked him even better than the other black stallion. Where had the Sen Duneans found him? Every step he took felt calculated. Each stride was perfectly even as the next and he was agile as a cat, not stiff-backed as so many other horses. She waited for him to sprout wings. He was so well trained—he responded to the slightest change in her seat like he read her mind. They cantered all the way to her clearing and took a few laps through the grass. He was perfect.

Slowly Gellia dismounted, took out her books and let the horse do as he pleased and hoped he wouldn't run off. She spread out on the grass and watched him for a while. He stood there and seemed uninterested in grazing. She opened the great tome.

"....Our Moonseeker is a strange one. I hope someone besides me can see all his facets. I suppose that's why we get along so famously. He does have qualities that no one else sees. ...Mystic assures me Moonseeker will be appreciated in the future. I wouldn't be surprised if he takes over the world, unless his energies burn him to a cinder. At least I can rest knowing that he promised to protect my family if they were ever in need and I know that he will keep this promise to me, as he would to my father..."

Another journal of Quenelzythe. He wove such interesting stories that she reread them often. He wrote of adventures searching for the "Key to Zenobia" and casting spells to preserve old magics, dragon watching, unicorn riding and other exotic escapades. She put it aside and opened the next. A dragon chronicle this was, filled with pictures and places and names. Half way through the book she found a particular drawing that she liked very much of a black dragon who had no horns or spikes, it was just sleek and black with great wings. She read the writing at the bottom of the picture. "...this is the great Amarynth, one of the Black Moon Dragons of Lunara. I say this with such respect because I know as well as our Moonseeker and certainly Amarynth, that this religion is dying and with it, so will the dragons."

"What an imagination," Gellia said to herself. She knew whom he was talking about, the cause for this fabled destruction. Quenelzythe's uncle was a great hero who was set against evil and who seemed to sometimes hate Quenelzythe very much... It was a long story and she wasn't sure if any of it were true. But that name was lovely... "I shall call you Amarynth," she announced to the stallion, "from now on, that's who you are. What do you think?" It felt right.

The horse ignored her.

She leafed through the book for a while longer, probably longer than she realized then finally pulled out the little book she always had with her. It was the first time she was alone in a long time with the opportunity to look at it. *"Dearest little one,"* it began; *"So much has happened to us…"* she realized this use of 'us' in Xzepheniixenze meant he and his entire family in all times. She found it rather peculiar used in this context. *"…so much has already come to pass with so much more still on the horizon. Only we understand the truths in the Silver One's words. Only we hold the power to help things be as they should. You must carry on in our efforts despite all else."* She heard a noise and jumped to her feet.

"May I join?" Currain walked up the path and grinned at her.

"I'm not going to read aloud for the likes of you," she said and smiled.

"Oh, stop that. Not like I haven't heard you before."

"Excuse me?"

"Oh sure, I've been around but I never bothered coming out into the open." He came towards her and looked at the new horse but kept his distance.

Gellia smiled as she noticed how Currain admired her mount. "I've named him Amarynth," she said.

Currain laughed and she glared at him. "It suits him," Currain said. Gellia sighed and waited for the boy to move out of the way so she could collect her books. "Something's bothering you," he said.

"What does it matter to you? Servants always gossip."

"I'm curious, and I never gossip with anyone but horses," he replied. "It's Cassius isn't it? It's always him."
She looked at him and scowled. "My thoughts are beyond your comprehension."

"Oh, I don't know about that. I might understand more than you think."

Gellia looked at him for a moment longer. She'd never had much luck trusting others. She'd never had a bosom friend, and didn't know if she really wanted one. However, there was no one else she could talk to. She started to speak, but slowly. "I don't understand why he's here, why he's invested time in me. Everyone thinks he's a suitor, and that would have made sense before all this training. Now there's a rumor about a new suitor, and he's said nothing... I suppose it's the business of men. We poor womenfolk have little to say in the matters of our own paths in life." She sat in the grass and pulled single blades from the ground. "Corrah thinks he's hesitant because of my foul disposition. I honestly don't know what I think anymore."

Currain thought for a moment then answered. "Did you ever think that it's not what he wanted from you?"

She looked at him with disbelief. "Surely you jest. It appears that's all I'm worth. I'm merely a woman, barely better than a broodmare, and often treated worse. The only reason I'm of any value is because of my family tree." Her mind was jumbled with thoughts in all directions.

"I think there are better questions to be asked. I hear he wishes for an alliance, that is why he came here."

"You are being very strange," she said. "An alliance with Fuarmaania will do little good for anyone. Fuarmaania has nothing to lose and everything to gain, I'm sure."

"I don't think he's here for an alliance with Fuarmaania. I think you need time to accept things that you could not accept before, then you'll be ready for change. You need to make decisions no one else can make for you."

She rose and brushed off the grass sticking to her clothes. Speaking in such a way to such a person had finally set off warnings in her mind. Gellia turned away and strode to her horse. "I should get back. I have to go. Good-bye."

Gellia shoved her books in her saddlebags, swung onto her stallion and rode away. Maybe she wouldn't talk to Currain any longer and try to avoid him as well. "I don't know what's wrong with that boy, but I'm sure I don't like it," she said to Amarynth. It was then she realized she'd been speaking Xzepheniixenze all afternoon.

***

The princess trotted through the gate and saw that wagons were in the stable yard and she wondered if she should stay away, but still entered the stable and took care of her new beloved mount and said hello to Tempest. Cassius stood near his horse's stall, she said nothing to him. When she walked back out into the yard she thought her heart stopped. Servants carried armfuls of books to the wagons. She felt dizzy. "No! Stop!" she shouted.

The king strode from the castle. "You can't have them back and that's the end of it! Your betrothed is arriving in a few days with your grandfather and I won't have you avoiding him with this nonsense. Is that understood? You're to be present and modest!"

"You can't do this!" Gellia shouted. They had emptied the library, had they found the secret room?

"You will marry this man and produce heirs. Don't think I won't have you beaten!" King Hugh hollered.

"The smartest thing my mother ever did was leave here," Gellia said. She knew this would enrage him, but she didn't care. Everyone found places to watch from in windows and doorways. Gellia felt her legs shake as she stood for all their judgment. Her father watched her angrily. She was alone. No one would come to her rescue.

"Take them away!" her father said, trembling with rage.

"No! I won't let you!" She jumped off the stair, ran to the horses to take the lines. If only she had her sword. She could fell a dozen before they'd even realized what she'd done.

"Get out of the way!" the driver shouted.

Guards grabbed her while the driver whipped the team through the gate. Gellia struggled in the grasp of the two men who held her and glared at the king. She did manage to get a few good hits in before they subdued her. A wind swept the yard and clouds billowed over them. The princess felt the strange flutter within her burn through her veins and the channels in her mind as it built pressure. Dizziness swept over her. Gellia barely felt the hands that held her as she slipped into a semiconscious world. A dark cloud rolled past them and drops of rain splattered on the cobblestones. The king stood before her, backhanded her. Gellia hung her head for a long moment; she watched red spatter across her dress. The flutter grew fiercer. Voices of the ancient past called to her. Her breath caught.

There was something in the air, something cracked in the torrent of her mind. Gellia's eyes flashed for a moment before she finally went limp. "L-leave her there. Let the rain c-cool her temper," Hugh stammered. He glanced at her one more time before he left.

Guards and onlookers followed him into the castle. Rain started to fall. Only Cassius and Currain remained. "Go back," he told the boy. Cassius picked up the muddy princess and carried her to Amarynth's stall lay her in the straw. After he draped his cloak on her, he leaned over and wiped away the blood. "How could you let your lineage fall into such disgrace? Did you expect it wouldn't in such a place? Why did you not stay in Demf where it was safe? ...At least one is finally worthwhile..." There he left her to sleep with Amarynth and returned to his own chambers to contemplate.

The servants uncorked a bottle of his own wine that he kept in his chamber, and there in his room he stayed for the rest of the evening. There were few options for the misplaced princess—escape or death. Hopefully she'd make the right choice so he didn't have to make it for her. With her all the secrets of her heritage would die and forever be lost... And he had made a promise. There would be no more need for the Welcoming Festival.

***

Gellia awoke in the bed of straw, Amarynth in the straw next to her with his muzzle on her stomach. She quickly realized her left hand was grasping his ample mane, and when she released it her fingers were cramped. She felt for the wound she knew she had but found nothing; her face was completely unmarred. Was it a dream? She remembered being about to burst (somehow) and then she couldn't move but she was carried—it was Cassius—and he touched her, yes, that was it, and it didn't hurt anymore, then she fell asleep. This was his cloak, covered with straw. It was morning. Cassius was there; she looked up at him as he stood in the stall door and Amarynth carefully rose to

⅋⅋96ଓଷ

his feet and shook off the bits of bedding. "What happened?" she asked.

"I wonder if you already know," he said. "If you cared to look."

"I don't know about that." She felt she would kill them all…

"You didn't have a weapon." Something was extremely different about him—he was older or taller or greater somehow. "The idea of... it's so ridiculous that I can't even say it." She wasn't even sure if she said things aloud or in her mind anymore. What would Charlotte say if she was there? Charlotte would support her.

"Say what, exactly?"

"I can't—it's completely absurd." She pulled herself up off the floor and brushed the straw from her dress, handed him the cloak. Why did she even have these thoughts?

"Keep it."

She put it over her arm and walked from the stall and almost tripped in her hurry. She felt the same strange sensation in her stomach that she felt when she first saw him. None of what she loved did anything but hurt her, and she wondered what she should do. Run away like her mother? But to what end? A girl alone on the road would be an easy target for anyone else out there. And what did she know about the world, anyway?

Cassius was next to her. "Don't dismiss your thoughts so easily, princess."

He was acting very strangely and she wasn't sure how to react. Her mind had become even more confused than before, and she felt she didn't have all her faculties. Part of her was screaming inside, screaming so loudly in pain and confusion she barely felt she was still in this world, and hearing him talk to her was just adding to it all.

"It is something you understand, you feel it in your soul. That is why you can barely tolerate me, princess. Take the first step to a new world. You will find it more difficult to hide in the future."

"I don't know what you're talking about." She turned away. In the past she thought he referred to the concept she had feelings towards him but she realized there was something else.

It was absurd. She felt her book bump against her leg in her pocket and she thought of the words she read there. Those words were for her.

***

The next few days were quick and confusing. Gellia numbly went about her day without her books or horses. There were always extra guards nearby, and they followed their orders. The most Gellia was allowed was to visit her horses, but not even enter a stall. They brought her to the empty library so she could see that everything was gone, even the tapestry—but there was stone there, not a door—she was sure of it.

She'd been presented to her new betrothed and he was just as vile as she'd expected. He looked at her lustfully, and he smelled of old smoke and filth, like so many others. Luckily he spent his time with the king and she was in her room for much of the day. He was some noble her grandfather dug up from somewhere. He was a man of vast property in Cambiga, and one of grandfather's hunting companions.

Cassius watched Gellia pet Amarynth's velvety muzzle as he stood in the shadows down the aisle. Currain stood nearby, silently. Her guards put their hands on her to lead her away but she shook them off and went on her own. She was too busy fuming to notice him.

Cassius spoke in a low voice. "She's close. If she goes off here, if she loses control, then this place will be crawling with every scout in the empires to search the crater. Be alert."

Currain gave a nod.

The official news came soon enough. "Well, Gellia, Lord Blake has agreed to take you as a wife despite rumors of a curse," King Hugh said with a smile. "If need be he'll always travel with guards and a tether. His added forces will be an asset in our war against Sen Dunea."

Gellia stood obediently before them in her best grey frock as they discussed her life. It had crossed her mind that they may have drugged her. She felt more sedate than usual. She should have paid more attention when they were serving the wine. It would have been a smart decision on their part, for they knew how she could be and they didn't want her scaring away her future husband.

It seemed she lost time, for suddenly she was in her chamber on the floor and her aches seemed all too real although her mind was numb. For a moment she wished that her life spark would flicker out and leave her in peace, but that strange feeling welled within her and the thought was banished. Her spirit rose once again even though her body wouldn't obey her commands. Within the next few days she was confined to her room and was only brought out to be displayed. Gellia's ever-faithful Corrah came and dressed her and spoke with her but never said a word against her father's behavior.

"He seems nice enough," Corrah said about Blake. "I think he'll give you a nice home." She continued, told Gellia of all Blake's possessions. "I'm sure you'll get used to being married…It's a man's place to take, a woman's is to submit. Once you finally learn a woman's place you'll have an easier life. And once you're running your own household you'll realize contentment. Then one day his highness will pass and you'll return here to sit next to your husband as queen." She pinned Gellia's hair she continued, "If you're pleasant, they might let you say good-bye to your baron. He's been fixing on leaving, although I haven't seen him in a while." Corrah seemed distant. Gellia decided Corrah didn't care for Blake either, but was making the most of the situation. No different than what was expected of all women. "…it seems the baron's negotiations are done. We'll miss him."

***

"Ah, so you're the baron I always hear about," Blake said.

Cassius turned and stared a hole through the lowly man's skull. "The only baron worth speaking of, but few are worthy of speaking of me," he replied.

Blake looked around and licked his lips. "I think I've heard of your type." He shivered and wiped his forehead. His neck was starting to ache from looking up at Cassius.

"My type?" the baron rumbled.

He rubbed his meaty hand through his pale, thinning hair, shifted his weight and laughed a little. "Zefferzenzee."

Even though he tried to look impressive, Blake shriveled beneath the baron's wintry gaze. "What gives you that idea?" Several young ladies of the court hurried past in silence and without glancing at their favorite foreigner.

Blake laughed but stopped abruptly and cleared his throat as he saw the baron was not amused. "Uh—where are you from?"

"If you are so familiar with my empire—Tintagel is my family's home."

Blake regrouped and puffed himself up like a peacock, tried to shrug off the unblinking gaze. "Oh, yes, I know Lord Meliot, he came to our town once, are you one of his people? He told us about his home. He is from a powerful family."

A smirk unfurled across Cassius' face as he answered. "Ah, yes, Meliot. Yes. So then you should have the capacity to comprehend that Meliot has been a servant of mine for many years—and not an impressive one."

Blake's face changed to the color of snow. His breath was labored. "You are Meliot's master? The baron of Tintagel? The one they call the Dragon? What are you doing here?"

"Yours is the castle halfway between the Winterlands and Yzelle, isn't it? The motte-and-bailey cottage near a pond. You were attacked not long ago, were you not?"

Blake looked at the baron, dumbfounded.

"Hmm," Cassius stared down at Blake. "Her betrothed are cursed, you know." Cassius walked past and Blake could do little but scurry from his path, knocked over a table in the process.

***

Gellia felt sick. "Has the baron left yet?" she asked Corrah. In all the haze of the past few days he was all she could think about, but not exactly him, his world.

"I heard he was preparing the other black horse not long ago. I suppose he's taking it with him because to kill it would be a waste of horseflesh. Your father seems to think that horse is bewitched. Thinks it's the same horse that carried your mother away."

How could he? How could he do this to her? Wait. "Saddled them both?"

"Yes. Sir Blake has taken ill, you don't have to go out tonight."

Her breath caught in her throat. "Corrah, in the library where the tapestry used to be, there should be a door. I know it's there, you just have to look. Inside are saddle bags that I need. They're heavy but they're very important. Please don't tell anyone about the other room."

Corrah looked fearful, but she was dutiful. "If they let me through with them."

"I you never do another thing for me, please do this." She was certain the door was there, that the wall she'd seen was just in her imagination.

Corrah looked at her with her chins quivering, but nodded and left.

Soon after the king and grandfather appeared in the room. "Plans have changed. He's marrying you in the morning. He's anxious to go home," the king told her. "We'll celebrate without you," he said with a smile.

Gellia's resolve was being restored. "I'll never go with him. Do you understand? Never." Gellia pulled herself to her feet with the last of her strength and glared at the king. "I promise you that." She straightened and raised her head, a calm falling over her as she felt some sort of strength come from within.

"Why do you never learn?" Bellowed Hugh, whose face changed colors again but there wasn't only anger in his eyes— there was a look she never saw in him before—fear.

"I hope I never learn how to lick your boots like all the others do," said she.

"I thought you said you had her under control," grandfather said. "All women need a good beating to remind them of how good they have it. You've spoiled her, heir or not." Grandfather had become frail over time, but his mind was still sharp. "If I were well enough, I'd do it for you."

"I'm the king, you old goat," Hugh said. "And she'll learn respect." He cuffed Gellia, who took the hit well and glared at him. With fear in his eyes he hit her, a solid hit. She spit out blood and continued to glare. It was then he grabbed her by the shoulders and threw her to the ground to kick her. "Defiant witch! You do as you're commanded!"

Gellia went to that place in her mind again. If she could only feel out how to do it, she could kill them both. But with the beating her resolve was once again leaving her. The men left from the room sputtering curses upon her as if she was the entire reason for their miserable lives.

She didn't know how much time had passed when she heard Corrah. "These are some of her things to be organized, yes, I'm coming right out." The door closed again. "Oh lamb," she said as she came to Gellia's side.

Corrah, faithful Corrah... "You've always been so good to me," Gellia said. "I wish I could take you with me."

"Oh my poor child," Corrah said, tears in her eyes. "It will be alright. It's not easy being a woman, but it will be alright. Live for your children."

With the nurse's help, Gellia pulled herself to her feet and staggered to her bed. From where she lie she could see the twilight sky through the window and her cup with the rose in it... the rose. The rose was in full bloom, the color had changed to a vibrant purple like in her dreams. She felt herself drift. She wondered if she would die then, and the music in her soul started to glimmer. It was so familiar; she heard it so many times before. It curled around her, didn't touch her, but it showed her that the self she didn't know would give her fortitude to leave this life, for this life was not hers. This life was not hers. She belonged elsewhere, not in this barbaric little country, she had no connection to these people, her people were elsewhere... A story lost in through generations.

It wasn't a silly fantasy. Maybe she had finally gone mad, but there was nothing left to hope for. She couldn't stay. Did her mother feel the same way? If she were broken, would she even know it? How would she ever make it out of the place alive? How would she survive out in the open alone? Her mouth opened, but she didn't know if she spoke, she couldn't hear her voice. Would anyone hear? *Cassius... Cassius... don't leave without me. Please...* The glimmering feeling wrapped her in its warmth, in its strength, it gave her the energy she needed as it spoke to her in whispers and shimmers. She wrapped her arms around herself to hold it to her, and it took her into itself, taught her own song, understood her and gave her wings.

The door to her chamber opened. The guards were asleep outside.

***

"She's quite the beauty," Blake said as he pushed his food around his plate.

This was a small dinner between the three men, a private one so Blake wouldn't feel pressured and back out of the engagement. They were in the king's chambers where it was cozy and quiet.

"She looks like her mother," Hugh replied.
Grandfather shook his head. "She looks like her father, that fiend," he mumbled.

"Well soon she will be off your hands and into mine. I'm sure once she's been mounted a few times she'll fall into place." Blake smiled. "That's what we do to calm our women where I come from." They all chuckled and raised their cups. She was exquisitely beautiful and was ripe to be plucked. He thought she was even more beautiful when she was awake and wicked. It gave him a chill when he thought of how much she resembled the Zefferzenzee kind, a chill that was a mix of fear and lust. She was such a prize; perhaps the king didn't realize it. He was confident his knowledge and power would keep him safe from a curse.

"I am surprised the baron wasn't able to join us tonight," Hugh said. "I invited him. He's been a most excellent advisor, I have to say. Thought maybe he was unwell. The servants have seen him pacing around here and there."

Grandfather spoke, his mouth still full of food. "I should like to meet him."

"This is a fine dinner," Blake said. "Goose is my favorite."

"She might try to bolt in the future like her mother," Hugh said to Blake, pointing at him with his knife. "You might want to be careful about that."

"I will. I'll make an honest wife of her. If I have to lock her in her room or keep her in irons so be it. No more riding, that's for certain."

"Now there's a reason for celebration," Grandfather said raising his cup.

From the great hall came crashes and shouts. They looked at each other, and the king asked: "what is it?" of whatever guard was available.

In a few moments they led the princess through the door, dressed in her armor and purple cloak. "It seems to be the princess, sire," the guard said.

"Indeed it is," Hugh grumbled. "Where did she get that armor?" She didn't look like he remembered.

"None of you really want me so why don't you let me go." She was filled with pain but her mind was acutely sharp as she contemplated her escape. She was nearly out before the guards subdued her.

"You must learn to submit, girl," Blake said and rose.

"My submission is something you'll never have," she said. Without her wimple her black curls were unruly, she had to look through them to glare. She could see the fear in Blake's eyes but she wasn't sure of what he was afraid.

"So," Hugh said. "You were running off with the other whores like your mother."

"My mother was a noble woman; a whore would have stayed with you out of greed." Gellia was surprised at the force of her words. She almost didn't feel like the same person she was moments before.

The king looked horrified. "You're lucky I didn't feed you to the hounds!" Hugh roared.

"If you keep me you'll regret it, I give you my word," she growled.

The king strode towards her. Thunder shook the castle and echoed through its corridors. It stunned the men enough that she struggled free and kicked both the guards, bolted for the stable. Gellia jumped down flights of stairs. She could hear the shouts of the guards. They probably knew she would head for the stable. Tempest wasn't saddled... Amarynth was. Amarynth was saddled. Were they still here? If she could make it out she might be able to catch up with them...

The stable yard was filled with guards. Gellia's breath was heavy in her lungs. Hooves clattered through the aisle in the stable and a massive black horse leapt through the door and galloped across the yard to her, people scattered out of his way. Amarynth! She jumped onto his back from the stair and he wheeled towards the gate. People closed in on them with weapons.

From the dark Cassius rode, she hadn't even seen him there. There was a cry from the battlements. They were under attack. Gellia, confused and scared, looked at the baron. She wasn't sure if he was the same man she knew. No, she didn't ever know him.

Grandfather yelled something at Cassius. "I know you! You're one of them! Decius was one of them!"

Cassius' voice resonated through the stable yard but he didn't shout. "Decius was a fool." He raised a crossbow from his side and put an arrow through grandfather's throat. The old man's arms flailed as he gurgled and fell. There were screams and shouts from all around. Soldiers and courtiers alike seemed to be everywhere.

Blake ran towards to stare up at the baron. "I—" Blake started.

Gellia didn't wait any longer; the gate couldn't be an obstacle now, not when she came this far. They galloped towards the gate and she kicked the soldier who was lowering the bar. Amarynth reared and knocked one of the great doors open. She was free. They sped away, the enemy beyond the gate paid her little attention as she fled.

"I—" Blake said again. He looked at the fleeing princess and back at the baron.

Cassius said, "Pity you aren't worth my efforts to make you suffer as you deserve. None of you animals ever were. Now for the curse." Before Blake could say another word his head was neatly detached from his shoulders. Nighthawk lurched forward, and the two of them were swallowed by the shadows and were gone, Blake's head rolled slowly after them.

Gellia galloped across the fields, trusted her horse's sight in the dark. Night was cool, quiet, welcomed her as she continued. This time she could never go back. She galloped headlong into a world of which she knew nothing. Stars above her shone brightly, smiled down at her, it was the first time she looked at them. Where was Cassius? She could feel his presence even though she couldn't see him. They must have been close to the end of the kingdom; this horse was so fast.

Amarynth kept his pace, and she was almost numb when she felt him collect himself as if to jump, but he didn't rise up into the air but straight out into nothingness.

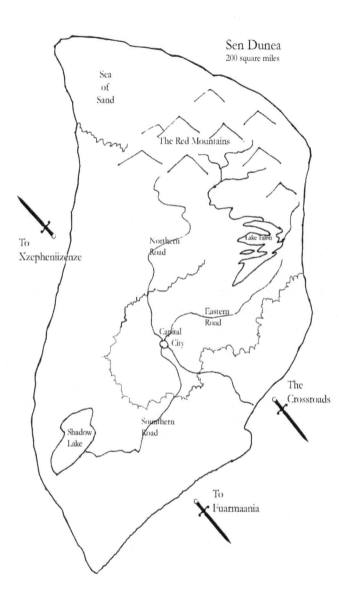

4

Gellia blinked as the sunrays warmed her face. She didn't remember how she arrived there, and didn't remember dismounting and deciding to sleep on the ground. She lie on the cool, damp earth for a moment more; let her eyes adjust to the morning sun. What had she done? She had run away from her life, a life that now seemed very much like a bad dream. She blinked away remaining sleep and looked into the treetops and the cloud decorated sky high above. Her mind was quieter than usual. Yes, she had no idea what to do or where to go, but she was no longer part of that life.

A breeze rustled the trees. She hadn't thought to bring any money, nor did she pack clothes or anything else. Her body ached from wearing armor all night. Where would she go? Had she made a mistake? Somehow as Gellia lie there she sensed someone near; it could only be one person. "I feel strange," she confessed.

"Of course," came the Xzepheniixenze reply. Cassius' silhouette loomed above her.

She decided to speak in Xzepheniixenze as well. "I'm lost." She sat up and sighed. The forest was old and grey, and smelled like moss and dew—so did she. Nearby the Great Cliff towered above them as it silently watched the forest. Above them was Fuarmaania. They were now in Sen Dunea. She expected to be attacked, or to have angry soldiers all around her, but there was no one. Nothing but her traveling companions and the old forest. It was so peaceful.

Cassius frowned. "Hardly. You aren't that old princess of Fuarmaania any longer; you're something far more interesting. Welcome to your new life."

"You're talking nonsense again like that fool, Quenelzythe."

"Quenelzythe Zapheny may have been many things, but he was not a fool."

Gellia gazed at the trees around them. Their two black mounts were observing them from nearby. "So where are we going?" Gellia asked as she rose to her feet and picked the leaves from her armor.

"We?"

"Yes, I'm going with you. I've no other place to go." She certainly didn't know where to go on her own, which direction, where to avoid...

"Oh. So you're coming to Xzepheniixenze with me?"

"If that's where you're going, yes." Gellia watched him as he checked Nighthawk's equipment and noticed Cassius was rather plainly dressed, especially for him. Doublet, cloak, everything was just plain black. He frowned at the poorly cleaned tack and the tangles in Nighthawk's tail.

"Yes," Cassius said suddenly. "I'm in disguise."

"Pardon?"

"You were wondering why I'm not very stylish today." He smiled. "If I was dressed in my usual way, our experiences on the trip would take a different twist than what I want. Luckily a more elaborate costume isn't needed, for we Xzepheniixenze all look alike." He took a sword and scabbard hanging from his saddle and handed it to Gellia. It was her sword.

Had she spoken out loud? She took the sword and was thankful. Amarynth nickered as if summoning her. Gellia checked her tack as well, started to hum a little tune. She didn't need to act proper anymore, she thought. She didn't have to do anything for she was completely free. But was it such a good thing? The world seemed very big and very frightening. As she adjusted her stallion's breastplate Amarynth chomped the bit. "You knew," she said quietly.

Cassius smirked as he always did.

Gellia rubbed the leather of the breastplate. She wasn't exactly angry, just a little maybe. She was more stupefied than anything. "You knew I was going to leave?"

"I knew that you would refuse to stay in that place for much longer," said he as he mounted Nighthawk. "You'll learn soon enough that life is an orchestration. Shall we?"

Gellia mounted cautiously as if she climbed onto some sort of strange dream that she imagined before, perhaps in another life. "Are we going to Xzepheniixenze to live?"

"No, to an iceberg in the Winterlands," he replied.

They made their way down a narrow path. As they rode in silence Gellia tried to imagine what her future would hold. Anything was possible now. Something told Gellia that this new place was a culture vastly different than her own. If it were acceptable for women to act as she did then what other strange experiences would lie ahead? She stared at Amarynth's mane and listened to his hooves thump rhythmically on the ground.

"You have much to learn, princess. We've only just started."

She watched the black clad rider ahead of her. She was alone. With him. Possibly forever. Although he was a man and as a rule not to be trusted, she felt if there were anyone in the world it would be he she should trust. Not because of the goodness of his heart, but because he had too much time invested in her to throw her away.

"There are many things I must teach you before we reach Xzepheniixenze. We're going to stay in Sen Dunea for a time; we should reach the King's City in a few days."

"Won't they kill us?" Or drink their blood or feed them to the dogs...

Cassius didn't glance back. "The first thing you will learn is a new perspective on most everything, including stereotypes the pocket kingdom has created. Luckily you already realize that Fuarmaania is a backwater heap of human compost."

She agreed about the comment about her kingdom and wondered what her life would have been like if she went with Blake. It gave her the chills.

"You would have killed him." He sounded cheery. "Not right away, but eventually, I suspect."

"I don't know if I believe you," she said out of habit. Had she spoken aloud again?

"You really think you would have tolerated that pig for any amount of time? You're much more intelligent than that oaf could ever fathom," Cassius said as he waved his hand, "even if you are young and inexperienced. I'm sure your wedding night alone would have made you start plotting."

Gellia blushed and was quiet for a long time. Cassius was the first person to ever say she was intelligent. It was a compliment she liked, and didn't know anything about the world so she couldn't argue with his other comment. There was some underlying enigma within herself that she couldn't even begin to understand. "Where are we going right now?"

"There's an inn a distance from here."

"No place to buy clothes? I don't think I can live in armor forever."

"We'll find you something."

"I don't have any money," Gellia said. Leaving was a priority, not packing.

Cassius glanced back at her and smiled. "From now on finances aren't an issue. I'm sure we'll find a way for you to repay me." She looked at him with anger and fear and he returned her gaze with one of disgust and said, "Nothing like that, don't be absurd," and muttered something about it happening a long time ago if he'd wished.

***

The Grey Goose Inn was not as far as Gellia expected; they reached it before nightfall. She had never been to an inn. The boy who took their horses was dirty and thin. As Cassius gave him orders in Sen Dunean Gellia stood looking at the front of the main building. It was a smallish structure; dark wood and dusty windows, which gave it the same aura of the rest of the forest. While she stared up at the smoke rising from the chimneys, Gellia felt him near. "Shall we?" Cassius said.

Inside was rather quiet, only a half a dozen people sat at the many tables. The smell of old ale and greasy cooking filled the smoky air and the smooth floor boards creaked under her feet. Gellia followed her companion towards a vacant table where she seated herself as primly as her armor would allow. She would at least still maintain some decorum even if she was now a vagabond. Gellia glanced around at the rough faces and swallowed. A harsh voice hailed them. The woman who approached was big and burly with a gravelly voice, but Cassius didn't seem to notice as he spoke with her. She seemed respectful despite the way she looked, and nodded often. In a short time after the woman left she returned to the table with two bowls of stew and two cups of what must have been wine. The woman and the Xzepheniixenze spoke again, and the woman looked puzzled and went on her way. Gellia watched this exchange silently as she delicately sipped the tepid liquid.

"She's leaving some clothes for you in your room," Cassius said as he eyed the stew for a moment before he continued. "Up the stairs and to the left, the last door."

Gellia swallowed the sour wine and looked at him silently.

"You're quiet," said he.

"I'm afraid one of these people will come over and smash me," the girl said.

"You needn't worry about that. These people don't usually bother Xzepheniixenze, certainly not two Xzepheniixenze."

"Two?"

"Have you ever looked in a mirror?" Cassius smirked. He picked up the cup, sniffed it and returned it to the table. "Exquisite. I'll have to save it for a special occasion," he muttered.

She slowly made it through her stew and noticed that Cassius didn't touch anything the woman brought him. "I think I'm going to go to bed," Gellia said after she finished her meal. "As long as no one tries to kill me as I leave."

"Would you like an escort if you are so afraid of the locals?" he offered.

She thought for a moment. Even though Gellia wasn't sure how talented Cassius was at tavern brawling she was still happy he would at least try to protect her. Not that she knew anything about tavern fights other than what she heard. So Gellia pursed her lips, swallowed her pride and blurted out a tiny, "would you?" And waited for ridicule.

"Certainly," Cassius said as he rose.

They walked up the creaky narrow staircase. Gellia spoke. "I think they might have the idea that..." she didn't finish. Why did she even think such a thing? But she didn't want others to think she was a common whore…

"I doubt it," he didn't need the rest of her sentence. "They all heard me ask for two rooms."

"Wait a moment." They were at the top of the stairs. "Two?"

"Well yes. You've already established I'm a scoundrel, but what you've failed to realize is indecisive youngsters like yourself don't interest me," he said. "You certainly are preoccupied with the subject, aren't you? I suppose it's what rustics teach."

The door to her room was nearly a big chunk of wood with a handle on it. She opened it and peered in. A lantern was lit on the lone table.

"You're safely here, now," her escort said. "Don't forget to bolt the door."

"I'll see you in the morning then." She stepped into the dim room. If he didn't decide to abandon her. Even though she knew he thought she was valuable in some way, there was always the chance he'd change his mind.

"I'll be in the next room on the left towards the stairs."

The door closed and Gellia was left alone with her thoughts. She found the new clothes as well as a nightgown on the threadbare blankets of her bed. Indeed the room was sparse and old, but tidy. She shed her armor onto the floor with a thunk and clatter and she picked up the gown and pulled it over her head. There was a window in her room that let in pale moonlight. After she blew out the single candle Gellia lie on the lumpy bed and stared up at the dark ceiling. He said that the Sen Duneans would not harm them, and they hadn't yet. Then, what was it that he would obtain by being kind to her? Why was he so willing to take care of her? Maybe she would ask him in the morning but she doubted he would give her a decent answer.

***

"Tonight we will likely sleep on the ground."

"Lovely. But I don't know how much worse it would be after sleeping in that bed. Ugh. I felt that I was sleeping on a rock the whole night."

"You are a true princess," he teased. "Perhaps you needed more mattresses."

"I still would have felt it."

They were on what turned into a proper road, one wagons could use. The two stallions could walk side by side with room to spare. "Where we'll be staying in the city will be much more acceptable," Cassius told her.

Only the sounds of birds, rustling tree branches and hoof beats could be heard for a while as Gellia's mind drifted off into her own peace. In the distance a hawk called. The world was so big. She was already far beyond where she had ever travelled. "Why are you helping me?" The question didn't seem as forceful as she wanted, but it was out. Both horses stopped. "There has to be something for you to gain to take all this time with me. I refuse to believe you're helping me because you enjoy my company. You aren't going to sacrifice me to some deity or something, are you?"

Nighthawk pivoted to stand nose to tail with Amarynth and Cassius looked at her. "This is as good a place as any," he said mostly to himself. It was a completely different answer than Gellia expected, not that she knew what she expected. There was something in his eyes that made her stomach flip-flop. "The goddesses are indifferent to sacrifices, even if they had the strength to notice. I think it's time I showed you something, especially when you're finally open to new concepts."

Gellia was apprehensive to say the least. "I hope it's nothing horrific."

He shook his head. "Perhaps to a true Fuarmaanian like you've tried to be and failed. But against all better judgment you're going to have to trust me."

She frowned. Gellia sighed and fidgeted with a loose hair, tucked it behind her ear. She didn't have a choice. "I—go ahead. But don't think this means I'll trust you any other time."

"I wouldn't expect you to." He smiled. "Close your eyes." Gellia did as he bade and heard the leather of his saddle creak. She felt the coolness of his fingertips on her temples. "I will be amazed if this doesn't come easily to you…. I want you to center your concentration on yourself. Forget the world around you... Now, feel for ground, the anchor, that which holds you to this earth. Very good. See? It does come easily for you; it takes hours, even days for others. That strange feeling that you didn't understand before, that strange thing that's always there, I want you to look for it."

It was there. How did he know about this? "It's big," Gellia said, "It might swallow me." Her words startled her. Something was there that could harm her but she didn't know how, but she wanted to know what it was... It swirled before her, within her, she could felt it, saw it in her mind and soul. She felt at any moment she would careen into chaos, but somehow he held her there.

"I won't let it swallow you; you can tell that I'm still here. I am far too large a presence for you to lose me..." Cassius said. "I want you to embrace it."

She felt that she was swimming in it, like it was a lake of violet-purple light, and seemed never-ending. Gellia bathed in a blissful tide. She felt free. In this strange awareness she could tell Cassius was still there, his part in this guided her with a song of green energy.

She could see the world around her. Gellia scrambled for her seat, her horse dropped his shoulder to keep her mounted. That presence she felt before, it was not unknown to her. In the castle. The day he arrived. "It was you," she said softly. He was with her even more that she had realized, this strange feeling.

He merely smirked and withdrew.

"There were times… I remember when the king took my books away, I felt... I didn't know what it was."

"I prevented you from leveling the castle... you aren't helpless, see? Just a wild talent with myriad gifts yet to be explored."

Tears rolled down her face. She couldn't help the torrent. That thing she had, that—power—it could kill her. Where did it come from? Could she control it or did it control her? It frightened her with the idea of this development inside her... she would have killed herself with the… How would she control it?

Was this what she and Charlotte always talked about? Was this what made her feel insane?

"You were never meant for Fuarmaania, princess," Cassius said. "And they insisted you were one of them. You aren't mad. Not in the least."

"I don't know why I'm crying," Gellia whispered. Perhaps it was the fact she felt her soul had been open to him, he could see every flaw she ever had. He could see her weaknesses, her vices, and her secret thoughts, her memories. Everything. He was there amongst it all, walked through her being as one would walk through an untidy garden. She felt herself tremble in the saddle and expected Amarynth to bolt, but he stood as calm as a lake under a summer night. His calm helped her. Gellia wiped her eyes.

"It happens. The Awakening is a disturbing time," he said with certainty, then added, "I still remember my Awakening, I was four. You're luckier than you realize." She blinked at him, fought the rivers that poured from her eyes. He continued. "You knew it was there, you didn't want to admit it. In the world you lived in I can understand why… and don't worry, I didn't look. I don't need to."

She rubbed her cheek with her hand. "I'm tired," Gellia said. Cassius seemed even more different. Perhaps more familiar—she wasn't sure if it was for the better or the worse. She could sense it now, how enigmatic he really was. She sensed his volatility even in this moment of serenity, realized her true ignorance, understood what she felt when they first met.

"Of course you are. I would imagine you're in a bit of a fog. Maybe we should camp in the clearing ahead?"

"Yes." The whole world felt different, she could sense things all around her unless she suppressed this power deep into herself, and that she did instinctively. Gellia could feel him near, like an adult helping a child walk.

Cassius watched her as she tried to regain her bearings, and spoke mostly to himself. "Only Zapheny could have that much control with so little experience."

Nighthawk turned on his haunches and they walked down the road until they came to the clearing of which Cassius spoke. It was there he tended the horses and produced a few blankets to sleep on. At dusk they sat near the fire, which Gellia conjured (with much concentration) through her new found power. She huddled next to the fire, her arms wrapped around her legs and with her chin rested on her knees. Even with the unknown ahead of her, she felt more content in this moment than she ever had in her life. She wondered what happened at the castle, if they were looking for her, how Corrah and Cresslyn fared. She supposed she may never find out. She twirled a leaf with her fingers while Cassius rested on a blanket, his head on his saddle as he stared at the sky. "You're quiet," she said finally, wondered what his thoughts were, wondered what he meant by 'Zapheny'.

"Just allowing you to sort out your thoughts." He shifted and sighed.

Gellia stared at him. He was expressionless as he gazed at the rising moon. She recalled something about moon gazing in the books she read. "I don't know where to begin. I don't know what my options are. You're my teacher, I'll listen to your advice."

"Am I? Didn't know if you were still interested since you ran off from everything you knew."

"Don't tease me," Gellia said.

Cassius smiled. "It's an option. There are many other instructors out there."

"I wouldn't know how to find one."

"You wouldn't have to. They would find you. There are others already looking for you, even besides our friend Zyendel, of that I'm sure."

For some reason the statement gave Gellia a chill. "I don't know what to do... are you... are you like… me? You know, strange... with..."

"Magic? Is that the word you cannot pronounce, princess? You are a magical creature."

"And you?" She watched a lock of hair fall out of his face.

"Yes," he seemed amused.

"Well."

"Well what?"

This power was still there as it always had been, but now she wasn't so afraid to look into it and see herself. He was right.

She still wasn't sure if she trusted him or not. If not him, who? How would others find her? Maybe it wasn't as difficult to believe as she had once thought. If she had remained in Fuarmaania, then what? Never would this power been discovered. Power. Gellia had power. Even if it was just a little, it still was. "I want you to teach me."

"We'll start tomorrow." Cassius listened to the dried leaves rustle as she put herself to bed without further comment. Still he stared at the sky. Gellia had chosen correctly, as he knew she would. To remain a wild talent meant self-destruction. "Others" would not be to her benefit, and certainly not his. There were sages in Xzepheniixenze who could potentially teach her, but she was his secret and no one else's. Not until she was ready, and that would take some time. She was already more at ease, had shed her false bravado, and was certainly less conflicted. Indeed, she could be herself, the self she was destined to be.

5

"Is this it?"

"It isn't the barbarous horror you expected, is it?" Cassius asked. They gazed over the King's City. "Or perhaps you expected to see a kingdom under a curse where all the people are now cats?"

They stood above the city on a hill giving them the best view of the main gates, and the road that led to their destination. Everything seemed to be made of sandstone, and whoever the city planner was did a great job of making the city open and easy to navigate. Streets bustled with people and animals, wagons of every shape and size. She could hear the shouts of merchants and the noises of animals, and people as they greeted one another. The castle was in the center, on a bit of a rise and higher than the rest. It looked exotic and well kept.

Gellia spotted a group of mounted men on the road moving rapidly towards her and Cassius. "There are riders approaching," Gellia said. She felt the energy bubble around her and almost panicked as she tried to needlessly suppress it. Cassius already had it clamped down. She was again thankful he was near.

"Our escort into the city, no doubt," he replied.
"I don't like the looks of this. There must be dozens of them." She looked from the riders to her liege, who adjusted his cuffs and gave his hair a finger-comb, and back to the riders. He wasn't concerned at all?

"They keep a very close eye on the road. If someone of interest approaches they send a few guards up to inspect whoever it is. It's a rather dangerous job considering they're charging me. I wonder what kind of manners they have. The prince should be civil."

Gellia had the distinct impression he was mocking her. "What you don't know, princess, is that indeed the roads are dangerous. The average man does little travel due to brigands and terrain, even with the better roads here. It's strange that we should be here."

"We didn't see any brigands," she said.

He smirked. "Yes, well, even the most uneducated here know what a Xzepheniixenze looks like. We have quite the reputation. The few of them on those remote roads kept their distance."

There were less than a dozen soldiers, ten to be exact. The riders cantered up the hill towards them and called some sort of greeting. Gellia prepared herself to run for her life but her companion didn't budge. Gellia took a death grip on her stallion's reins who promptly took the bit in his teeth and jerked his head towards the ground, nearly unseating her.

Cassius spoke a few soft words. He looked so calm; he even smiled a little at them. To Gellia's amazement, the Sen Dunean men changed their demeanor. The one in charge, a young man, maybe a little younger than Gellia, spoke cheerily then laughed. Soon the two travelers followed the warriors down the path and towards the city.

"What did you tell them?" Gellia asked.

"I told them who we are."

"And they just forgot to attack us, just like that?"

Cassius chuckled. "My agents have already been here to let them know we were coming. Don't be afraid, princess, no harm will befall you while we're here—in fact you're safer here than you ever were in Fuarmaania."

Throughout town people in the streets parted like the sea before a great ship. Hundreds of weathered faces gazed up at them as they passed, their expressions changing to awe. Never had she been so admired. Children smiled and pointed, women stared, and men seemed to forget everything but the two visitors. When she glanced at her companion Gellia realized that he didn't seem to care about all the excitement. She found herself noticing odd things—there were carved gutters in the streets to manage run-off, not like the poorly tended streets of Fuarmaanian towns.

No, these were clean with plenty of room for wagons and people on foot. There weren't emaciated people in the streets, there were minimal beggars; great care was given to these people. She took a deep breath; the air was full of spices, not the smell of filth.

At the castle the king himself greeted them. A robust man, he was, with simple loose clothing embroidered with gold. He had dark hair that was cropped short, a tidy beard and laughter in his eyes. He smiled and spoke rapidly in the halted Sen Dunean language. "He's pleased to have us," Cassius told her in the more familiar Xzepheniixenze, "and quite honored. The king himself has made all the arrangements. We'll be staying here in the castle."

"He doesn't care that I'm the enemy's daughter?" Gellia said.

The king laughed heartily.

"He knows a little of the language," Cassius explained as the king continued. "He says that you aren't... he's going to try to talk in Xzepheniixenze for your convenience. Speaking Fuarmaanian is no longer an option for you."

The king led them through the castle to the great hall with its grand tapestries neatly hung, and an obviously well-kept dining table. There the three of them sat for a time and spoke of many things while they enjoyed refreshments. The food was hearty and flavorful. Gellia stayed out of most of the conversation and listened to the soft creaks in the beams above them as the chill of night approached.

About the time Gellia thought of sleeping in her chair someone sat across from her and spoke to her. Not hearing what he said, Gellia looked up to see the boy-warrior they met on the road. She now saw the family resemblance.

The king made the introduction. "My heir apparent, Prince Lucifer."

"If you want you will train with us," the prince said in Xzepheniixenze, his thick Sen Dunean accent chopped the words. "Milord Vazepheny, may she train with us?"

Cassius glanced over his shoulder at her. "If she wishes, young highness."

Prince Lucifer looked at her with a glimmer in his eye. Lucifer was a lithe version of his father. He was handsome, but not any more than the girl would have thought a Sen Dunean would be.

For a moment longer Gellia watched Cassius then turned to the young man. "All right," she said, "what are we training for?"

He chuckled. "I'll see you tomorrow in the yard."

The king smiled. "My other son, Mervrick, is with the horses." He continued to speak with Cassius.

She listened to the king and Cassius continue in Sen Dunean for quite a while, but she entertained herself by watching the large hunting dogs chase cats through the room. Servants refilled her cup every time she emptied it and she had to turn away the spicy food they continually brought her. Gellia swallowed some more wine from what must have been her fifth glass. The room spun merrily. Her confidence was at its best and she had a question burning in her mind, so she blurted, "Why did you attack my castle?"

The room was silent but for Cassius' chair creaking as he turned to look at her. Their host smiled and leaned towards her, but not before he glanced at Cassius. "Perhaps a mystery you'll have to solve for yourself."

Cassius raised his eyebrow at her.

Gellia sank into her chair until she was sure she would fall off the seat. All at once she felt ignorant and foolish. There was something else afoot here, but her foggy mind couldn't decide what.

"I think she's had enough," Cassius said.

"It is rather late," the king added. "I have assigned ladies to attend to her."

"I'm sure she'll appreciate your thoughtfulness." Cassius looked at Gellia, who smiled crookedly.

"Her women can be woken up to aid her to her room," the king offered.

"That won't be necessary," Gellia announced. "I can go myself; just tell me where my room is." She rose to her feet and teetered a little. "All my servants need to be warned of my temperament."

"Out into the long gallery, into the great hall and take a right, go through the library, the next hall, into the trapezoid gallery, across the open gallery take a slight left to fourth door from the left side." the king told her with a smile. "And don't worry; we've heard plenty of stories about you already."

"Fine," she said with a smile and a nod.

The two men watched Gellia take a step, trip over her own feet and fall face first onto the ground. "I'll take her to her room," Cassius said as he rose.

"Don't worry about me, I'm fine," she insisted. She couldn't tell if Cassius was angry with her or not. He didn't sound angry but any move he made could be false.

The king laughed. "Sen Dunean drink is a little stronger than what she's used to, eh?"

"Well, your majesty's stock is palatable, whereas Fuarmaanian is not." Cassius walked around the table and assisted Gellia to her feet. "Shall we," he said.

He helped her towards what would be her chamber. "You're going to have a busy day tomorrow, princess." He watched her lean on a pillar for a moment.

"Oh?"

"Yes. You're training with young Lucifer in the afternoon; you're training with me in the morning. Early in the morning. I should make you stay up and practice your calligraphy, it's still deplorable."

"You're a slave driver."

"I've never condoned slavery. I don't suppose you're able will yourself sober?" he asked as they reached her door.

"No. I suppose you can."

"It's something I'll have to teach you some time."

"Very well. I have something to tell you," she smiled.

"I'm a bastard and you hate me."

"Yes, that's right." She'd wanted to tell him that for a very long time.

"I wouldn't expect anything different." Cassius opened the door and helped her in, lit a candle with a wave of his hand on the way. A sleeping gown had been placed on the bed for her by her servants. She started to pull the gown over her day-clothes. "That will be wonderfully comfortable, princess, especially with your boots in the bed."

"What do you know about women's apparel?" she asked.

"Quite a bit, actually."

"Do you dress like one?"

"No, I've just known a lot of women." He smirked at her and watched her face redden.

"Go away. I hate you."

"No you don't, you wish you did."

"Yes I do. Don't try to compromise me."

"Don't make me ill, you foolish child. Go to bed. Rest while you can."

***

Her practice with her most affluent teacher was in a decrepit amphitheater that had likely been nothing but a weed garden for the past hundred years. Much of it was falling down, and if he ever got around to teaching her combative magic there might be less of it. However, so far Cassius would only discuss defensive magic in all its variable forms.

Cassius seemed annoyed by her impatience. "If you can shield yourself correctly it will save you in a fight where you cannot win—but you'll be able to make it out alive."

Gellia reached for the energies around her and wove a spherical barrier around her while Cassius watched—not completely patiently. "There's an uneven spot, can you find it," he asked.

"Why is it you can find these things so quickly when I'm the one making it and I don't even know? ...There it is... is that better?"

"Yes. I can find weak spots because it's part of my job and I've worked with magic for a very long time." He picked up a rock and lobbed it at her.

Gellia instinctively ducked but the rock hit the invisible barrier and bounced off. "Why don't you hit me with magic?"

"You aren't ready for that. Pick up that book and put it with the others. No, not physically."

Slowly Gellia gathered the energies to lift the book off the stack while attempting to keep the barrier. The truth was she felt like a child. She was frustrated and wondering if she would ever learn any of this to his liking.

80124cs

Don't lose the barrier, Cassius said into her mind. *It seems to be a common misconception in beginners that one must drop the barrier to accomplish other tasks. It isn't the case.*

Him speaking to her in her mind didn't help.

The book floated a few feet off the ground and inched along towards the other pile. After struggling for a while, Gellia felt the mystical presence of Cassius guide her. Once the old tome was above the pile he released her and the book started to fall. In a wild attempt to catch it Gellia drew more power and tried to bend it to her will. The book flew past the two of them. Gellia squeaked in panic as it plummeted towards her. She felt the barrier drop and quickly she built it up again to avoid getting bruised. It bounced of the shield. Gellia hit the ground. The book was neatly closed and placed on the pile for her. She looked up at her teacher. Cassius sighed.

"I'm sorry," she said.

"At least you almost managed to keep your barrier. Luckily most mages wouldn't have noticed. I did because I'm me. We have accomplished something today. I want you to practice every waking moment. You can make barriers as large or as small as you want so you can do it even walking through the marketplace. Someday you'll be able to use your magic without thinking. You have an appointment with young Lucifer."

Gellia climbed to her feet, dusted off her clothes and sighed. "It has to be easier than this."

Cassius smirked and produced a vial of amber liquid and offered it to her. "Drink this."

"Why?"

"It will give you back your strength."

She took it, looking at him with uncertainty.

"When you're with them don't be disrespectful—Sen Duneans are some of the best warriors the Outlands have to offer. They're not what the Fuarmaanians think. In fact, I quite prefer them."

"The Outlands?"

"Yes, all these rustic little kingdoms. They're called the Outlands."

***

Gellia spent the afternoon with the princes, and other young men, in the stable. They brushed horses, cleaned stalls, distributed feed, and filled water buckets. By suppertime she was exhausted. Lucifer explained that chores were part of the old ways, which their father, the king, preferred. No pampered royals here. "Builds character," Lucifer said, quoting his father. There were regular stable hands as well, but the young nobles living in the castle did much of the heavy work. She had to admit that she'd never seen a tidier stable. Here in Sen Dunea horses were highly prized and therefore even more selectively bred and very well-tended. In just one afternoon she learned how to treat a sick horse and how to ease the pain of a lame one.

Gellia surprised herself with her own willingness. Perhaps it was because she was treated as an equal, respected. The two chestnut horses nickered to her as she entered each stall and dumped the oats into their troughs. They weren't pretty horses but they were sturdy and their coats gleamed and their stalls were spotless. As she looked up the aisle she noted that the two princes had gone about their other tasks. She smiled. Lucifer was her favorite. She supposed if there was an arranged match between her and him, she would have agreed. …Actually, it might have saved lives with a match like that…

Gellia tossed her braid over her shoulder and walked down the neat aisle to replace the bucket on the stack by the oats bin. She paused to look at the blisters on her hands and smiled. She would need gloves tomorrow.

"Helloo!"

"What?" Gellia spun towards the voice, a familiar voice. "Currain?"

The boy leaned out of a stall, smiling and waving.

Gellia blinked a few times. "This is too strange," she announced. "I'm most certainly mad. No doubt about that now." Her heart was telling her that he and Nighthawk were one and the same, but she didn't want to believe it. Although it would certainly explain a lot.

"I didn't mean to startle you," he said. "You aren't mad." He leaned on the manger.

"It seems that it would be easier if I was."

"No."

Gellia fussed with the hem of her tunic.

He took her shoulders. "You are a very fortunate person. You cannot realize just how fortunate you are—very few receive such effort. You may never realize it. These are very exciting times. Gellia, as I do, learn all you can from him."

Gellia stared at him; he backed into the stall and could not be seen in the dim light. "Goodnight Currain," she whispered. It gave her more proof that she had always been right about Cassius. He even had a magical creature to ride, and to be a spy for him. However, Currain was right, she should learn all she could from him while he still thought her useful.

***

Gellia was having her daily luncheon with the king, learning how to better her table manners. There was no queen, for she had passed years before from an illness, and since the king had two healthy boys, he didn't see the need to take a new wife. Apparently he'd been to Xzepheniixenze and stayed long enough to learn about them. She was quickly finding that Xzepheniixenze was filled with protocols enough to confuse her for the rest of her life. However, she came to love her time with the king. He was a good man, forthcoming and worldly, even with his gruff exterior. There was warmth in him that she had never felt from a man before.

"Even as the daughter of royalty, you're still and Outlander, to those people you'll appear very coarse. Milord Vazepheny insisted you be schooled to perfection and I told him I would do my best. Their culture is a society of subtle subversion and meticulous details—I've studied what I could, I wish I knew more."

She thought it strange that a king would refer to a baron as 'milord'. "Who is he, exactly?"

"I don't know much about the nobles of Xzepheniixenze to tell you the truth. I only know a few of them and not the details of their stations. He is the only one who treats us with respect. Xzepheniixenze are a people not to be trifled with, all of them are powerful in one way or another." He took a sip of wine and set the goblet down on the table with great care. "All I truly know is that his title says he is baron, and he treats me as the king I am."

"I thought he came to Fuarmaania for an alliance, or," she almost blushed. "...as a suitor... but it seems neither..."

The king smiled. "A suitor? No. An alliance? That would be with you, not your king, I suspect. I'm sure the king is wondering what will befall them now that the rightful heir has left the kingdom. Our attacks were for reasons other than conquering, although I'm certain it will all work out for our benefit." He was silent for a moment while Gellia stared at him. "There are many barons and other nobles of the like, earls and dukes, kings and princes... Then there is the emperor. He is the one who sits on the throne of the empire, and of course there are layers of nobles, and there are many clans to keep track of— nobles change all the time from what I understand. Some have cities they care for, others don't. Often they fight each other for territory... they're a volatile people—this I know. It seems that Xzepheniixenze is in a perpetual state of civil war in one way or another. You'll find all extremes while you're there. Another thing you'll notice is the way they treat women. Unlike our cultures which are patriarchal, in Xzepheniixenze it is might that has control. It matters not if you are man or woman. That is why you are treated as a prince here, not a princess. It is difficult for many here to comprehend, nor did I until I saw the might of the Xzepheniixenze women for myself."

No wonder Cassius was willing to instruct her. It was normal for his kind. She was filled with excitement and fear. Xzepheniixenze was her destiny. What she'd be doing there she had no idea, but she would be there. A place volatile yet so many opportunities, certainly more for her than back home. She surprised herself how eager she was about going to such a dangerous place, and looked forward to doing so. "What does it look like? Is it dismal and war torn?"

He thought for a moment. "There is no other realm in existence that can match the beauty of Xzepheniixenze," the king said. "You can only see it for yourself. Legend has it that it changes for everyone, ever so slightly. That it gives a different feeling to different people and it will change a person forever. It's why there are sixty different words for 'beauty'."

She could see it in her mind, her wild imagination had its way. Everything was vibrant and full of life. "Why is it that I'd never heard of this place when I lived in Fuarmaania?"

"It was kept from you, no doubt. There are strange stories about Fuarmaania and Xzepheniixenze but I have only heard of them, never heard them told… I should also inform you of something else, something no Xzepheniixenze would or could think to explain to you. You will not be bound in any way to another as we do with marriage. There is no marriage. Nor is there the concept of affection towards one another like in the stories here." He shrugged. "But for the human cultures there I suppose. All the strange behaviors you had would make perfect sense to our baron. As I've said before, your temperament is well known, and that comes from your blood, the instinct to trust no one. Don't lose that instinct."

***

For months Gellia went through vigorous training with the princes and with Cassius. Lucifer and Mervrick oooed and aaaahed over Gellia's sword when they first saw it and were quite amazed and impressed that she saw battle before. They smiled and were silent when she asked about that battle; and when she asked them about her horse they said there was never a black horse in their stable so there was no possibility it was formerly Sen Dunean. None of them could figure out his age by the traditional method—looking at his teeth—which Amarynth barely tolerated. Anyone who had any dealings with the stallion was under the strong impression that he could turn on them at any given moment, although he never nipped or kicked or made motion to do so.

The arms master was a difficult instructor for he didn't see the value in teaching a woman, but he did so for the king. She was happy she had at least some previous schooling for he was at times harder on her than the young men. He was ordered to cover as much information as possible with her, so she wasn't honed in anything in particular but was learning the basics from hand to hand to fighting on horseback. It didn't take all that long for the other young men to realize that in fact, women like her were women to be respected and potentially feared, unlike their own native ladies. Gellia was feeling freer by the day. She certainly enjoyed the liberty of wearing tunics and breeches instead of overly long dresses. Being able to stride about instead of the stiff and careful walk of a lady was an amazing boost to her mood.

After her lessons with the arms master Gellia chose to still help with chores. Cassius told her it was tradition from the times long ago when the Sen Duneans were nomads and their chieftains and their families took part in such tasks. He said he doubted the Sen Duneans remembered where such customs originated.

In six months Gellia could magically shield herself from all angles, move objects around at will and could speak to Cassius in his mind when he didn't block her out. She also learned to shape her magic, started to learn its truth. Cassius told her she was coming along nicely but sometimes Gellia wasn't sure about it herself. "It's a long process," he told her. "Give yourself time. Most study most if not all their lives." She was impressed how what a gentle teacher he was. As long as she maintained focus, he was pleased.

Every day some follower of the baron's would arrive to deliver new books to read and return what Gellia had already been through. It was the highlight of her stay there. Cassius insisted she be reading at any available moment. He said she would likely forget much, but even retaining a little of it would help.

They were sitting at a table together as they often did, and she started to read a newly delivered book. It became instantly clear that this book was one she had read before. "...'and I wondered if the realm would ever recover, I somehow doubt that it will for the one thing that bound it is gone...' Where did you get this?" Gellia held up the old book.

He didn't look up. "I think you already know." Cassius toyed with a pen, twirled it between his finger and thumb while he read a letter.

"Don't play games with me."

"If I were playing games with you, princess, you wouldn't know it."

Gellia looked at him from across the table with skepticism. "Only I knew where that room was," she said. "I found it. No one had been in there for years. Did my father find it when they took all my things out?"

"He isn't your father," Cassius said. "He never found anything. I knew where that room was before you did."

"How?" She wasn't sure if she should feel violated, betrayed, amazed, or curious so she felt a mixture of the four.

"You needn't worry about it."

"Of course I'm going to worry about it. You know too much…" Gellia felt there was no use in continuing for he wasn't about to tell her. "You saved them for me?"

"They're valuable to me—including the one you keep in your pocket."

Before Gellia could respond a porter announced a visitor and a slender Xzepheniixenze entered the room with a slip of paper. These people are very strange, Gellia thought. All very lean and graceful and quiet, always dressed in greys and black. This one had been here before, but she didn't know his name. He handed the folded paper to Cassius who opened it and scoffed. "Tell that blundering fool cousin of mine that I have business to attend to, namely killing the princess of Fuarmaania because she's useless, and then I'll be by to visit him. I won't waste good ink writing to him."

Gellia shrank in her chair and paled. The man left her and Cassius alone again. He wouldn't have spent so much time on her if he was going to kill her—what strange circumstance had she found herself in? Some barbaric Xzepheniixenze tradition? "You're going to kill me?" she asked.

"Don't be ridiculous. You aren't the princess of Fuarmaania."

"Yes I am."

"No, you're Zapheny. I suppose you could take the name Iolair if you really wanted to. The princess of Fuarmaania didn't have magic, did she? And she lived in a castle the size of head box with a loathsome oaf who the local rabble called a king. It took a long time to kill her, actually." He shrugged. "And it was a mercy killing."

It started to make sense in a perverse way. "Where did you get those other names?"

"Iolair is your father's name. The man from whose loins you came. Zapheny is your greater ancestor's name, Quenelzythe's name. You're not some person from some wretched little country," he finished. "...of course I didn't tell my cousin that I was assisting in the birth of your true self, the one who has been locked away for all these years. All of this will be terribly confusing to him…" He smiled at her. "I will be the one to mold you into what you should be."

He really was a scholar. "How do you know these things? Who is your cousin?"

"I know a great many things about you, I know far more about your lineage than anyone … My cousin is the person who insists he is the emperor." Cassius waved his hand and rolled his eyes. "There is not a word or comparison I would insult in using it to describe him."

Gellia was silent as she thought, and Cassius grew distant with some vexation that was unknown to her. For some reason she had a clear picture of the emperor in her mind, but she wasn't sure where it came from. He was tall and dark like all Xzepheniixenze but he lacked the grace she would have expected of someone in his position. In fact, he seemed very destructive and obscene. Primarily he laid waste to cities and took joys in genocide and chasing women. But he wasn't an old drunken fool like Hugh—no—he was very powerful. A creature like that didn't deserve the throne. The people should be cared for, not used for sport. There was so much to do, and really none of it was her business, but perhaps Cassius would help. "Cassius," Gellia said.

"Hmm,"

"How powerful am I? What I mean is, how much potential do I have?"

"Your magical talents do you mean? Your ability to withstand the use of them?" He was looking at her with renewed interest. He was reading her—she could feel it. She almost liked the fact that she could tell and enjoyed his gaze. What a strange thing.

"Yes."

"You have vast magical talents that can be compared to very few of this time, but your strength to use them is limited by your human blood. You could easily kill yourself by using only a fraction of your power. It is a problem we'll have to solve. But yes princess, you could be quite powerful."

"Quite?"

"Quite."

She wasn't sure where her words came from, and she surprised herself. But if Xzepheniixenze was her destiny... "Then I think, some time, when I'm better at my magic, I think I should like to help the people of Xzepheniixenze, save them from a bad ruler, I would suspect. I would like to be useful. I feel a bit foolish to be saying it, for I know little of the world, but..." Cassius leaned back in his chair and smiled. A wave of black hair started to slowly fall into his face.

"I mean, if Xzepheniixenze is as great as I feel it is, then why leave it to be ruled by a pig?" There was some part of her that said it was fate. She'd never been more certain, even with all the conflict in her heart. Quenelzythe.

He laughed. Could she have a concept of what she was saying? Why she said it? Cassius wondered. She wasn't jesting, he knew that; she was very serious. Unsure, but serious. Perhaps naïve as well. "You've just insulted a very noble creature, the pig," he said. She improved much over the months away from Fuarmaania. Her confidence gave her a whole new posture, one that befitted her ancient bloodlines.

"I know that I probably can't be taken that seriously right now but..."

"When I'm done with you they'll take you seriously. The whole world will have no choice but to take you seriously. Wait until you meet him, then make your final decision." There was laughter in his eyes.

"Don't mock me. I almost sure I know what I want."

"I'm not mocking you, princess, but you aren't ready for him, nor are you ready for Xzepheniixenze."

"I also want to learn about the Zapheny."

"Then I shall teach you everything I know about them," he said and smiled. "They tend to be a mysterious lot, even more so than most give them credit, and the more someone might know about them the more enigmatic they become."

"Yes, teach me everything you know."

He chuckled. "Actually I was hoping learn from you."

***

"No, I'm taking a day's rest today," Gellia told Lucifer. "I think I might go mad if I don't go out today, and luckily his lordship has given me leave."

The prince nodded and smiled.

Gellia walked through the gates of the castle into the crowded streets of the city. It was the first time she'd been out since she'd arrived, and being able to do so on her own felt wonderful. Although in the back of her mind she wondered if she would end up lost in the hustle. All around her the people went about their business and only stopped a few moments to stare at her as she slowly made her way down the main street of the marketplace. The king had given her some money to spend but she didn't find anything that tickled her fancy. Certainly nothing that she thought she would want to take on the road with her. Weapons and armor shops, jewelry, fine fabrics, all sorts of food, paper, harness, wood and a vast array of objects she had no idea about were presented as she meandered through the people. It seemed to her that many of them thought she was rich even though her plain clothes showed them otherwise. The merchants in the finest booths held out their goods for her inspection while the people in the cheaper booths seemed nervous when she approached.

She wandered for most of the day, didn't buy anything for quite some time until she came to a little shop that's shelves glittered but not from jewels. As Gellia moved closer she found that it had tiny sculptures made of shiny stones. Her eye was drawn to one in particular, a black horse no taller than half her little finger. The shopkeeper gave her an odd look when she smiled at him, but he seemed to know which one she admired without her saying a word. He set it on the table between them.

The little horse stood on its hind legs, the tail helping the balance. Every hair in the mane and tail was detailed. "One to match yours," he said in Sen Dunean.

Gellia wondered how he knew she had a black horse or how he remembered seeing her riding Amarynth when they first arrived. The local language was just another thing heaped on the pile of knowledge she'd been learning. "How much?"

The shopkeeper thought for a moment. "Two silver," he said.

Gellia thought about it and the man waited. "I'll take it." She dumped out the contents of her purse and counted the coins. It was the first time she ever handled money.

The merchant slipped the horse into a soft pouch and handed it to her. "Thank you," she said and started to walk away. Not far from the booth she thought about how she might earn money so she could afford to buy Amarynth some new equipment. Tack was expensive no matter where one went.

It was time for her to return. Cassius would want her there for lessons that evening. With a sigh she started towards the castle but she didn't walk very far before something down a side street caught her attention. Amidst the earthy tones of complexions and colorful clothing of the locals stood a silver-haired youth whose beauty rivaled all whom she knew. It wasn't just a physical attractiveness, his light seemed to radiate outwards. No one else seemed to notice him, but Gellia was frozen in his gaze. He smiled at her. He reminded her of a dream she had once, of a silver unicorn she saw there. Goosebumps spread across her skin. He was only there for her, it was her moment, and she felt her magic respond.

Someone bumped into her, nearly knocked her over. "What are you doing?" Gellia said as she regained her balance. When she looked again, the silvery man was gone.

A boy, maybe eleven years old, stood near her. He looked up at her with reverence but didn't seem afraid. "Sorry, I need help—they're after me," he huffed. He had dark, unkempt hair and was in need of a good scrubbing; his clothes were little more than rags. "Don't suppose you would help me?"

"Who's after you?"

"Some men. Big men. They want to kill me."

"You're joking,"

"Here they come!" The boy pointed and hid behind her.

"What is this?" Gellia demanded in Sen Dunean. "How dare you threaten a child?"

Three large, well dressed and armed men stopped before her and looked down at her. "This boy is a thief"

"I'm not!" he called from behind her.

"He says he's not," Gellia said. Thief or not, Gellia decided that she would stand her ground; truly stand her ground for the first time. And she wouldn't lose. She would work this out.

The leader looked at her coldly, but perhaps a little nervously. Another spoke. "He is, and if you don't move, we'll have you off too."

"How dare you threaten *me*." She took a defensive stance.

One of the men drew his sword. Another held him back, mumbled: "Xzepheniixenze."

"Let's go, come," the boy said and grabbed her hand. Before she could say another word the boy was pulling her. He was far stronger than she could have ever imagined and she stumbled after him. The two of them ran through the marketplace while shoppers shouted and intimidating men gave chase. Under wagons, through booths, over fences, around horses, through tight spots Gellia was sure she wouldn't fit. "Hurry!" the boy shouted at her.

"I don't think—"

"Just go! Here! Here!" They dove under a very low wagon. "They didn't see us, see?"

Gellia looked at her companion in disbelief. "I wasn't the one in trouble!" she said.

"You are now." He smiled at her with a charm she'd never seen before. Some of the men who chased them climbed nearby scaffolding for better view while others looked under the tables and in anything that could hold a person or two. "They'll find us soon if we don't leave," the boy told her and started to wiggle.

"Wait a minute, I have an idea." Gellia focused herself. Well, she was in trouble anyway.

"We don't have time for…"

"Be patient…." She could feel the guards with her magic, used it to lift them into the air and fling them into different parts of the market. There were shouts and crashing. Gellia smiled. It worked!

"I don't believe it!" The boy exclaimed and giggled wildly. "Imagine my luck running into a mage! A friendly one at that!"

"Let's be off," Gellia said.

Together they squirmed from under the wagon and were on the move again. "I'm starving. Do you want something to eat?" she asked as she noticed how skinny he was.

"Sure, you're buying it though."

"I offered, didn't I?"

They came to a bakery where Gellia purchased two big pastries. One she handed to the boy who thanked her repeatedly. He was not an average child; there was something a bit different about him, something that felt familiar. His eyes were bright and mischievous.

"So why are you here?" he asked.

"What kind of question is that?" Gellia replied and picked at a flaky layer of pastry.

"You're a Xzepheniixenze, you don't usually come around here unless you're up to something."

"Oh, well I wouldn't assume anything. You look rather dark yourself."

"I'm three quarters Xzepheniixenze. One-quarter human. My mother was half human half Xzepheniixenze; my father was a pure blood. My mother tells me all sorts of things. My parents didn't have a successful association. There aren't many of us here, very, very few in fact and no purebloods to speak of. Most don't believe I have the blood in me."

"You probably know more about them than I do," she murmured. "I don't understand why you say human and Xzepheniixenze like they're two different creatures like dogs and cats."

"Because they aren't human. You're very odd."

"I know I am." Gellia snacked on her pastry in silence for a few moments. "Where is your mother?"

"I'm not sure. I haven't seen her in a few days."

"You're by yourself?"

"You could say that... oh no."

Gellia looked up to see one their pursuers down the street from them, pointing in their direction. "We better be going."

"I think that's a good idea," the boy said.

Both of them turned on their heels and ran. "Where are we going?" Gellia shouted.

"I usually run around until they get tired," he laughed. "This way!" They scooted under a horse's belly and jumped over a vegetable cart. The boy lost his footing around a corner and Gellia grabbed him and dragged him along until he regained balance, but almost took her tumbling down with him. Gellia squealed, grabbed a nearby wagon and pulled them around it, nearly toppling the fruits that were piled in the bed.

"These guys aren't giving up!" the boy yelled to her as they ran and laughed.

"I wish I had my horse!" Gellia called.

"Of course you do! I wish I had mine too! In here!" Diving head first into a tent wasn't the best idea, but with all the chaos they were creating in the city, what was a little more?

"Where are we?" she whispered between breaths. Luckily for them, no one was in the tent.

"Don't know. You wouldn't fit down the routes I usually take. I think we should keep moving, though."

"You're right. This way."

"Do your trick again," he said.

"What? It takes me too long to do that unless I can stay in one place and concentrate for a moment."

"You aren't very good, are you?"

"I saved your life you little weasel."

"Not yet you haven't. You never know, I may save yours."

They made their way through the dark tent, which, judging by the sparse furniture, was someone's house, and peeked out the other side. "It's the castle," Gellia whispered harshly.

"So? We don't want- hey!"

"Come!" Gellia grabbed his hand and dragged him along at a run.

"You're strong for a girl," he laughed.

"Stop your noise and run! They're right behind us!"

"I'd like to take my chances rather than to run into the castle—what are you doing?"

"I know people in there."

"Yeah, so do I—he does the sentencing."

But the boy followed as they skittered through the thinning crowd. The gate was so close, and the guards knew her, but the gate was closed for the night. "Any other ideas?" the boy said.

Gellia made a mystical grab for the power, and with rattling and clanging the gates shifted, the portcullis started to rise

"The gates are opening! I still don't know if I want—" They were in the castle walls. The portcullis plummeted to the ground. With sparkling eyes they looked at each other and panted. The men shouted at them through the gate but the guards inside ignored them and watched Gellia and the boy.
The second Gellia had breath to spare she started to laugh and toppled to the ground.

"I-I- I...don't know...what you're laughing at.... but it isn't hah-hah that funny," he sputtered. "We... we're in th' castle. We're dead now." But still the boy was doubled over in wheezy laughter.

"I don't think I've ever laughed this much," Gellia said. "Hello your highnesses." The two princes stood above her. She could barely rise to her feet with all her laughing.

"What's going on?" Lucifer asked.

"We escaped certain doom," Gellia said as she sobered.

"Your majesties! That boy's a thief!" the men called from the gate.

"Search me, I don't have anything," the boy said. The princes took him up on the offer, all but turned him on his head and found nothing.

"We'll go talk to them," Mervrick said and left with Lucifer.

"Come on, we need to find Cassius," Gellia said.

"Cassius, huh? Is he the real thing or an imposter? Is he from Tintagel?" the boy asked.

"He's a companion of mine. My teacher. He'll be expecting me. You said you had a horse too?"

"Not yet but mother said I should be getting one any time now."

***

"You're late," Cassius said when she entered the hall. He was sitting at the end of the table and scowling, he hadn't touched the food the servants brought him.

"I know, I'm sorry, but you see—"

"You have an excuse? And what about this urchin you've brought with you?"

"I'm Saquime," the boy said. "I'm three quarters Xzepheniixenze."

"Saquime?" Cassius suddenly smirked. "A market thief?"

"I'm not a thief, I'm just fallible," the boy said.

Cassius chuckled.

"What kind of name is that?" Gellia asked. "From now on you're Skip. It's easier."

He shrugged. "Fine," Skip said, smiling.

Gellia continued. "This is my new pet. May I keep him? Please? He could be my page. I've never had a page before." Her liege inspected the boy; there was a glint in his eyes. "I suppose it would be acceptable. Now send him away. We have matters to discuss."

Gellia gave Skip directions to her rooms and sent him on his way. She sat next to Cassius in one of the well-loved chairs. For a moment she tried to tidy her wild curls, but quickly gave up.

"Don't make a habit of coming to dinner covered in dirt. Look at you, frazzled, filthy and undignified," Cassius said. "You're lucky I let you sit with me. And you've disrespected our hosts. Starting trouble in the city, taking advantage of the king's good will is no way to keep allies. You broke the gates, destroyed stalls in the marketplace, injured those hired men as well as innocent bystanders and created overall bedlam. People will need to be compensated and repairs made."

Servants set plates in front of her; she smiled and mostly ignored her teacher's words. Not that she intended on appearing like she did again nor causing any more trouble. It really was in poor form. "I brought you a present," she said and rummaged through her purse. "It's not much but I had to buy it for you."

"The seekers were here again."

"The who?"

"Seekers, the people who always come to visit from Xzepheniixenze?" he said. "I have to return."

"Am I going with you? ...Where is that thing?" Did she drop it?

"You aren't ready."

Gellia stopped her digging and looked up at him. "You're leaving me? Who'll teach me while you're gone?"

"You'll teach yourself and read while I'm gone. You'll survive, I'm sure. Practice in the arena or outside the city, understood? And don't attempt anything we haven't studied before. Be respectful of our hosts." That's when she saw for the first time, a flash of anger in his eyes. It was enough to sober the sloppiest of drunkards.

"Yes. Here, I bought this for you." Gellia placed the horse on the table between them, desperate to clear the air. "I thought it looked like Currain, uh Nighthawk. So I bought it." She shrugged. "Just a little something. I mean, I like him and you've done a lot for me and..." Cassius picked it up and looked at it. Gellia waved her hand. "Just a little..." She felt her face get hot. "I just."

He looked at her.

She cleared her throat. "Well, I'll be going wash up and go to bed now. Will you be going in the morning?"

"I'm leaving tonight."

"Tonight?"

He nodded. "I like it," he said.

"Pardon?"

Cassius held up the horse. "I like it, I said."

"Oh, good." Gellia smiled.

6

The pale globe whirred around the boy and faded. "Is it gone?" he asked.

"No, it's just invisible now," Gellia said. She rolled over on the giant rock and stretched her arms, dissolved the shield around Skip, who stood nearby in the deep, windblown grass. Gather, disperse, gather, disperse—that was her practice with magic. Shields—up, down, up, down, shrink, grow, shrink, grow, layer, layer, layer. That and lifting things—lift, drop, lift, set down, toss, drop. Skip liked being lifted and shielded, was always fascinated by it. "Oh, this is dull as tombs," Gellia complained.

"You've kept me impressed for days," Skip said. He was downright pretty now that he was cleaned up and in proper attire. Being that his body was young and androgynous he could easily put on a dress and be a very pretty girl.

"I've so much more to learn—I feel there is so much more I don't know." She stretched and sat back down on her rock. The boy dropped down next to her. For a few moments Gellia just took in the scenery, the brown grasses and forests, the city below them. Oddly enough it felt more like home than Fuarmaania ever did. She looked up to the sky and watched the clouds for several moments, wished she could be among them. Maybe she could move them. It was very quiet. The clouds started to shift, started to slowly swirl together above her. Gellia found if she didn't concentrate as much it was easier. The wind rushed down around them, dust devils appeared in the grass. Skip looked at the city from where several shouts and screams came. Well, causing the suspicious commoners to react to her magic was enough bedlam for the day.

She felt her magic wear thin. The clouds slowly returned to their former course. He worried too much. "I don't know how to be more effective. I tire too easily. I guess my body can't handle the stress." Why couldn't she try greater magic? How could she know what she was truly made of unless she tried?

"You'll figure it out."

Skip, he was such a dear. Every day he followed her out to the fields or to the ruin and served as a target. He never once complained. Even though she felt she could say anything to him, she never mentioned her past life and he never asked. It was an odd understanding but perhaps it was part of the Xzepheniixenze. They were friends and that was all that mattered.

Her sensitivity to magic awoke, there was something in the air; she felt something new, foreign. Something magical, powerful—it came into her senses like a bolt, set off alarms in her mind as it burned into her.

Skip jumped to his feet. "Someone's coming." He looked down the path. It was the only ridable side of the hill; the other sides were cliffs covered in forest. Its seclusion was why she liked it.

Gellia rose to her feet as well. She had a terrible feeling in her stomach. It wasn't Cassius who approached, but some other person or group that felt completely alien to her. Whoever it was, they had arrived by magic.

"Heavy horse," Skip said. "They're wearing armor, hear it?"

"Amarynth." The stallion already stood by his mistress. "We better go," Gellia told him and mounted.

"You're right. How are we going to get back to the castle?"

"I don't know." Gellia pulled the boy up behind her. Amarynth rolled his eyes and struck at the air with his forefeet. "Oh rot. Where to go?" Gellia said as she tried to stay calm. If she could reach the castle she wouldn't want to bring an enemy force there and endanger the Sen Duneans. Her hosts had little they could do against magic. Her mind was a whirl of indecision.

Skip stood on Amarynth's rump. "White horses, expensive armor. Maybe they're friendly, but they're Zephrons and I doubt it, not to us anyway," he said. "They're not charging, at least." He almost fell as Amarynth moved.

Gellia could then see them. "There are more of them," Gellia rasped. She directed Amarynth across the top of the hill, trying to decide what she should do.

The dust concealed the enemies' numbers; but their armor glittered in the sun. Amarynth must have been mad with fear; he seemed to want to go over the cliff. She was sure she heard shouts from the city. Would there be battle?

Skip hung onto Gellia's baldric. "Use your magic on them," he said.

"I wouldn't know what to do. Are they going to attack? They have us pinned." She stroked the stallion's neck to try and comfort him to no avail. What's wrong with him? Gellia thought. He seems so angry. I don't know what he wants me to do. She'd left her bow in the castle, and even if she had it, attack would undoubtedly be futile.

"Here they come!" Skip called. "When in doubt trust your horse!"

The black horse backed up against tree and shrub covered cliff behind them. Amarynth tore up the ground with a fore hoof, sending clumps of dirt flying. A man on a white horse appeared before them, others behind. He looked very serious. Gellia reached back and shoved Skip into the bushes and charged.

***

Everything seemed so bright. Too bright to see. What happened? Gellia forced herself to open her eyes. Everything was white around her. This wasn't the hilltop. She flailed under an unfamiliar weight until she felt herself fall and hit a very hard surface. Wait, a bed? Yes, she had been lying in a great bed and now she was on the floor, and she wore some sort of nightgown which was tangled in blankets. There was no one else with her. It was a large room, walls of white marble as was the very hard, cold floor. One tall window. A table, a chair, a door. She struggled to her feet to try the door. It was locked. The window. It was open and she looked out. Gellia found that she was in a tower of a very, very large castle. No, a palace, stretched out before her with walls and rooftops. It was the most beautiful thing she'd ever seen, and it took her mind several moments to realize it was real.

The structures beneath her were all gleaming white, their simple shapes elegant and appealing—never did she think that such beauty existed in the real world. Past the palace was a city, then an ocean of golden grasslands that went on forever. There were people below. She called to them but they either didn't hear or ignored her.

It hadn't been long since her capture because she still felt mystically drained. There was a signature around her. Magical signatures, Cassius had told her, can explain a lot if you know which is which, and of course she didn't. After centering herself she could feel more magic in the palace, what she decided to be old magic—it was the first time she was in a place that was innately magical. It felt so different from Fuarmaania and Sen Dunea—they had very little mystical energies. This felt so much more natural, but the amount of power here terrified her. She already knew any mages here would no doubt out-class her. Gellia paced the length of the room. If they let her be for the night she should be back to full strength, for whatever that was worth. This person though, this person who held her here would know that. Whoever it was had to be clever enough to figure that out. Where was Amarynth? What happened to Skip? She hoped they were safe.

Someone spoke to her. Gellia spun around and saw a young woman in the doorway. The woman wore a white dress styled unlike she'd seen before, and had hair the color of sunshine. Blondie placed some blankets at the foot of the bed, ignored the door behind her. Gellia crept towards her escape. The woman turned to catch the final glimpse of Gellia as she closed the door and locked it behind her.

The woman shouted. Gellia ran, her bare feet stinging as they hit the marble floor. She heard shouts, but she only paid enough attention to them to figure out which way she should run next. Great stairways and gaping doorways. Men in armor, palace guards. The tall passage went on forever. Guards raced towards her. Gellia ducked down another corridor. There were shouts coming from everywhere. She skittered down staircases, through the kitchen, through a sitting room, down some more corridors and through some large empty rooms. Every so often she caught a glimpse of the outdoors and tried to decide if she headed in the correct direction for escape.

If only she could find something to hide in. It soon seemed that she ran in circles, and she hurt all over. Gellia ran into a large rectangular room with a long side completely open to a huge platform outside. There was a corridor in front of her, the one behind her and one on the opposite long side that had stairs. People were everywhere. The only place to go was over the edge. If she had been stronger, she could lower herself down to the ground or even over the walls, but at this time her magic wouldn't hold out for that long. Gellia stopped in her tracks. But maybe she could use the last of her magic to surprise them enough to slip by them. In desperation Gellia reached for the unfamiliar energy around her and cast a sphere at the men who chased her. The globe of purple energy surged down the corridor and because of her panic did more damage than she expected and the guards crumpled. She wasn't sure if she had killed them or not.

When the repercussion of her draw hit her, Gellia fell to her knees and coughed uncontrollably, spit up globs of blood. She knew better than to exceed her limitations. Cassius would scold her. Attacking guards was surely a death sentence. She should have thought this escape through better, he would say. Should have remained calm for days and got to know the castle, but what if they never let her out of the room?

In agony Gellia pulled herself to her feet and called on another magic that wasn't exactly her own. "Xianze!" Her sword appeared in her hand.

The first of the knights charged. Gellia waited. In a flash of enchanted steel Xianze slipped across the first man's midsection and thrust into the next man's gut. Another man didn't make that mistake and quickly disarmed her. Xianze disappeared. He backhanded her with his gauntlet but didn't knock her over—hits from Hugh were worse. Gellia retreated. Even though her legs felt they would no longer propel her, somehow she managed to spin and flee once again, but this time her flight was short lived.

She hit a wall, a rather large man. The battle was over as she bounced off him and landed on her backside with a thud. Guards ran to grab her, but the man stopped them with a wave of his hand. He was taller than her teacher, wore an impressive uniform and a long white cloak. Gellia could only sit and gaze up at him. His handsome face was mature, he probably early into his fourth decade by human standards, had shoulder length platinum blonde curls and calm, ocean colored eyes. Something in those eyes made her shrivel inside—she wasn't sure if she felt she was judged or that he looked at her with disgust or perhaps many things—she was riveted just the same. Guards ran up behind him and he put out his arm to bar their approach.

He looked at her for a moment then spoke with the command of a supreme leader in a language she understood. "You'll be given amnesty considering the situation you found yourself in. However, if you give me further reason to dispose of you, I won't hesitate."

As she wondered about his flawless Xzepheniixenze, Gellia managed to speak. "Where am I?" He was still measuring her, she could feel it.

"Zephronia. Dournzariame more specifically... far from where we found you."

"Where is my horse?" She didn't mention Skip, hoped they didn't even see him when they took her. She finally thought to wipe the blood off her chin.

"Your horse is in the stable. You may visit him if you like." He started away.

"You're not locking me up again?"

"If you act like a normal guest, no."

"I'll try." Gellia almost said something else but he silenced her with a look.

"You'll find Dournzariame's defenses will work well to keep you in as well as others out; if that's what you're planning."

Gellia said nothing. He was powerful, his magic ran exceptionally deep and strong and it was unimaginably old. She knew better than to challenge him. Actually, she was lucky he didn't end her right there.

"These women," he said, motioned to a group of timid looking ladies, "will attend you." He strode down the corridor and left her with her servants. She noticed many bowed as he left.

Gellia followed the blonde women. They fidgeted and glanced at her while Gellia ruminated. This man had been listening to her thoughts, or tried to. She had grown into the habit of keeping herself protected. He didn't threaten her mental defenses, and she did her best to ignore him. To let him know she was watching him would have been a sort of challenge, and Gellia didn't know her opponent well enough to carry through. So why had they kidnapped her? She would have to be patient. She scolded herself for panicking. Stupid, stupid, stupid.

The women drew Gellia a bath. She'd learned from Cassius that the "Great Empires" preferred bathing often, unlike "the Outlands". She sat in the tub for some time, letting the steam dampen her hair into ringlets that stuck to her skin. …Maybe these were the same people who sent their boys to visit her in Fuarmaania. It would make sense, they all looked like family. Gellia's new women, five of them, ran in and out to bring clothes for her.

One of the women approached her and motioned her out of the tub. "What? What do you want? Me to get dressed? Eat? I have to go to dinner." Gellia guessed from the gestures what was going on. That man might be the only one who knew Xzepheniixenze.

They dressed her in men's clothes, but much to Gellia's disliking they were all white. And to make matters worse they tried to make her wear a veil. None of them wore veils. "I don't think this is to my taste," she told them and removed it. Since abandoning her wimple she had little use for head dresses.

They led Gellia into a very large dining room where her host waited with one other person—someone who looked familiar. She spoke before the servants had a chance to close the doors behind her. "I know you," her voice echoed off the walls and arched ceiling and startled her.

"Of course you do," they young man said in Fuarmaanian. "I came to visit you once." He smiled at her. "Come have a seat."

He was too friendly for Gellia's taste. "I'm sorry," she said, "I've forgotten your name."

"Zyendel," he said. "Prince Zyendel of Dournzariame, which is where you are," he said with a smile and a motion of his hand. "But you can just call me Zyendel. My father, the emperor," he gestured to the man, "agreed to have you join us for dinner."

"Thank you, your majesties," Gellia said. She still spoke in Xzepheniixenze. Fuarmaanian seemed such an abrupt, brutish language. She noticed another place setting but no other entered the room to join them.

Zyendel and his father had a conversation in Zephronian. Gellia picked at her food with her fork but she tried to remain as true to her etiquette training as possible. The prince then turned to her. "We can talk after dinner if you wish."

"Why did you bring me here, majesties?" Gellia asked but didn't expect an answer. Some of the sounds of the Zephronian language seemed familiar, as if Fuarmaanian borrowed some of the words.

Before Zyendel had a chance to speak his father did. "It is to your benefit. You were a magical entity we'd been watching for a while. When your magic was felt from all this distance we went to investigate to find if you were a threat. On finding that you are barely better than a wild talent we decided to bring you home with us and then decide what to do with you."

She hadn't expected such a straightforward answer. "And that's for my benefit?"

He continued, "As you are, if you were found by certain members of the Xzepheniixenze aristocracy you would have been exploited and used as a weapon and eventually burned out without consideration for your basic rights as a living being."

"Oh." Gellia felt more awkward with every passing moment. "Don't reprimand the maid in my room, it wasn't her fault," she said. "I tricked her, sire."

The emperor paused. "Only a fool would punish someone for such a thing. It will not happen again… Since you do know a bit about your magic, you are at a slightly less risk to yourself, but your obvious naiveté puts you at dire risk from the Xzepheniixenze. Here we'll assess your magical talents and your inclinations."

"And then?" she asked

He sipped from his goblet, his son remained silent. "You might be released, trained or executed. Much depends on your character. You certainly aren't helping yourself with murdering guards and tricking serving women, especially when you woke to find yourself unharmed and well-tended."

They why treat her this well? Why keep her around at all? Why wasn't she locked in the dungeon? Or already executed?

Zyendel spoke again. "She's the daughter of Decius Iolair. I did some research. He visited Fuarmaania years ago and she's what came of his visit, out of a human woman who became the queen for a short time."

"Never heard of him," the emperor said. "He must be mortal. It's looking up for you... You may burn yourself out before we ever need execute you—especially after your performance earlier."

Gellia could say nothing.

The prince swallowed his food. "Was she out of control?"

"Almost. She was spent when she arrived."

"That isn't good."

"I'm not hungry," Gellia said. "But thank you for the meal, sire."

Zyendel smiled. "Well, let's go for a walk. Goodnight, father."

The way the emperor watched her made Gellia uneasy. She never experienced such a look of cold, like she wronged him in some way. A grudge from a thousand years ago.

In the corridor Zyendel spoke in Fuarmaanian again... "I don't think he'll kill you," he said. "I don't think he is as fierce as he seems to be. Besides, I won't let him harm you."

She glanced at her servants who were always near. "You're trying to be my friend, aren't you?" Zyendel had to want something from her, didn't he? And why did she feel as though she was his new pet?

He paused. "You need one, don't you?"

"It's possible I suppose." She managed a smile. "So all Zephrons look alike?"

The prince chuckled. "Not as much as the Xzepheniixenze. You lot are easier to distinguish by magic than by appearance."

"I'm only half Xzepheniixenze," she corrected. Xzepheniixenze, she thought, and liked the feel of it. Zyendel took a step closer, far too close for her comfort; a mere hand-length was between them. She leaned back a little and started to move her feet across the marble.

"That's the strange thing. Even though I know you're not, you seem very much like a pureblood except in personality." He paused to look out a window at a courtyard filled with fragrant bushes.

"I'm that odd?" She slid her foot back a step.

"Extremely. You are a total enigma. But I like you just the same."

"I thought as much." She leaned over the window and inhaled the perfume that rose from the flowering branches. "So you have magic as well? Like your father?" She turned to watch him as he spoke.

He smiled and stared at guards as they patrolled the corridor, then took another step towards her. "I have magic but whether it's like my fathers or not, I don't know. I have reason to believe that we are not related by blood."

"Really. But you are prince and heir?" Gellia heard him sigh. "Have you ever asked him about it?" She was surprised he told her this much.

"Yes, and yes. I asked him about my mother and he only tells me that I am his son and the prince of Zephronia. That's all he will tell me. He doesn't speak of my mother. He's also not the type to have illicit relations with women."

Her "father" didn't like to talk about mother, either, but she wasn't about to share that with him. She was impressed he was so willing to talk to her. She also amazed herself at her outward calmness. No matter where she moved, he was nearly on top of her. Did he intend to make her feel that uncomfortable? She suspected Cassius would say she gave Zyendel too much credit. Well, Gellia wasn't as experienced as Cassius, and she was doing the best she could.

"It doesn't take much for a conversation to stop when Gallylya is involved. Or anything to stop. I'm sure you realize that already." He glanced at her then looked away, then put his hand on her forearm. "He could command the tides to cease if he chose—and without magic."

She nodded and continued to watch him, resisted the urge to yank her arm from under his hand but she desperately wished she could. The emperor's name was Gallylya.

"In the olden days and some people even now know him as the Phoenix. He is the leader of the legendary Vega Knights. You should read the stories some time. I'm not nearly as impressive as any of them to be sure."

"Perhaps you haven't come into your own yet," she said and wondered if the compliment would take her anywhere.

He smiled at her. "I'm over three centuries old. I think I've reached my potential. Unlike you." As he said it Gellia recognized the look of admiration in his eyes. It made her skin crawl.

She looked away. "I don't know anything about that."

He brushed her dark curls from her face. "I do."

Gellia quickly spun away and smiled. She hoped her flirtatious display would keep him talking and that he didn't notice she didn't want his other attention. "Do you have siblings? Other relatives?" She would do her best to keep the subject off her.

"I'm an only child. I do have an odd aunt, though." He motioned for them to walk again, offered his arm, which she hesitantly took. As they started to move Gellia noticed a few ladies who stood together in a nearby corridor. It was then she realized it must be a cultural habit, for these women spoke very closely to each other but not so much as people whispering or telling secrets. Perhaps that was why Zyendel always stood so close to her—not that it made her any less uncomfortable.

"To tell you the truth, I don't exactly know what causes her strange behavior. She's been that way for as long as I've been alive, probably even longer. She doesn't really talk to anyone, especially not my father. I think it's something he did, but I don't know how he could do anything that would disturb her that much. She stays in her chambers by herself most of the time and every so often comes out and wanders around."

"Sounds odd," Gellia said and sat on a nearby bench.

"Quite." He looked away and would not continue further. "You have my father's honesty. You don't know how rare that is for one of your kind."

She forced herself to stay put when he sat next to her. "Tell me about your relationship with the Xzepheniixenze," she said. "I know so little about them." It was the truth, too.

Zyendel raised an eyebrow and smiled a little. "They haven't bothered us in years. They haven't even been in the Outlands for ages—but for the Crossroads of course. I try to keep track of big events over there to keep an eye on when they might attack."

"You're at war?"

"Not anything that's been declared as such. The bitterness runs deep. I haven't been around long enough to understand it all, although it seems there's really nothing to understand. There are only a few great powers still in Xzepheniixenze. My father knows more about it than I do, certainly in older times. I do know the modern powers, though."

His gaze made her uneasy. "Thank you for talking with me," Gellia said. "I'm tired and I think I'm going to bed now." Gallylya was obviously too powerful for her to be opinionated. But if Zyendel would give her information…

Zyendel nodded and smiled. "Sleep well, princess." He watched her leave with her servants. "You do not know how astonishing you are."

As she tried to sleep in the strange bed Gellia thought of something Cassius said once. Didn't he make mention of Zyendel and his father once in Fuarmaania? It was a long time ago… The night felt so different here. She rose and went to the window to feel the breeze and remembered her wind chime that hung in her room in Fuarmaania. It always helped her sleep.

The city below was so serene. The lanterns were lit in the tidy streets. She wished she could explore. Zyendel might tell her otherwise but she was indeed a prisoner. Beyond the city, beyond the plains, the horizon beckoned her. For long moments Gellia stared at the distant darkness and prayed that she would not remain here forever, that somehow she could escape.

Something fluttered in the pit of her stomach. She instinctively looked at the dark sky. No one else stirred. Did anyone else feel it? There was a streak of color through the stars, just above the horizon. Several appeared parallel to the first; each reminded her of a wound. She could almost feel a strange twist in the air, like something cried out all around her but it was so weak. The streaks faded in and out and changed color, almost seemed to smear across the sky. She clung to the windowsill and tried to regain her breath. It was such a faint feeling yet it frightened her to the depths of her soul. Cassius, where are you? What is happening? She thought fiercely, but could not allow the thought to travel beyond her own mind.

Before her legs wobbled too much she darted back to bed and pulled the covers over her head. She was certain Gallylya would protect her if there was real danger.

***

"Well she doesn't know anything about the realm but does know a little magic, and they certainly wouldn't have taught her," Zyendel said.

"Not unless someone wanted to spare the effort to create an ally—she speaks the language very well—and what makes you think she knows nothing of Xzepheniixenze?" Gallylya drummed his fingers on the table. "Luckily she doesn't reek of Xzepheniixenze mage so the chance of her being in contact with one is less."

"Well, let's see who might be interested. All the Azqebrynes are homeless, the Grian are on raids, Alasdairs and Rintaro won't come out of their libraries, most clans are doing their usual... the Lorkiegns are on a spree and even though I stay away from Ravengate I know he wouldn't sneak about like that. I've never seen hide or hair of anyone near her. The only thing that would suggest that someone was with her was that Fotryn was never found. Seekers do you think?" He noticed his father was distracted. His father was never distracted.

"I wouldn't doubt it... What do you know about Tintagel?"

"They're loyal to the emperor. Not much to say about them, really. Why?" Could his father have a hunch?

"Used to be a very prominent family but they haven't been anything to see for over nine-hundred years, maybe even longer. They were loyal to Zenobia. Zantedeschia Adamina was a nightmare." The emperor fell deep into thought before he spoke again. "She caused more destruction than any two armies. You would do better to find out all you can on them—and anyone else of any talent."

"Zenobia," Zyendel repeated. Gellia belonged there if it was as fantastic as the stories claimed. She didn't know what he she did to him, her beauty was far beyond the physical, he could feel her magic but not see it, and it drew him in like dragons to treasure… He could tell his father nothing of his feelings. Not yet at least.

***

Gellia spent three days exploring the palace. The residents were unfriendly, but she was used to that. Luckily the architecture was astounding. The palace was so clean, so pure and yet she could tell from the many halls and stairways and anything else made of stone that it was used for countless centuries. Some things were replaced while other parts were worn from so many years—but this was not run down Fuarmaania castle—this was beautifully aged. She wondered how many walked the same path before her. She visited Amarynth daily, who was surviving in the meticulously kept stall, but they would not let her take him out.

…She thought she might fall asleep as she lie across her bed. Lazily she created empty barriers off her finger and thought of Skip. From what she gathered, the Zephrons hadn't seen him when they captured her. Would the Sen Duneans come rescue her? She didn't want harm to come to them. Would they send word to Cassius? Gellia rolled over and climbed to her feet. She needed to find something for entertainment.

So Gellia did the only thing she could and watched people. She walked up and down corridors, through gardens and halls. They seemed to be a quiet people, probably because they were always standing so close to one another. She wondered if she would have a chance to observe the emperor, and if she had the opportunity if she would be too frightened to do so.

It wasn't long before she spotted a group of ladies, likely in the service of another noble. They were all a fluster when they saw her. All but one. This one approached her from the midst of the group. Gellia wasn't sure what to do but stand there, entranced. As the woman came into the light Gellia noticed how fragile she looked, like she had lost much, as if her age was measured by the weight on her soul. She was Gellia's height and shape, but Zephron. The princess glanced at the other women who quickly ran away.

"Gellia," the woman said.

Gellia felt a shiver up her spine.

"You are Gellia." The woman spoke Xzepheniixenze like Cassius did; it had some sort of quality to it that Gellia had yet to master.

"Who are you?" Gellia asked. She tried to ignore her goose bumps.

"Someone who has been waiting a long time to meet you." She put her hand on her bosom. "I'm Connylia, but call me Conny. I have no use for formality."

She had the same blue-grey eyes as Gellia, and the same ringlet to her hair. There was something else… Something strong pulled them together. "How do you know who I am?"

"I know Zapheny."

Something in Connylia's eyes warmed her, there was something between them Gellia always desired. "I feel that I know you as well," Gellia whispered.

Gallylya's voice shattered the moment. "I should have known that a bloody Xzelki would bring you out of the woodwork, sister." He strode towards them from the other end of the corridor. With him were Connylia's serving women. "Your women feared for your safety but I see they over-reacted."

"They learn from the best," Connylia muttered. Something flashed in her eyes as her brother approached, and she walked away without another word.

Gallylya watched his sister storm away. "What did she say to you?" he asked Gellia.

"Nothing, sire."

"Surely you don't mistake me for an idiot."

"I heard she's a lunatic, sire," Gellia replied. Being near him made her start to wither.

"How skillfully worded," he said. "My sister hasn't been herself for a very long time." He looked at Gellia and she shrunk away, but she gathered enough strength to speak.

"Have I wronged you is some way, sire?" she asked.

Gallylya chuckled; it was not a warm sound as laughter usually was—it felt more like daggers piercing her. He walked away. Gellia watched him disappear down one of the arched corridors. She took a deep but shaky breath and started towards the stables. She wondered if she could find Connylia again at another time.

***

To Gellia's surprise, Connylia was already there with Amarynth, visited him as if he was an old friend. He had his head over the stall door. Her pale hand rested on his forehead, partially covered by his cascading forelock. "What do you call him?" she asked.

"Amarynth."

"Amarynth. Amarynth." Connylia whispered, and told him something in yet another new language and smiled a little. It didn't look like happiness came to her easily, for the smile quickly slipped off her face as if she was too tired to keep it. As her hand ran down his sleek neck under his thick mane Connylia's eyes closed. Gellia just watched curiously. The Zephron sighed and opened her eyes. "An honor. I shall have fine tack made for you," she told the horse. "What do you say, Gellia?"

"If you wish." She was stunned; it was unlike him to be so amiable. Usually he stood in the back of the stall and glowered.

"We have much to talk about," Connylia said. "And it looks like we have the time. My brother isn't going to let you go, ever, if he can help it."

Gellia followed Connylia through the stable to a very large box stall that contained two large horses. They were majestic and glowingly white, heavy boned but elegant. Connylia spoke as she petted them. "I'd like you to meet Justin and Jutham," she said.

They were obviously bond horses of some kind, for their stall door didn't have a latch. Each reached his head over the wide door so Gellia could touch them. She'd never seen anything so beautiful. Their manes were so full they fell on both sides of their necks, their tails thick enough for several horses, and their coats were soft as satin. When Gellia's fingertips touched a velvety muzzle she felt a wave of something strange and powerful. It make her choke with emotion. It seemed strange, but all she could feel was love. Pure love. Their gentle, wise eyes, their souls were perfection.

Connylia leaned her head on one's neck. "They're all that keeps me alive, it seems," she said. "And they're very pleased to meet you. Welcome, Gellia."

7

Connylia dismissed her attendants and invited Gellia into her royal chambers. The first thing she noticed was what had the most color, an old wooden trunk that looked like it had been through a war. Everything seemed blank and white; plain furniture was scattered through the three rooms. Even though it was light, the starkness was dreary. They passed the trunk on the way to the long balcony where they sat on a satin upholstered sofa. The landing overlooked the vast Zephronian countryside of golden brown grasses and distant trees.

She didn't look like an emperor's sister, Gellia thought. Connylia was dressed more like a servant. Her dress was plain and pale and was barely better than a nightgown. She wore her hair in a very long braid, a few wispy ringlets escaping around her face. Connylia must have been beautiful at one time, unimaginably beautiful. But now her face was tired and sad, her whole body seemed to sag with some sort of invisible weight. "Tell me about yourself," she said. Gellia watched as Connylia tried to smile a little.

Gellia didn't know where to begin, really. "Well, I was born in Fuarmaania."

Connylia nodded. "The New Land, as it translates into Zephronian. Although I've heard it called the Pocket Kingdom as well."

Gellia smiled. So much she didn't know about her own kingdom. "I was the princess there. I was raised by my nurse, Corrah. I ran away…" She wasn't comfortable giving details quite yet.

"You've told me nothing of yourself," Connylia said. "And I haven't had any news about the world outside in a very long time. Please continue." Servants brought tea and biscuits.

"Well, I was in Sen Dunea when the soldiers brought me here. I made some friends there." She wasn't sure if she would ever see them again. She knew it would be easier to bear now that Connylia was in her life. Somehow.

"I know what it is to miss people," Connylia said.

Gellia nodded. "All those years I felt my life was already over but now I realize I was just sleeping. I feel like I've just opened my eyes."

Connylia smiled. "Ah, there's something."

Gellia shook her head in thought. "I had to be woken up."

"Who woke you? It couldn't have been a Fuarmaanian, that's for certain. One of your friends?"

"Friend? Well I suppose... a teacher really... well I guess he's a friend. Travel companion too I suppose." She sipped her tea although her hostess hadn't touched her own. It was flowery and sweet with honey.

"Oh?" A dim light arose in Connylia's eyes.

It came out Gellia's mouth before she could stop herself, as if under a spell. "He's a baron. His name's Cassius, from what I gather he isn't very well known." Gellia could barely believe she said his name in this place, but now it was entrusted with Connylia. She hoped she wouldn't regret it.

"Cassius?"

Gellia looked at her tea. "Yes, you haven't heard of him—I'm not surprised..."

"Is his aura a perfect shade of green that seems to permeate to the core of all that is magic?" Connylia asked. "And is he a meticulous creature? Mutters his complaints? Smug?"

Gellia never heard it described so closely to the truth. "Y-yes."

"Then I know who he is. Well I'll be. He still lives." Connylia beamed. "I haven't seen him in a very long time... Kept his promise I see, although I'm sure it's to his advantage as well... Cassius Vazepheny of Tintagel for I doubt he would let anyone have his mother's castle."

Gellia sipped the tea as she weighed her situation. "I don't know if you'll ever see him again. I don't know if he'll come rescue me," Gellia said. "I have no idea how I'll get out myself." It wasn't wise to tell so much, but Connylia felt so familiar. Not knowing what else to say, she tried to ask questions of her own. "So you have been secluded for twenty years or so? That's an awfully long time." Gellia was puzzled by Connylia's look of surprise. "If Cassius is only in his thirties, then..."

Conny looked at her for a moment then broke into a giggle. "Did he tell you that?"

"I don't understand."

"Don't worry yourself about it, just details... I haven't laughed in so long..." The Zephron woman calmed after a moment. "How long has he been with you?"

"Oh, a while now, years..." It had been a long time.

"And he woke you up."

"Y-yes."

Something in Connylia's eyes sparkled. "He'll come for you Gellia, you needn't worry about that. Just give him time." She smiled widely with her lips pressed together. "Perhaps he wishes you to spend some time with me. Perhaps he waits for the right opportunity."

Gellia set the teacup down. It was late afternoon and she didn't want any trouble with her host. "I should be going to dinner soon—"

"Oh don't bother." Connylia waved her hand.

"Won't his highness be angry?"

"He isn't going to kill you for missing dinner." A servant she must have mentally summoned appeared. "Tell his highness that Princess Gellia will be spending time with me tonight." The servant nodded and left. Connylia turned back to Gellia. "My brother is harsh, but he does what he thinks is best, but he lets his righteousness get in the way... I don't hate my brother, Gellia, I just hate what he's done. He'll never understand us."

Us. As in she and Gellia. That's what Connylia meant. "What about Zyendel?" Gellia asked. "I, I almost think he's fond of me." They were odd words coming from her. She'd never really spoken of fondness, certainly not involving herself.

"I have no doubt that he is fond of you. How could he not be? Trust that you don't trust him."

"But if Gallylya—"

"You're young, so even though you're a Xzepheniixenze and an enemy, you will receive mercy. There is a long history of distrust, and those like my brother have the most distrust, even when evidence of virtue is in plain sight. Zyendel is not the man the emperor is, unfortunately."

Gellia just looked at her.

Connylia smiled and it was obvious there was going to be a change of topic. "My goodness, Gellia... So he taught you a bit about magic?"

"Yes. He's teaching me how to be Xzepheniixenze too. I've been learning protocol and what not from him and the King of Sen Dunea. He has books of magic sent to me to read, not that I understand the complexities of it all."

Conny continued to smile. "I know what that's like. And while you're here I'll continue your education. What else is there to do?"

"How?"

"A long time ago." she looked to the horizon. "I was an ambassador. I spent many years of my life in Xzepheniixenze and have learned much of the details of their culture. I also have a bit of magic of my own—I had a very, very talented teacher...." She grew distant for a moment. "I think for the time you're here I can help you. I doubt that the King of Sen Dunea knows how to teach you to dance or how to be a lady of Xzepheniixenze." She smiled and was silent with thought for a moment before taking Gellia's hand. "...I know it may be difficult for you to believe... but I am the mother of the founder of Fuarmaania, Quenelzythe Zapheny. And you, as all of your royal family, are descendant from him, from me."

"How is that possible?" Again, Gellia was curious but not completely surprised, for she was discovering that everything about her heritage seemed to already be within her some place.

Connylia shook her head and smiled. "I'm very old."

"My life has changed so much in the past months I don't think anything will shock me anymore." Gellia said slowly. "In Fuarmaania they called me insane but it all makes sense somehow."

"And you are with company that proves it to be true. You are Zapheny, Gellia. Zapheny are not like other people, they are more separate from all others—even those of the same race—but they are closer to the others than any Xzepheniixenze could be."

Connylia smiled and shook her head again. "You have given me a reason to continue to breathe for a little while longer. I never thought I would see anyone ever again. It becomes clear why I'm still here."

They were silent for a time, admired the night sky and the half-moon that had risen above them. What happened to her? Gellia wondered, but decided if Connylia wanted to tell her she would. It was peaceful out there in the world. The breeze was refreshing, and for the first time since her arrival Gellia felt truly relaxed. Her new companion had put her mind at ease. She'd be able to fill her days with activities here and perhaps she'd still be rescued from this gilded prison. She'd been given hope.

"I see you found my ring," Connylia said.

"Pardon?" Gellia looked at her new friend and thought perhaps her eyes were welling, but she didn't shed a tear.

"That ring you wear, it was mine. I gave it to Quenelzythe. It is yours now. I certainly don't need it. Would you like to know its magic?"

"It's magical?" Gellia looked at the ring. She hadn't taken it off since the day she found it in the secret room.

"Oh yes. If you say the word written on it you can understand any language spoken around you. It was given to me because I could never keep all the languages and dialects straight when I was in Xzepheniixenze. Its other magic I'm sure is lost now."

It was a Xzepheniixenze word written on the band, she realized.

"But be careful where you use it. Sometimes you're better off not knowing. Knowing too much can be difficult on the spirit. Someone told me that once. I wonder where he is now."

Gellia felt a chill. "I'll be careful."

Connylia smiled. "There are some things about Xzepheniixenze only a woman can teach you. And yes, it's very important."

Gellia smiled.

***

The very next day Gellia had the misfortune of meeting the emperor in one of the corridors. "You've been speaking with my sister," Gallylya said. When she'd spied him from the other end she tried to come up with a way to avoid him. Unfortunately there was no corridor to escape down, and if she'd turned on her heel he would have called to her and she would have been mortified. In the halls of Dournzariame she was back in Fuarmaania. At least there were no beatings. Yet.

"She's very nice, sire," Gellia replied, beamed to hide the fact that he intimidated her to no end. Her mind wanted to wander anywhere but here. There were people walking by, bowing as they went and shooting glances at her.

"At one time..." he rumbled.

"I'm going to see her now, sire. Would you like me to give her a message?"

"A message is useless to someone who is deaf and blind." He went on his way.

Gellia scampered through the palatial castle to the out-of-the-way wing to her friend's chambers. "I'm here!" Gellia called as she burst through Connylia's door. When she saw the look on Connylia's face she knew she'd been a bit to exuberant on her entrance, but after escaping the emperor she couldn't help it. Safe at last!

"We do have much to accomplish, don't we?" Connylia said as she smirked. She began to teach anything and everything she could think of, and not always in a rational order. Information would come back to Connylia's mind at odd times, and would be conveyed before she forgot it again. Connylia was a demanding teacher, but Gellia didn't mind. It was a good distraction from her other worries. It certainly passed the time, and before Gellia knew it, she's been at Dournzariame for several weeks.

Gellia found that she could even rise extra early, have breakfast with Connylia and avoid everyone else for most days all day. There were certainly times when she had to face the emperor or deal with the prince, but for the most part she was happy, and left alone. An added joy was Connylia would smuggle books from the library when she could, when a book wouldn't be missed. Gellia was denied access to the library so had never seen the inside. She was certain it was glorious.

It was late one evening after a day of reading, dancing, and discussion. They were having supper in Connylia's room and Connylia was speaking of cultural tidbits. "Their hair is of significance. There are old stories about these traditions, but I'm sure most don't know or care about such things any longer." She took a sip of wine. "You can tell how old they are by the length of their hair; it's really the only way to tell such things. Immortals such as them always look young. But most importantly, don't touch their hair unless you're making a proposition. It's not looked down upon, and you're very beautiful so your proposition would likely be accepted, so know if you're making one." She shook her head as Gellia turned bright red. "Don't blush, Gellia, there's nothing to blush about. You didn't think such a culture of equal opportunities for all, no marriage, and alliances continuously being made and broken was going to have women submitting on their wedding night for the good of the country?"

Gellia wasn't certain what to say. "No one has ever been so straight forward with these talks. Is it the same here in Zephronia?" Her face was still hot.

"No no no. It isn't as bad as in the outlands, but it isn't as free as Xzepheniixenze." She was thoughtful for a moment. "There used to be a practice—many centuries ago that is thankfully not widely used today—of keeping young women and their bond horses from being together. Young women were basically prisoners, and any white horse that was wandering around was chased away until it gave up. Sometimes it would take years, but without physical contact the bond couldn't be made." She smiled sadly. "That's why I never had one. I was a handmaiden to the queen, and my parents sought a good marriage for me. They didn't need a bond horse mucking things up."

"How would a bond horse muck things up? Aren't they good things?"

Connylia smiled. "Yes. But bond horses only think about taking care of their person, and bringing that person to their full potential and happiness. A bond horse would encourage a girl to disobey her family and find further education, adventure, wonder. That wasn't always desirable for a young woman in Zephronia."

Gellia was sad for Connylia, and sad for herself that she wasn't born in Xzepheniixenze.

"But," Connylia said with a happy smile. "I have Justin and Jutham, and they're companionship and loyalty have been invaluable. I am one of tens of thousands denied bond horses, although I'm sure most have passed on by now."

"I think Nighthawk might be Cassius' bond horse," Gellia said as she digested the information.

"Nighthawk?" Connylia said. She was thoughtful for a moment and seemed distant. "Nighthawk is a foster, a young bond horse who was lucky enough to find a mentor. He'll move on at some point. Right now he's learning all he can, like you are."

"The more I find out the more I realize I don't know much at all. Will I have a bond horse? Or because I'm from the Outlands…"

Connylia giggled. "Oh Gellia, you silly child. You have one already. And you waited long enough to find him, after your years of yearning while with your trusty Tempest."

At first Gellia didn't comprehend, but when she did she scolded herself for being such an idiot. Amarynth. "But he doesn't speak to me and do all those magical things like Nighthawk."

"They all have their own personalities and abilities. Now that you realize and accept that Amarynth is what he is…"

Gellia nodded and knew she'd have to visit him as soon as she could. Looking back she could see it now. He came to the Outlands to find her. That was a long way away from Xzepheniixenze. No wonder Cassius had him saddled for her… She had to push this new joy from her mind, she wouldn't be allowed to see him tonight because it was too late, but perhaps tomorrow.

"Xzepheniixenze is a strange and wonderful place. Anything is possible for those who want it and are willing to do anything to attain it."

"How long did you live there?"

"Oh, not long enough." Connylia seemed to drift away. "That was a long time ago. I had to learn everything in a hurry as well..."

Gellia wasn't sure if she should continue to ask questions or to keep quiet so she merely sat there focused on her meal.

"My brother would be wrong to keep you here, Gellia. I see you. I see your magic, your soul, as few others can. Most miss exact splendor of your life, but I have seen it before and recognize it. Others only know that there is something different about you, something unseen. I am so happy you're here with me. There is so little time for us."

***

"I understand the grape harvest was wonderful last year," Gellia said in an attempt break the maddening silence. Zyendel smiled at her. It had been months since she first met Connylia, and it was the first time the emperor's sister came to his supper in that time. Even though Connylia might have been insane, one could never tell by her manners, for in public everything she did was graceful. Gellia did her best to imitate what she saw and tried desperately to remember everything she was taught.
The emperor watched his sister who was seated next to Gellia. "It's good to have you here tonight," Gallylya told his sister.

Connylia ignored him.

Gellia spoke. "Excuse me, sire, I was wondering if we could have a party here sometime? It would be so lovely..." She knew it was rude to change the subject but she wished to take his attention off his sister. Furthermore, a party would give her a chance to practice her new skills under pressure.

"I don't think we've had a party here for a very long time," Gallylya said and leaned back into his chair.

"It might be fun," Zyendel added. "I'm sure everyone would enjoy it. I could start the arrangements tonight..."

Gellia forced herself not to roll her eyes. Zyendel still smiled at her, watched her. Just that morning he cornered her in the stable and asked if she wanted to go riding. Of course, she refused and told him she would ride none other than her own horse, which wouldn't be allowed. So instead he introduced her to his own gleaming white bond horse and tried fruitlessly to sneak more information from her. However, Gellia was too distracted by being angered of girls' treatment in the past concerning their bond horses.

"Only if my sister promises to attend," Gallylya said. Connylia dabbed her mouth with a napkin. Zyendel seemed braced for something, and his father continued to look at Connylia.

"Ah…" Gellia started. She wished she could come up with something better to say.

Connylia rose from her chair and as strange aura flowed around her. As Gellia shrank from the tension, she felt the magic energy zip past them as Connylia grew more enraged. She still had her napkin clenched in her hand and she drew herself up regally. "How dare you! How dare you do this to me! How can you be so cruel?"

Zyendel looked as if he is used to this, Gellia thought as she almost crawled under the table. Connylia drew so much energy that it radiated around her, billowed her clothes and blew her hair.

"We've had this conversation already, Connylia." Gallylya seemed calm, even a little bored.

"And you still don't understand." The energy fell. "You never will. Not even after all you care about is dead," she said. She finished with a sentence in a language that neither Gellia nor Zyendel, she judged from the look on his face, understood. Gallylya knew what she said. He slowly rose from his chair. Gellia slid down in hers and watched the prince do likewise. So this wasn't something Zyendel saw before, she thought. She hazarded a glance at the emperor. She swore that the look he gave could have struck someone dead. Gellia peeked over the table and watched her friend storm from the room.

His highness seated himself and the meal continued.

"I tire of this," Zyendel said in Zephronian.

Gellia continued to eat and tried not to look like she understood what was going on. Magical rings were wonderful— all she need do was mouth the word when no one was looking. It was too late to catch what Connylia had said, but it still proved its usefulness.

Gallylya spoke. "Creator of the Golden Age or not, Razhiede was an evil, scheming old bastard. If he had his way dragons would be living in Dournzariame and laying waste to the countryside."

"I'm sorry about the ball, I didn't mean to start anything," Gellia interjected.

"You didn't know," Zyendel said. "It's one of the strange things we have to deal with."

Gallylya spoke in Zephronian, "I have my doubts. I wouldn't be surprised if she knew what we are saying."

As he watched her Gellia tried to keep her composure. He only has conjectures, she told herself.

Zyendel continued in Zephronian: "she hasn't had any cultural exposure and you think she has it in her?"

"She's Xzepheniixenze, that's all we need to know. Have you ever in your centuries of travel met an honorable Xzelki?"

"True." Zyendel nodded.

"In all my years I've met maybe two… Have your people found out anything yet?"

He must have meant Gellia. Did he know? Gallylya eyed her. What would she tell them? She always lived with the fear that she would be questioned. In her wild imagination she often thought she'd be interrogated by someone from the dungeon with the threat of an iron maiden or skull crusher. However nothing frightened her more than the emperor himself. Logically it was doubtful she would be tortured, and she felt she could keep her calm when talking to others. But Gallylya… his mere presence was enough to make her doubt her courage, even after all her time in the palace.

"Everything is about the same in the empire. Raven is doing his usual ignoring of the country and wenching, Kaymaria is rebuilding. From what I just found out Raven had been looking for this one but he hasn't found her. He sent Decius to find her mother, but well, you know the story. What's wrong?"

"As we speak she has mental barriers up to keep us out."

"Can't you break them?"

"I don't yet have reason to. They're quite skillfully made." Gallylya leaned in into his chair and mused over her.

Gellia tried not to beam with pride. They were both looking at her so she smiled at both of them. "This is a wonderful meal," she said. It was the truth.

"Gellia, who taught you to speak Xzepheniixenze?" Gallylya asked.

She tried not to panic, and kept barriers at full strength, started to push her food around on her plate. "Sire, I found a book that translated it. It took a very long time. I like to read. It's all I ever did in Fuarmaania, that and ride my horse. It was quite the scandal." Cassius was a book, a book of infinite knowledge; she made herself believe the lie for safety's sake. She set down the fork and picked at a thread on the cuff of her sleeve.

Gallylya almost seemed greater somehow. "How did you find your horse?"

"He just appeared one day, sire." It was the truth.

"And how did you manage to get as far as Sen Dunea on your own?"

"Sire, my horse is very fast; we're able run away from most danger." Gellia smiled, but wasn't at all convincing.

"And where did you learn your magic?"

"More books. I told your highness that it was all I ever did there."

Gallylya's eyes narrowed. "Quenelzythe had a collection of magic books, did he? I'm sure they came to good use for a country filled with magicless humans," he said. "I'm surprised they didn't use them as kindling for they certainly couldn't appreciate their worth."

This. This was her fear. Maybe if she gave him a little... "I found them in a secret room."

"Ah, I see. And you ran to the enemy of your country with all your books and you weren't worried they'd attack you? Why aren't you asking me who Quenelzythe is? Connylia certainly doesn't speak of him."

Zyendel spoke in Zephronian. "I couldn't get anything out of her, how do you do it?" Gallylya didn't answer him.

Gellia wiggled her toes in her shoes. "Well I know I'm a little naïve but I thought maybe the Sen Duneans were different from what we were always told they were. Fuarmaanians are the true barbarians." She tried to think of a reason why she didn't ask about her forefather other than blaming books for everything.

Gallylya's eyes narrowed. "How fortunate for you that the Sen Duneans decided not to take you captive and hold you for ransom or act out their revenge on you. Fortunate indeed that you blended in so well with your black horse that they didn't recognize you, or that they saw you as a Xzepheniixenze and decided you were too powerful for them."

"What's your horse's name?" Zyendel asked, smiling at her.

She was grateful he changed the subject. "Amarynth."

"I haven't heard that name in a long time," Gallylya muttered. "Study dead cultures, do you?"

"I found it in a book, sire." The moment it left her mouth she felt like an idiot, and started to panic. She forced herself to breathe and quickly rose and scurried from the room. No one stopped her. Gallylya would destroy her if she stayed another moment. It reminded her that at one time she thought she was the strongest person alive. Not anymore.

***

Gellia was unable to contact her mentor—her door was locked and if there were servants, they wouldn't answer either. With no place to hide Gellia was forced to either stay in her room or wander the palace. Her room was far too boring to remain there all the time.

So began Zyendel's full-fledged courtship. Zyendel spent most of his time trying to encourage her to talk about her life and experiences and showering her with small gifts like flowers and sugary treats (which she fed to the servants). Gellia was certain he had seduced many a Zephron maiden in his day, but she was skilled at avoiding capture in such circumstances. She was also aware that he might be acting out a plot to find all her secrets for his father. His mind was always listening, she could feel it, but she kept up her defenses and waited tolerantly for him to go away. Her ability to be patient was improving daily. Eventually they would break her down, this she knew, but she would hold out for as long as possible.

For once in too long, she was by herself and able to visit Amarynth. She rested her chin on his stall door and sighed. Her paranoia forced her to stay up at night concentrating on her defensive magic, which was surely reported to the emperor. The added stress of Zyendel following her around didn't help. Gellia started to wonder if she would ever see Connylia again, or if she would remain a tortured pet of the prince for the rest of her life. She'd have to start thinking of an escape plan, which from this place and these people would have to be very involved.

Amarynth was in the back of his stall, coat gleaming from a fresh grooming. "What am I to do?" she asked him. "How will I ever escape when I'm always drained?" She started to feel defeated. Amarynth wasn't a garrulous horse like Nighthawk, and she'd accepted that. She was pleased just to be in his presence and have someone to talk to. She certainly could recognize their connection, now.

Something closed down around her, something magical but not threatening, and familiar. Gellia thought of it as being in a friend's arms, warm and protected. Amarynth sighed. *You will escape,* came a voice into Gellia's mind. It was just a glimmer at first, but she could feel it coming closer.

Amarynth, you spoke to me, didn't you? Her heart leapt with joy.

I am not going to make it a habit of speaking with you. It's imperative you learn to think on your own. His mind's voice became clearer to her, a wealth of masculine tones and depth and color. It was beautiful and elaborate. The stallion watched the men go about their business outside the stall. *These are desperate times.*

You have something important to tell me?

I see your exhaustion. You cannot hold out Gallylya forever, not on your own. Yes, he waits for you to tire. I can shield you from them as long as you're near. The palace's defenses are strongly against you and I cannot break through without them seeing it as an attack. Sleeping in the stable hasn't bothered you before...

Gellia almost cried. *I don't mind at all. Amarynth?* She sighed. The conversation ended. She had so much to ask. Why was he silent for so long? She hugged his arched neck and sighed. "You're so wonderful. And you can talk." Perhaps he wasn't ever going to be chatty, but her love for him grew daily. Amarynth munched on some hay and looked around outside. Gellia pulled herself from under his mane. "I'll take you up on your offer." She curled up in the corner of the stall. The straw was comfortable enough. Perhaps if he spoke to her again she could ask him about her mother, he might know something. She even grew a little excited with the prospect that her mother was still alive somewhere…

She was awoken by the clatter of galloping hoofs on stone. When she jumped up to look over the stall door she saw several knights galloping from the gate. *What's going on?* She asked Amarynth.

I'm sure you'll hear about it very soon, he said.

It was like and answer from Cassius. "In time," was a common reply to many of her questions. She left the stable and made her way back into the palace. Nothing seemed too out of the ordinary until she reached one of the larger corridors. She still didn't know the place well enough to know how to avoid such public places.

She heard Gallylya's footfalls before she saw him. That sound had always stuck with her, for there was no other like it. It echoed through corridors, a steady, even pace, faster than a march and more determined—as though he was going to single handedly win a war. When he finally came into view, Gellia figured out why people called him "the Phoenix." He was a god of light and fire as his golden armor reflected sunlight onto the walls in pools of brightness. Despite herself, she stopped and stared. Never could she have imagined such a thing. As Gallylya passed her his fluttering cloak whipped by her in a blue and white blur. One of the many who followed him carried a sword almost as big as she, a golden sword, the hilt a fiery bird. A ruby the size of her fist was the bird's body and seemed to married the handle to the blade. Gellia was filled with fear and admiration. Once he was out of sight she broke her trance and scampered through the halls to try Connylia and perhaps find some answers. After the servants let Gellia in, she found Connylia sitting in the sun on her balcony with her eyes closed. "My friend, hello.

There seems to be some excitement," Gellia said. "Have you heard anything?"

"Excitement?" Connylia said. "Nothing exciting happens around here, but for you."

"I saw his highness in armor, and there were people rushing about in the stable yard."

Connylia opened her eyes and stared into the sky for a moment. "That is strange. But we won't find answers here." She rose, dismissed all but one of her servants. That one helped Connylia change into tunic and breeches. "There's only one way to find out. They aren't going to tell either of us anything."

Gellia stepped aside when Connylia crouched near the wall and tugged at the grate there. "What are you doing?" Gellia asked. She couldn't decide if Connylia had come out of her mood or become zanier.

"It's a hypocaust," Connylia said. "Mostly unused these days. Built by kings long ago, back when we still had harsh winters. Long before my time, certainly. But now it serves in other ways. Come." Connylia crawled into the space. "My brother meets with the council members immediately upon news, and word from the stable says there's been some."

Gellia sighed and followed, took the small lantern the servant handed her. The hypocaust was full of cobwebs and dust, but she dutifully followed her mentor. Nothing soap and water wouldn't fix. "How do you know where you're going?"

"This isn't the first time I've done this," she said. "There aren't many access points, but I know where they all are. Soon we'll be in the walls, and sometimes we'll be under the floors, just stay close and do as I say."

Soon they were indeed standing upright once more and Connylia spoke. "It would have been unbearably hot in here in a different time," she said. "But now it's not anything anyone thinks about. My son shared these routes with me. It's how he snuck into the castle to visit. You'd think he was part seeker…"

"Quenelzythe," Gellia said. She would have to revisit his journals. He seemed to be quite the character.

"Yes," Connylia's voice became a whisper. "Prince Quenelzythe Zapheny, heir to the throne of Xzepheniixenze."

After what seemed to be hours of sneaking, Connylia put her fingers to her lips and bade Gellia set down the lantern. They crawled under a floor and waited. There was noise, movement and muffled voices until finally the commotion calmed and single voices could be understood. It was a council meeting, as Connylia predicted. From what Gellia could gather, it had taken some time for the entire council to assemble, and everyone was finally there. The emperor was there, as was the prince. The enemy had crossed into Zephronia at a remote location. They were deciding what action to take. So far the Xzepheniixenze force was in farmland. No one really seemed to know why they were there. Most of them couldn't remember the last time they were attacked by Xzepheniixenze. They said it was a small, fast moving force. Gellia heard her name. It was Zyendel. "Do you think they're after Gellia?"

There was much discussion, during which Gellia strained her ears further. Was it a rescue party? Would they find her? Could she escape and make her way to them? After thinking for a moment, she realized Gallylya had likely already decided what he was going to do.

"I will go," Gallylya announced, and the others fell silent. "From all this information it seems that loss of Zephron lives is unnecessary when I can take a small force and deal with them. However, this seems highly unusual."

"They might be testing our strength for a greater war, your highness," someone said.

"Perhaps." Gallylya said. "Alert the other Vega Knights, if they don't already know."

There was scraping chairs and creaking floors once more as the meeting ended. Connylia touched Gellia's shoulder to signal their departure as well.

Once back in Connylia's room, and having time to digest what she heard Gellia said, "Do you think Cassius sent them? Do you think I'll be rescued?" It was likely a foolish hope.

Connylia chuckled. "Cassius wouldn't have sent his own men. It is possible he tricked a party from another clan, likely an enemy of his, into coming. He would know that he cannot win a battle against my brother in such a foolish manner."

Gellia wasn't expecting such an answer. The servant started brushing the dust and cobwebs from their clothes and hair.

"He might have tricked them into coming so it throws off the scent—that makes sense to me." Connylia smiled. "Gallylya may not understand certain things but he is very correct about them. They aren't jovial people from children's fairytales. Never forget that. If Cassius is ever unkind to you leave him. Come back here if you wish, where you are safe, where we can protect you. And certainly don't trust anyone else." She chuckled. "You, of all people, might be the only one with the capacity to rule the likes of Cassius Vazepheny."

8

Several weeks passed, and when Gallylya returned it was easy to find out the details of his victory. Gellia had picked up some of the local language in her time there, and could understand parts of the servants' gossip. She wondered how the Xzepheniixenze force could be so foolish to attack such an insurmountable foe. The servants were telling tales of a massacre, and she knew that in the telling battles could become grandiose, but it seemed that it might actually be true. Connylia believed it to be so. "There are few who can stand against my brother," she said. "But I believe you will escape. Cassius will come for you. I'm sure he has everything planned."

"You haven't seen him since he was a child. Maybe he isn't as honorable as he used to be," Gellia said.

"Honor has nothing to do with it."

"I wish I had the faith you have." Gellia felt she had already been in Zephronia for an eternity. She loved her new friend but this place with the Zephrons wasn't hers. …Although she supposed she could learn to lead a useful life here, and it would likely be better than any choice she had in Fuarmaania. Being Connylia's pet was certainly a decent life, even if a bit boring at times.

Later that day, after she'd left Connylia's side once more, and had time to think, it finally dawned on her that Gallylya was the uncle who Quenelzythe wrote about in his journal, the one who chased him and his friends for decades. Gallylya was the uncle who was out to destroy all dragons and crush

Xzepheniixenze. He was also the one to protect his country from countless enemies for over what she calculated to be a thousand years. Quenelzythe's writings of his uncle were not tainted with hatred or admiration—but her great ancestor respected him.

Gellia stopped in front of Gallylya's study's great doors. They were thick wood, ornate but not overdone. She listened for sounds within, the two guards ignored her. She didn't want to disturb him if he dealt with more important matters. Nothing. After a moment of hesitation, she steeled herself and knocked. If he were an emperor more concerned with etiquette, this would have been a terrible breech. While her heart pounded and her legs shook she glanced at the guards. She heard an acknowledgement from the other side and one of them let her in.

"Sire, it's just me, Gellia," she said and peeked around the door.

"Come in."

She hadn't really expected to gain admittance. All at once she had no idea what she was going.

The emperor was sitting at a large wooden desk from a time long ago. He was writing something. His study was spacious and full of things. There were maps on walls, shelves full of books, elegant chairs here and there. She expected the office to have a more decoration since it belonged to an emperor, but it felt more like an elaborate war room with some touches of palace.

She waited just inside the door until he motioned to a chair on her side of the desk. Gellia sat there, the desk between them. He still wore his armor. Finally he looked up at her and put his quill down. He leaned back into his chair. He tapped his fingers rhythmically on the desk.

"Thank you for seeing me, sire," Gellia said.

The emperor regarded her for a moment, nodding slightly. "I wonder what brought you here."

Gellia didn't have an answer.

"You don't know, either," he said. "You have a privileged life here. You may not think so, but most of the palace does. We'll have to find a purpose for you."

For a moment Gellia felt a touch of welcome, a future. It was the first time she'd ever felt such from the emperor.

Although, his gaze still made her feel uncomfortable and judged. She glanced away, her eyes found his sword nearby. With a fleeting thought she wondered how many Xzepheniixenze and others it had cut down. Thousands, for certain, after so many years.

"Contrary to what you might think, I don't enjoy killing," he said, "even Xzepheniixenze."

It seemed he never missed a motion or glance. He couldn't have meant to defend his actions to her; he must be trying to measure something else. He also knew she would have found out. "I didn't know them, sire," she replied.

"Of course you didn't. We've already established you don't know a single Xzepheniixenze." His sarcasm cut her to the bone. He raised an eyebrow. "That makes their death so much easier, doesn't it? I suppose it comes easily to one of your blood... Killing people who have obviously been misled is irritating." Gellia kept silent, not sure what he meant or what he knew and did not want to give anything away. "Half of them probably didn't even know why they were there. Dying for a cause that's rooted in someone's imagination."

"Sire, you should give them some recognition. They probably can think on their own and decided to be where they wanted to be." She stared at the beautiful carved edge of the desk.

His eyes narrowed and he waved his hand. "You really think so? You think their leaders let them just leave whenever they want to go about their merry way?"

"Sire, I'm sure they could if they wanted to, it just depended on how simple they wanted their life to be."

There was something very bitter in his voice. "What a childish answer. You believe that if you want something enough you can reach it, hmmm?"

"Yes, sire."

"And I suppose that's something you've done."

"Well, not really, sire." Any hope she thought she'd felt was gone.

"Ah, finally the truth. Lies are the most abhorrent Xzepheniixenze trait," he said.

"I only lie when I really have to and I don't do it to harm anyone, sire."

He laughed. "Imagine, a Xzepheniixenze who doesn't want to harm anyone. How absurd. Even if you tried there is no way for you to not hurt someone at some point—especially on your previous course." He paused for a moment. "So why would a princess from Fuarmaania chose to be making her way ever so carefully to Xzepheniixenze? ...Do you think I'm cruel to you and you would never want to stay here? You don't know where you want to go. Do you think you can just go and play princess with them? Have some romantic idea for you and whoever it is who whisked you away from Fuarmaania? You have to change that idealistic mind of yours. Gellia, you'll be eaten alive— unless your liege has substantial power and chooses to continually protect you," He gave her a bitter smirk. "And let me assure you, whoever brought you out of Fuarmaania is out for his or her own gain, you are merely a pawn. That is what they do... Be thankful of your human half, it gives you hope here. The Xzepheniixenze would find it a weakness and take advantage of it to their best ability. I'm surprised this mysterious person taught you any of your magic. The easiest way to exploit a wild talent is to send them into the middle of a battle with no training and watch them self-destruct, taking half the battle with them. He's likely grooming you for something else, something special. I'll assume it is a man, I don't see you running off with one of their women. Yes, Gellia, make no mistake, exploitation is their specialty."

Gellia shifted in her chair. She had to move the conversation away from her before she burst into tears. Her mind searched for a bigger target. "Like the emperor, sire?" she asked.

Gallylya glared at her. "So you've heard of his reputation? He wouldn't be in the books you had in Fuarmaania."

Gellia froze and cursed her foolishness.

The emperor slowly nodded, smiled slightly. "He's a lecherous tyrannical idiot. He jumped on the throne by luck and brute force. There used to be far more formidable people out there than him. There still are, someplace."

"Like who, sire?"

"I don't even know if they're still alive. Zaphaniah Zanthus for example. I imagine he wouldn't be so easy to kill. Why, are you planning a war?"

Gellia wiggled her toes in her boots.

"He is a prime example of how easily they betray each other—he was our 'ally' during the wars, helped us with the slaying."

"Slaying, sire?"

"Dragon slaying."

A shiver ran up Gellia's spine but she didn't want him to talk about her. "Dragon slaying, sire?" Under pressure she couldn't think up anything brilliant to say.

"Some were barely a battle, some were much more, and the cost was great." Gallylya held out his arms and Gellia watched the light from the candles dance over his armor. "This was the most infamous of the dragons, the most feared of all time, and it took many years to bring him down." There seemed to be graveness in what he said, he wasn't bragging. "It was a mirror dragon but for some reason it had been born gold... It is a reminder of those horrible days, and is priceless because of the thousands of lives it took to destroy the beast. Knights and others willing to give their lives to protect their country."

She looked at the quill on the desk, anything to avoid his gaze, and more ridiculousness came from her mouth. "I don't know how you could hate an animal so, sire. Animals don't do things out of being evil..."

"You cannot know what you say. Dragons are not animals as you think they are. They are not dogs or cats or horses. They are not fairy story dragons, giant lizards that breathe a little fire. These entities are giant creatures of spite, magic, and greed. The great ones had armies of loyal followers as fodder for our slayers, idiots worshiping a beast who thought of them as we might think of ants. Expendable and worthless, all the while dragons having the power to level several cities in a day."

"If they're doing what is in their nature to do, sire, than can you call it evil? Nature is nature." Gellia said. She knew it was foolish even as it came from her mouth, but at least the topic wasn't about her.

Gallylya looked at her silently for a moment. It seemed to Gellia that he was thinking very intensely about something. "Can you be so naïve? I suppose it's easy for you to dismiss them as just animals for you've never had your family and friends, your people destroyed at their whim... For you it might be easier though, considering you cared for your family and duty so little you abandoned them for the road."

She shifted in her chair. "There are no dragons left, sire?" He didn't know her circumstances, either; he didn't understand why she left—although he would probably say staying in Fuarmaania would be better than following a Xzepheniixenze. How he hated them. But did she want to tell him what her life was like? Did she dare open that door? A thought sprang into her mind: when you're a Xzepheniixenze, no one comes to your rescue. Save yourself or die.

"Not that any of us can reach. In the height of the slaying some of them had spells cast to return them to nature so they could be reborn again. There is a key to the counter spell that was split in two. I have one half. The other is lost someplace in Xzepheniixenze. That magic is dead. The ruler before me made sure of it. They will never come back."

"How sad," she said, but mostly to herself. To annihilate an entire species of magical creature seemed far from a good idea. Naïve, perhaps, as he said, but it was what she felt in her heart.

"It doesn't surprise me you think so."

"You really do hate me, don't you, sire?"

"I dislike the evil that flows through your veins, the potential I see in you to become one of them. Your lies for the sake of protecting your ally are disheartening. An ally who will repeatedly betray you."

Gellia shriveled inside. There was some air around Gallylya that made her want to beg for forgiveness. But part of the time she still felt the desire to help. She wanted to understand. The frustration she had with herself was becoming unbearable.

He watched her. "Someone has taught you very well how to keep your secrets," he said. "No spellcaster could teach you what you've learned. Some mage has taken great pains in teaching you—*great* pains."

"I told you I read books, sire…" Gallylya glared at her with such ferocity that she couldn't continue.

"You must be the most disciplined person alive then. Youngsters such as you would much rather learn the fun magic, the destructive magic, before learning the rudimentary defensive kind, not matter how important it may be. Most self-taught mages are weak at protecting themselves and talented at obliteration." He raised his nose, "And I haven't seen much destruction from you. What could this person be training you for? A shield for himself?"

Gellia tried desperately not to fidget so in turn froze where she sat which wasn't any better. She wanted to shout, to tell him to leave her alone, to let her go… Her voice didn't come.

"There's no doubt my sister knows who it is, but she stopped talking to me long before she went insane. She certainly won't tell me now... I'm sure she's already told, that I am a tyrant and a horrible person."

"No, sire," Gellia said. "She's never said that. She just said that you don't understand."

"What is there to understand?"

"I don't know. I don't know what happened."

"She hasn't told you?" He was actually surprised; it was an expression that didn't seem to come often to him.

Gellia shook her head. "But I do know that she…" she thought for the right word in Xzepheniixenze and couldn't find it. Maybe a Fuarmaanian one would do: "loves your highness very dearly."

The emperor snorted. "Funny how you couldn't find a word for that in Xzepheniixenze. That's because there isn't one… Let's just say your ancestor, Razhiede twisted her to do his will, cast spells to turn her against her king and country. She's never recovered."

She didn't push the subject. Perhaps the Xzepheniixenze was horrible to Connylia and that was why she refused to speak of it. She wondered if Gallylya avenged his sister and brought her back here. Indeed, she had a lot of questions that would likely never be answered.

"...I can't say I'm glad to see you but she has seemed to be a little happier since you've come... you haven't deceived her either. I suppose it could be worse." The words he used in Xzepheniixenze hinted that he spoke to her as if he knew her from a past life or some other time. Gellia was silent and he continued. "I knew there would be a time when one of her lineage would appear—it was just a question of how long and how diluted the line became. It's obvious you have Xzepheniixenze in your recent past even without much information about you."

"My—father," she said. The words felt strange. Hugh was the only father she'd ever known, even though he wasn't related.

"Yes, Decius Iolair. And what would one of you be doing in an Outland where there was nothing of real interest? They were looking for you to exploit. We just want you to stay out of trouble. Obviously that didn't happen." He silently looked at her for a moment. "If what my son found out is true and you are without a doubt the daughter of Baron Iolair then it would have been Raven who sent him to find you. Something more important came up and he left without your mother or you but it wouldn't make sense for them to abandon their efforts so easily." ...Gellia looked around at the floor, she wouldn't say a word. She reminded him of his sister all those years ago, but she did not have the advantage of Connylia's training. "Perhaps you fancy yourself in love with this person and that is why you say nothing." He watched her shoulders tense ever so slightly as she tried to remain detached, but she was a child and her emotions were not that of a seasoned Xzepheniixenze. Who was it she protected? She seemed far too clever for the likes of most of Raven's agents and certainly none of them would spend so much time with her schooling. It would have been a straight forward kidnapping, not this careful extraction. Who else would know of her lineage? He doubted Zaphaniah would show himself at this date. Gallylya decided to prepare for the worst. If Raven came Zephronia would be ready. The Vega Knights were already warned. This girl was so foolish, so naïve.

...What Gallylya said hit her with more force than she could even believe herself. He would not give up on trying to

extract information from her. She could not give in. She
remembered a time when she felt nothing but hatred towards her
mentor... Why was she so important? Was he going to give her
to the emperor? There were too many things that Gellia felt were
out of her understanding and it constantly worsened. These
people weren't giving her any answers. At least Cassius told her
a little. Cassius.

Gallylya's brows pressed together. "You just thought of a
signature."

"What?"

"A signature just ran through your mind. I felt it. You
must be very close to this person if you can think of him by
signature."

Gellia willed herself to relax. If she clamped the shields
down tighter it might give her away. He didn't seem like the kind
of person who would chisel away at them without a first strike
from her. "I don't know what you're talking about, sire."

"Don't lie to me, Gellia. I can see through your lies as
one sees through glass."

Silence. She tried to keep her composure for she didn't
want him to see her cry.

He withdrew. "No matter. You're here and I can wait."

"If I'm such a no one then why do you want to keep me
here and why do they want to find me?"

"You are of Zapheny bloodlines, Duvray as well as much
as it irks me to say so. There is magic somewhere in your veins
that needs to be watched. Somehow the talents were bred out of
your family until now." He watched her for a moment, thought
of how childlike she was. "I know you're protecting someone.
It's only a matter of time before I find out who it is. They will try
to come for you; whoever it is, he or she has put far too much
effort into you to leave you here with me. When that time arrives
we'll be rid of this mysterious mage and you will stay here to
learn to purge yourself of their wickedness. In time you'll be
reconditioned for honor and the good of all, not for selfish and
malevolent pursuits. You were brought here just in time. You're
better off here."

"No she isn't." Connylia stood in the doorway behind
Gellia, who jumped in surprise. "Let her go where she wills."

"We are not having this conversation," he said.

"Funny how every time his name is said I hear it, no matter where I am," Connylia said. "Come with me, Gellia."

"They even managed to name her for the unicorn," Gallylya scoffed. "How fitting. Zapheny appear to be our curse."

"My mother named me," Gellia said.

"And where is she?" he asked.

"She..."

The emperor could read her mother's fate from Gellia's expression. "Your father undoubtedly killed her. Probably when she resisted him as he tried to drag her away to Raven."

Gellia felt herself crack, she wasn't sure if she would shout at him or if she would cry. Connylia dragged her through the door and closed it before the girl lost her composure. Gallylya was saying something on the other side of the door but they ignored him. "Come," Connylia told her and led her down the corridor.

In Connylia's room Gellia crumpled into a heap on the floor. "I'm sorry, I don't usually do this," she said and wiped her face, took a few deep breaths.

"I don't mind, Gellia." Connylia sat on the floor next to her and draped her arm across Gellia's shoulders. "Do as you wish, for you are safe here."

"Your brother is right. He'll never come back for me or he'll be killed in the process. I don't know why he'd want to... maybe I should go back to Fuarmaania and beg forgiveness. I left my Tempest there, who knows what will come of him... and dear Cress, who tolerated me for her entire life."

"Don't talk like that. Everything will be fine."

Connylia held Gellia in her arms while she sobbed. "I didn't want to cry in front of him but maybe I should have because I could have shown him I have a soul, but maybe he would have thought I was trying to trick him," she babbled. "Maybe he's right, maybe I'm a terrible person in the making, wicked and cruel."

Connylia shook her head. "Well, if you ever do decide Xzepheniixenze isn't the life for you, even before you go there, you have a place here. Gallylya can know you better and understand then. If not..." She shrugged. "But if you ask for help

in earnest, he will help you—that you can always trust."
Connylia pulled away and patted Gellia's hand. "Come to court
tomorrow."

"I'll have to be near him."

"You'll sit next to me... there's a pageant tomorrow, it
might lift your spirits. I heard it's going to be a wonderful show.
It will take your mind off your troubles here."

She wiped her tears with her sleeve. "You're so odd
sometimes, if you don't mind me saying so," Gellia sniffed.

"There is a method to my madness." Connylia smiled and
thought of her dear friends, Justin and Jutham, and the
information they had. "I've just given up trying to explain it to
anyone."

***

"Brilliant, my sister and her friend are joining us to see
the circus," the emperor said as he seated himself on the throne.
Zyendel sat on one side; the two women placed themselves on
the other. Connylia dressed a little finer that day and styled her
hair. Connylia even smiled a little. Gellia just wore the usual
white tunic and breeches—Zephronian servant issue. Her hair
she'd pulled into a braid.

It was rare such diversions were allowed in the high
court, and the fact that the emperor's mysterious sister and a
Xzepheniixenze were there added to the attraction. The entire
Fuarmaanian castle could have fit into the great hall of
Dournzariame. The tiers of balconies lined the walls where more
people stood and waited. There were hundreds. Of course,
everything was dazzlingly white with splashes of blue and gold.
The crowd settled down. The master of the show entered through
the archway of the main door. He spoke in Zephronian. Gellia
used her ring, but she understood much without it.

"...and you will be amazed at our main event, an event so
spectacular that I cannot put it into words..."

Gellia was bored already. She surveyed the attendees and
saw many of them stealing glances at she and Connylia. The
insane sister, and the Xzelki in their midst were probably more of
a show than anything. Not that Gellia wasn't used to being the

strange one at a court. In Xzepheniixenze she'd blend in magnificently, she suspected.

"...but first we have Marta and her amazing..."

Gellia ignored the show, not amused by dogs doing tricks or prancing horses or... Connylia looked very regal, a little smile on her face. Did she always put on the happy princess act for public appearances? The audience went wild around her with laughter and applause. She supposed the main attraction was coming out. She heard there might be elephants, which could be entertaining if it were true. She wondered if anyone else was as bored as she was.

Gellia sighed. Connylia was wrong. She soon found herself staring at her bootlaces. Gallylya, Zyendel and Connylia didn't seem all that impressed either. Considering their ages and what they must have seen in their lives, she wasn't surprised by their boredom. It was likely something they did just to entertain the courtiers. Zyendel looked over at her on occasion and smiled… Maybe tomorrow she would ride Amarynth in the courtyard if they would allow it, if he would come out of his stall. Or braid his mane. And as always, she would spend time with Connylia, time which she treasured. They'd spent so much time together, Gellia had learned so much, but so little about Connylia. She certainly didn't seem as crazy as everyone claimed. It was quiet in the hall... Should she ask Connylia to reveal her mysteries? …There was a steady beat of someone walking in a silent hall. One of the minstrels dropped a tambourine. The footfalls were familiar and sent a shiver up her spine. She snapped back to reality.

Standing out as would a black arrow against new snow was Cassius. At first she barely recognized him. The players had made way for him and all looked as astonished as the rest audience. No one knew what to do. Gellia tried to keep her composure. Gallylya glared down from his throne. Gellia wondered if the emperor would attack. It could be the end for them. She froze in her chair and couldn't even breathe.

"Greetings," Cassius said, wearing his smirk that was so familiar to her. He bowed to the emperor.

"You," Gallylya said. "…you should be dead."

Cassius raised his head. "Yes, you should have killed me in Fuarmaania. Ah, it was a long time ago, but the years have passed swiftly for me..." he looked at Connylia, "and so slowly for others."

The court was silent, but it was apparent they didn't know who had just entered, other than he was Xzepheniixenze. They all waited for word from their leader. Gellia looked at the emperor and was thrilled it was not she who received his glare, for it surely would have killed her. Cassius returned his gaze to Gallylya and held it, not intimidated in the least as the emperor spoke. "You should be dead by now," the emperor repeated.

"You'd think so, wouldn't you?" Cassius said. "I've brought you a gift, your majesty."

Connylia smiled.

Gallylya rose from his throne.

"It's just a little present, Gallylya, really now," Cassius teased, but handed it to Connylia's waiting servant.

"It's tradition," Connylia said and watched her servant carry the box away.

As usual Gellia didn't understand the exchange, but this time she didn't care. She did, however, take notice of the loathing Gallylya showed towards her instructor, as if he looked into the face of malevolence. Cassius never broke his intense eye contact with the emperor. Gallylya was thinking too much for Gellia's comfort. "Your past is catching up to you Gallylya," Cassius purred.

"You're not a child any longer, Cassius," Gallylya replied.

Cassius shook his head. "You don't want to start a fight here do you?" The look on Cassius' face for that instant was one Gellia never saw before and it shook her to her core. It was a look of pure malice. Gellia was sure something would spontaneously combust at any moment. "...Since now you have the stomach to finish the job?" She could tell he was coiled to strike, although his magic was at rest.

"Then why are you here?" the emperor growled. Guards ran up through the crowd but kept their distance, looked to their emperor for command.

"I came to see if our rising star wished to depart."

Gallylya glanced at Gellia. "Should have known," he muttered, then said aloud, "She lives here now, safe from your depravity."

Cassius smiled. "Does she? By her own choice? If I remember correctly you kidnapped her—took her against her will—and you speak of depravity." Whispers rushed through the crowd. Cassius tilted his head thoughtfully. "Well I suppose that's the way I like to be whisked away on holiday."

"She isn't yours," Zyendel blurted, standing proudly next to his father. "And we will treat her far better than you ever will."

Cassius ignored Zyendel. "This implies she's owned. I thought Zephrons were against slavery." He looked the emperor up and down. "I'm disappointed."

"Leave. I don't want your baseness soiling my palace," Gallylya said.

"Come now, Gallylya, old friend, you haven't heard from me in ages. I have far fewer notches in my baldric than you. Genocide has always been your specialty, not mine. I've been trying to put the world back together since then."

Gellia was sure Gallylya's people silently rallied around them—no one insulted their emperor. But what was Cassius talking about? Would there be a fight? No, she realized, not unless Cassius started one. For the moment, he had all the control.

"...Obviously you missed two of us in your killings," Cassius continued. "I think your sister would have preferred to die though," he added.

Gallylya seethed. "Get out."

"Not until our Zapheny has made up her mind," Cassius insisted. "Unless you decide that she has no will of her own." The crowd started to whisper excitedly, repeating 'Zapheny' over and over again and looking at Gellia. She felt goosebumps, and felt a flutter in her stomach. She had no idea what to do.

Gellia wondered if she could really leave Connylia now that the choice was before her. The two women regarded each other for a moment, Connylia smiling. *You don't belong here,* she mind-spoke. *Your destiny lies elsewhere. I'll see you again.*

I'll miss you, Gellia replied. For a moment she debated on freedom or friendship, then she hopped from her chair and joined her mentor.

Cassius didn't take his gaze off Gallylya. Zyendel stood near his father, jittery and speechless.

"Leave," Gallylya told them once more. "But don't think I'll forget you again."

"Thank you for allowing us to enjoy the pleasure of your company," Cassius said to the entire crowd. He gracefully bowed to the emperor. *Let's go*, he said, almost forcefully, into Gellia's mind.

Gellia waved to Connylia and they turned to walk from the great hall. She wanted to run. Her breath became deep and fast. *Composure*, Cassius said. They strode into the antechamber through the oceans of guards, and Cassius magically closed the door behind them. It took them some time to pass through all the armored men but somehow Cassius managed to turn down several corridors until there was no one but the two of them.

"Run."

***

Inside the great hall Zyendel shouted: "Get them, bring her back alive!" Why wasn't his father attacking them? The guards looked confused, looked to their emperor.

"Don't start a battle unless he starts one," Gallylya commanded. "Everyone find safety." The courtiers hurried away by magic or on foot.

Zyendel drew his sword. "I won't let him have her!" Gallylya sat back down and sighed. Zyendel shifted his sword in his hand several times and looked to his father and to the door for he couldn't decide what to do. Connylia glared at Zyendel and left. Once Connylia was out of sight of her brother, she ran.

***

"Wha-?" Gellia blurted.

"Run." He grabbed her hand and towed her along behind him. They skittered around a corner; Gellia almost fell. "This way."

"What? Where are we going? Do you know where we're going? I've spent some time here and—"

"Princess. Like all castles, I know this one better than you do."

They ran down a servant's corridor and nearly toppled a confused maid carrying linens. "Why don't you use your magic?" Gellia asked.

"I like a challenge."

"Then why don't I use mine?"

"To tell them where we are? And what magic do you know that would help us? Use some sense, princess." Shouts came from up the hall. "They've gotten better I see." Cassius cheerfully muttered something about Gallylya being a bastard. They slid to a stop. "Over here."

"Where?"

He pointed to an opening to the hypocaust. Cassius grabbed Gellia and almost tossed her down the tunnel. "Go." Gellia slid down the hypocaust, her tunic ripped on something, her hands and knees were scuffed but she kept going. Cassius followed her. "Where does this waaah!" She found herself on her back, staring up at Cassius as he dropped from the tunnel like a cat.

"This isn't the time to be a weakling," he said and grabbed her.

It took her a minute before she was actually on her feet. After several rolls and hanging off Cassius' sleeve she pulled herself up to a run. Much like being dragged by a horse, Gellia thought as they bolted down the corridor. He had more muscle than she ever expected. When Gellia looked up there were more guards, but startled ones. This part of the castle was unfamiliar to her. Cassius scowled and they scrambled in the other direction. He grabbed her by the tunic and pulled her behind him.

A noise of surprise escaped her. If she hadn't known he was trying to save her, she would have thought she was being assaulted.

"What were you saying?" he asked as they took another corner. Gellia bounced off the opposite wall but stayed in his wake.

"We're going to die, aren't we?" she panted. She hadn't realized he was so nimble, either. He was not the pampered noble she thought he was.

"Rather dramatic, don't you think?" he said. "Think you can manage on your own?"

"Yes." She would manage. It was better than being dragged.

***

…Connylia stopped in front of the stall as her magic subsided. "It's time for you to get out of here," she told Amarynth. The stallion paced a lap in his stall as she undid the latch. He was already in his new tack, with all Gellia's equipment aboard—Connylia had taken it from the guards. It had been a long time since she used her power, especially one talent in specific. It did come in handy, that was for certain. "You know where they should be coming out...Thank you."

Amarynth galloped into the stable yard but paused and looked back at her. *No, thank you, Beloved One.*

Connylia called on her magic to clear the path for him, and none would remember as they stood frozen in her energies. She watched him gallop away. "Until the stars bring us together again," she whispered.

***

"Will you look at this," Cassius muttered.

"Oh no. How are we going to get out of here?" They had darted down dozens of corridors; numerous tunnels and now they were stuck in the laundry courtyard surrounded by Zephronian knights. "Now will you use your magic?"

"Not the right time. I have enough things to do besides deal with Gallylya." They backed against the large well in the middle of the yard. "He won't attack us when there are so many people in the way. You can always count on a Zephron. Of course, if it were a small city or a village their lives might be worth it to take a trophy such as myself."

Gellia swallowed and continued to pant. Her legs shook and threatened to buckle.

"I'm going to let you catch your breath for a moment," he told her. "They're waiting for me to make a move." He looked down at them with amusement and contempt. "This wasn't the route I wanted to take with you, but here we are."

She coughed in response. "Are we going to try and jump over them?"

"Don't be ridiculous. Perhaps you have me confused with Kellenvoss."

"Who? How can you be so calm?"

"Are you ready?"

"For what?" Gellia felt him grab her arm.

"Hold your breath."

A horrified expression was as far as Gellia came to protest before he sent them both careening into the well. The water was shockingly cold. She couldn't see anything, couldn't tell which way was up or down but bumped into the walls of the well as Cassius pulled her through the frigid water. She clung onto what seemed to be his clothes and tried to ignore the pain of her burning lungs and didn't dare open her eyes. She wanted to breathe. Her hands slipped off Cassius' wet clothes and she panicked. There was a current... it carried her...

"Breathe."

Gellia gasped and coughed and sputtered as she surfaced, still confused as she grabbed at the only steady thing she could find. Water swirled past them in the darkness. "You're fine," he told her.

She coughed a few times before she could speak. "I don't know abou th'." He was close, she could tell from his voice. It was so dark. She couldn't see anything and the water was so cold, her clothes so heavy.

"Take your time, we're safe for now."

"I'm going to catch my death," she blurted as she fought the current with fistfuls of his clothes and hair. Her whole body shook, her teeth chattered.

He replied, "You're just as predictable as they are."

"Where the blazes are we?" Even in her desperation she wasn't comfortable touching him, and felt for something else in which to grab. He was a lot warmer than her, though. He radiated heat like a fire.

"An underground river. It's very deep in case you were wondering."

"You're standing on the side aren't you?"

"I suppose you could call it that."

"I can't swim." She knew he was using his magic to warm her, but she couldn't sense the energy he was using.

"I thought as much. Some day we shall have to remedy that... we're going to let the current take us for a little while. You can try to go by yourself or you can ride, I've done this river both ways."

"I think I'll stay if it's all the same to you, and some day you'll have to tell me about the other times you've done this nonsense."

"I don't have to do anything."

He let go of the side and they drifted down the tunnel quickly at first, but then the river slowed down as it widened. There were several times they needed to submerge to clear rock. After what seemed to be forever passing through darkness Cassius dragged her onto some sort of flat spot next to the river. He dumped her halfway on the rock and moved away. She wanted to follow, but stayed where she was for she didn't want to chance falling in and she still couldn't see anything.

"Imagine," his said. "Still here after so many years."

"What?"

A spark. A small flame illuminated the pocket of dry land. "We put this here a long time ago to use on future trips through the river. I guess it finally came to good use."

"It isn't too damp?" Gellia asked as she pulled herself out of the river.

"It's enchanted, and not even real fire. It cost a fortune..." He sat on the other side of the log and rubbed his hands together. "...For two boys in the field living on what we could scavenge."

"Perhaps if you hadn't spent all your hard earned money on clothes..." Gellia straightened herself and tried to control her shivering. It took all the composure she could muster to keep her speech steady. "How is it you always seem in better condition than me?" Her fingers and toes were numb.

He looked at her and for the first time she thought he looked puzzled. It passed quickly. "Humans are notoriously fragile. If you were full human, you wouldn't survive this route, but you'll survive."

The two of them looked like beggars, their hair tangled with sticks and mud, their faces dirty, their clothes torn and completely drenched. Gellia started to giggle despite her violent shivering.

"What?" he asked.

"Good thing you weren't wearing one of your regal ensembles—we would have never survived." Her head wobbled as she shivered.

He chuckled. "I would have never attempted it if I was trying to be fashionable... well, maybe you're more than half human. Come here before you catch your death. I won't try and molest you, you ridiculous Fuarmaanian."

Gellia reluctantly tucked herself against him and he rubbed her arms. "You're thinking something very—not nice."

He was silent for a moment then chuckled. "Ah. Again you've confused me with Fuarmaanians and their apparently uncontrollable urges. Even if your thinking was warranted, you aren't very talented at deciphering what's nice and what isn't."

"No, I don't know specifically what you're thinking; I just know that it's something that I wouldn't like."

"What you're thinking would be entertaining. Perhaps not original. Your opinion I'm sure is jaded."

"I don't want to know."

"Don't flatter yourself. I wasn't about to tell you… and you have a flair for jumping to the wrong conclusions, but I've known this for some time. I assure you that youngsters such as yourself are of no interest to me."

Gellia listened to the quiet of the rippling water. If only she had dry clothes. "I think my clothes would dry faster if I took them off," she said.

"Are you trying to seduce me?"

She blushed furiously but managed to say: "Who would want to do that?"

"You'd be surprised," he muttered. "I promise I won't look. I'll turn the other way and you do whatever you need to." Cassius promptly did as he said he would. "Maybe I'll get some rest. That's what holidays are for anyway."

Gellia watched his back to make sure he was serious. Holiday? With some tugging she removed the wet tunic and splatted it against the nearest wall. "Can I move the fire stick or—"

"Go ahead."

She moved the branch closer to the wall and stood to remove her soggy breeches to place them next to the tunic. She was not taking off her underclothes. Under no condition would she do so. She sat very close to the warmth and rubbed her limbs. Cassius was silent. Had he fallen asleep? How could he do that? Gellia moved to where the fire had been and sat on the warm stone.

She already missed Connylia and wondered about all she had learned. It was also a moment to digest the exchange in the great hall. So Gallylya and Cassius knew each other? When Cassius was a child? What was the whole conversation about all the dead people? She felt herself start to doze.

Her stomach complained through the thin undergarment. Had it been that long? "You're awfully quiet."

"I was speaking with my mages."

"What?"

"My mages at court, I was speaking with them. I left them in charge of the castle."

"With telepathy."

"Something a bit more sophisticated, but yes."

"What are they telling you?"

"That the Lorkiegns are attacking Tintagel again. I leave for a moment and they run up to beat on the gate for a while."

"Shouldn't we be going then?"

Cassius snorted. "The likes of them could never take Tintagel. I gave orders that everyone in the castle should wait for the Lorkiegns to tire themselves and go away. I'm setting them up for something special. Not that any of my residents would be motivated enough to launch a counter attack."

"That's what you've been talking about?"

"I told them to prepare for our arrival."

Gellia shivered although she was considerably warmer. They would be going to Xzepheniixenze soon. Far from here, far from Connylia. What would it be like? She knew it had to be beautiful but how? Zephronia was beautiful—was it like that? What would her life be like? Or was Gallylya right? Would the people there destroy her? Would she ever return to Fuarmaania? See Cresslyn again? Would heartlessness take her over?

Soon enough the tunic was reasonably dry when she touched it. The tiny room was becoming surprisingly warm. Thank the heavens for the light fabric of the Zephrons—but it wasn't gleaming white anymore. She pulled it over her head. "I don't mind if you look now," What was he going to see, her legs? Not that breeches left much to the imagination.

"You're sure about that."

"Yes, I'm sure."

"Really?"

"You're mocking me. You always mock me. Why?"

"I find you wildly amusing… While it's fresh in your mind you need to tell me what you told Gallylya when you were interrogated."

"How do you know he did that?"

"He's Gallylya."

"I didn't tell him anything, he or Zyendel, I did my best to avoid their questions. I only ever spoke to Connylia. But Gallylya seemed to look right through me half the time and told me things like he already knew everything." She shuddered at the memory; did she want to admit to Cassius that the emperor made her cry? That his scathing words tore her to shreds? That he told her things that she didn't even realize about herself? "I didn't admit or deny anything he came up with that I can think of. I did tell him that I learned everything from books and not from you."

Cassius smiled curiously and spoke mostly to himself. "Nicely done although I don't quite understand your absolute loyalty to me." He shook his head. "Nevertheless all he had was conjectures, because he was certainly surprised to see me, wasn't he?"

She smiled.

"And he seeming to know things goes with his trade. He's been in the business of war for a very long time, and I'm sure could read your posture and your avoidance as easily as you read Fuarmaanian. Now whatever he thought he had to be prepared for is completely wrong and he has no idea what I'm really about. I'm sure he will spend many sleepless nights thinking about it." He chuckled a bit. "He is a worthy foe, not one to be taken lightly, remember that princess. I applaud your silence in his presence, for surely if you tried to tell him fiction he would have shattered you like glass. Now all we have to worry about is if Connylia can continue to withstand him." He watched her for a moment and saw how she struggled to stay awake. "You should rest," he said.

She nodded and tried to make herself comfortable on the stone. It was warm from the enchantment, it made it cozy enough for someone so exhausted.

He looked at her for a moment before speaking again. "You do realize you could have had a life there, yes? One of purpose? That it was your choice to go or stay."

"Yes."

He nodded. "Sleep."

Cassius watched her for a moment as she slept before he turned to watch the river. She was more like her ancestor than she could ever realize. Sometimes it almost unsettled him.

***

"Was it just me or was she walking next to him?" Zyendel asked as he swung his riding crop. "I thought she was sure to be behind him like a servant. Closely beside him too, like she was familiar with him. Xzepheniixenze are so territorial…" Like she was familiar with him. The idea turned his stomach.

Gallylya spoke, but mostly to himself, "He shouldn't be alive. By any force of nature he should be long dead by now." It was obvious now. He had too much time invested in her to leave her in Zephronia. Her fragile body couldn't withstand the abuse of the mystic, but her talent must be immense. Cassius would have to be very careful that she didn't burn herself out and take everyone with her. But the biggest disappointment was to see her follow him like a puppy. Perhaps they were too late, perhaps she was already too conditioned for the life of the Xzepheniixenze Empire.

The prince nodded although he really didn't understand. "Do you think he'll attack us? We need to get her back. I already miss her. Perhaps if we rack the seekers we caught they'll give us information. If we rack one and let the others watch…"

"Do what with the seekers?" Gallylya glared at Zyendel who smiled and shrugged.

"I was joking. I would never torture anyone."

Gallylya was silent for quite some time before he spoke again. "There's only one thing he would come back for… And I can only imagine what schemes he has…" Gallylya closed his eyes for a moment. Cassius had been quiet for so many centuries. So quiet they hadn't heard of him in Zephronia. What was he doing for so long? He could have the entire empire of Xzepheniixenze under his control by now. Gallylya needed to make a decision he didn't want to make. "He knows I have it, so I'm forced to give it to you for safe keeping now." From his shirt Gallylya pulled out the golden pendant he'd been wearing for many centuries. It wasn't a symbol the prince recognized but it seemed to be a character of some archaic language. "Keep this safe always, don't ever take it off."

"What is it?" Zyendel asked as the emperor removed the chain.

"Half of the Dragon Key. Without this no one can bring back the dragons."

Zyendel took the treasure and held his breath. "You think he'll come for you?" He was nearly overwhelmed by the responsibility and amazed it was he who received it, not one of Gallylya's compatriots.

Gallylya knew that it was possible for him to lose a battle to such a mage. An army would need to be gathered. From what Gallylya could tell, Cassius as a child had more potential than anyone he ever heard of, and to think that he could draw upon that now… and obviously he was filled with the cunning of his mother. No wonder Gellia was so enraptured. Cassius could likely sell sand to desert peoples.

"He doesn't stand a chance against us."

Gallylya rose. "He is the son of Adamina Vazepheny and Aurelian of Ellyndrien Rehara. I need you to send word to the remaining Vega Knights and tell them to gather."

"Pardon me for saying it but I think you're overreacting."

"You cannot appreciate who he is. Every precaution needs to be taken."

***

Connylia returned to her room. They would be safe for the night. Even if the Zephrons knew where to find them the underground river was no place to set up a battle. She remembered these runaway games they were forced to play. But now to her gift. Her old maid, who had been with her for ages, smiled at Connylia and handed her the box Cassius had given her.

It was shallow but long and wide, all covered with forest green velvet. Connylia remembered when presents were sent in sacks or wrapped in paper. She opened it and found a thin layer of purple paper, removing that her hand slid over the most perfect fabric she had seen in centuries.

"What's wrong, mistress?" her maid asked.

Connylia blinked a few times, sniffed, and turned the box so her maid could see.

"It's fine but not a very pretty color."

It was a pale eggshell color that seemed dull to the untrained eye. Connylia shook her head. "You don't understand," she said and grabbed a handful, ran out onto the balcony. "Come here." The old maid did as she was asked.

Her lady stood in the dark, held the shimmering fabric in the wind. As the moonlight touched the fine, now white, threads they changed from blue to green to purple in silvery beauty. Conny wrapped it around her body and went back inside. She scampered to the huge trunk that she hadn't opened in a millennium. The maid spoke to her, but was ignored as Connylia took out the key from her pocket and forced open the lock. The lid opened and from it rushed the scent of dried roses. Connylia ignored her tears and pulled out an old dress in tatters as if it were in a war. At one time it had been beautiful and soon it would be again. "It's the same fabric, Kayra, he's given it to me so I can mend this… you can't find it anywhere. Anywhere. It doesn't exist anymore. The people who made this have been dead for centuries." She held the cloth to her cheek.

The maid didn't know how to respond, but looked around the room muttering about her sewing basket. "There's something still in here," she said as she passed the gift box.

"What?" Connylia dropped the dress and returned to the discarded box. An envelope lie on the bottom. She picked it up and flipped it over a few times. The moonlight set letters aglow. She opened it.

'To Empress Connylia Duvray:
Your Majesty is respectfully invited to attend a ball in honor of the rebirth of old alliances. It would be a great honor if Your Majesty would agree to attend this event to be held at Shahyrahara on the eve of the solstice. Arrangements have been made for Your Majesty's journey.

Baron Cassius
Vazepheny of Tintagel'

Connylia smiled. "The Moonkeep," she said softly. "I thought it was lost." For the first time in far too long, she felt joy.

9

"I certainly took you long enough to rescue me. Did you not know where I was dragged off to?" Gellia asked. She tried to help them swim as best she could while she still held on to him.

"I knew who took you when I heard about white horses, but you weren't in immediate danger. I hope you did learn something."

"Lots of etiquette and cultural tidbits."

"Which is why I left you there for so long." Amongst other reasons. "Now all you have to do is use your new knowledge."

Gellia was silent for a time. She started to shiver again. "This water doesn't get any warmer, does it?"

"Not in a thousand years."

Blindly she looked around for any shapes in the dark. Cassius seemed able to see just fine. "This was the only way out?"

"Secret way, yes. Going back to the palace is much more difficult. Of course, we used to bring the horses with us but we didn't use that well."

"Oh my—Amarynth!"

"He knows where we're going and I'm sure he's headed there," Cassius said.

"Where are we going?"

"To visit another old friend of mine. This river will bring us to her manor."

"You seem to know everyone." Gellia commented.

"It's part of my occupation."

"What exactly do you do?"

"You'll find out soon enough."

He dunked her under and she felt herself swirling around. As long as she could feel his hand on her belt she tried not to be afraid. When Gellia popped up she sputtered and gasped for breath and didn't notice at first the group of people around them. Cassius hefted her out of the water onto the floor and climbed out after her. Sheets of water spattered on the stone tiles. They'd just come out of a massive indoor fountain.

"I've been expecting you, sir," a woman said.

"As always," Cassius replied with his usual flair.

A servant offered Gellia a blanket, which she was happy to accept. The woman who stood before them was much shorter than her, but grandly dressed in blue and gold. She was older, looked to be fifty in human years but with the way ages often turned out Gellia had no real idea. Her face was wise and rather snooty and not fully Zephron. After saying a few quiet words to Cassius, the woman turned to look down at Gellia, who still sat on the floor. Cassius looked at her as well. "Is this Quenelzythe's girl?" she asked.

"In fact she is. Although her blood-father is an Iolair."

"How droll."

"Quite," Cassius agreed. "Luckily all his blood did was unlock her heritage."

The woman turned back to Cassius. Gellia slowly pulled herself to her feet out of the puddle she created on the floor. It was a large room with vaulted ceilings and sunlight coming in through many windows. Everything seemed warm and gold, and there were many large plants in giant pots. Their host and her mentor were still chatting away.

"...It has been a long time since you've appeared in my fountain. How is it down there?"

"Oh exquisite, I plan to build a quaint summer home there."

Gellia was too busy shivering to say anything in agreement. Who was this person? Why wasn't she offering dry clothes and a fire? "...You have changed," the woman said.

This is Countess Delvaye. She runs a finishing school for Zephronian girls, Cassius said into Gellia's mind. *She has a wonderful appreciation of irony.*

The countess still spoke. "I've been following your career. I'm sure Connylia would be too if she wasn't avoiding life. I must say that I am impressed... but it seems that our little girl isn't used to such excitement," she looked at Gellia again. "My servants will show you to a room where you can bathe and dress. I'll see you at the meal." The countess flounced from the room, left them with a few servants.

Cassius strode before the attendants down the hall, Gellia followed with the blanket clutched around her. She didn't pay much heed to where they went but stopped when she was told to and entered a grand bed chamber, a hot bath already there for her. She found quickly that all the servants were fluent in Xzepheniixenze.

Gellia sank into the tub and took in her surroundings while the attendants washed her hair and served her warm drinks. All the furnishings in the room were finely carved mahogany and polished to a reflective finish. All draperies and linens were different shades of burnt orange, rust, and bronze. Her chamber was the most beautiful room she had ever seen.

Before she knew it, her hair had been hair pinned into an elaborate style and the maids encouraged her to step out of the bath. Had it been that long? They wrapped her in a dressing gown and sat her on a stool to have her face enhanced with cosmetics, which was a new experience for her. After that was finished they brought out billowy dress made of layers of pale blue silk with no other frills, just flowing fabric. Gellia felt quite silly but followed the maids through the corridors. From so much time spent in tunics the dress felt strange to her, and it was a full one at that.

The corridors they led her through felt unused. They were clean, but seemed out of the way from everywhere else. Gellia supposed it was good to keep the countess' secret alliances out of the way of teenage girls.

They led Gellia into a room with an open side to a beautifully gardened courtyard. There the countess and the baron sat together at a small round table talking. Some unseen manservant announced Gellia. She smiled shyly and tried to remember everything Connylia taught her. Her two companions watched her approach. "You didn't tell me how beautiful she is," the countess commented. "I like the blue on her."

Cassius snorted. "I disagree. It isn't her color."

Gellia wanted to verbally attack him, but refrained. She said nothing as she approached the table and neatly sat down with them. "She looks like a dark-haired Connylia," the countess said. "Although Connylia's brilliance has deteriorated over the years... so, dear Cassius, I would like you to meet my niece some time." Gellia watched as Cassius gave a subtle dirty look to the countess. "For one of your Mages perhaps," the countess said, "come now, I know you, I've followed your progress and I'm not going to pretend that I don't know what you are. You need something from me and I would like something in return."

Gellia nearly choked on the wine she had been trying to swallow. She looked at Cassius who smiled a little. "Connylia's happiness has a price?" he asked.

"Don't play games with me, you pirate," the countess said. "I would like her to go to one your mages so she's very far away from me but I know that she's with someone with a name. I don't want one of my family going to some pauper."

"Court mages or one of the petty mages?"

"Preferably a court mage."

"You realize that my mages have a very short life expectancy."

"Sounds lovely. If he dies then she can take up with the next one. It's her habit, anyway. And I'm too nervous to send for her in the realm," she winked.

"I cannot promise her happiness," Cassius told her. "And I certainly won't tolerate sniveling."

"You know me better than that."

"Fine. Send her along in a month's time to Tintagel. I'm sure someone will take an interest in her. And you will hostess the carriage when it comes."

"I enjoy being of some service," the countess replied.

"You never change, do you?" Cassius said and sipped his wine.

Gellia remained quiet. What just happened? Did they just trade a girl for a service? She wondered what Gallylya would think, after all, he thought Gellia would not survive in

Xzepheniixenze. How would some frail Zephronian girl survive there? Was it an exile?

"So, Cassius, have you any little ones running about? I hear your cousin has hoards."

"Good goddess, no. Don't disgust me. And as far as my cousin's children, I'm sure he'll end up killing them all before too long for fear they'll come after the throne."

"He never did know when to stop. And you, Gellia, do you have any children?"

Gellia turned red. "No, no I don't."

"You can tell she was raised in Fuarmaania. She has that distinct Zephron morality," the countess said.

"You'd be surprised," Cassius said.

"Well, if you ever want a suitable maia I have plenty of girls who would love to help. We have more girls here than ever before, it's the easy living of Gallylya's rein I suppose, you could take your pick." She smiled. "Not that a person of your narcissism would ever look at even the noblest-born girls around here."

"You're making me ill," he said.

"Yes, that's one way you and Quenelzythe differed. He settled and raised a family and you are the eternal bachelor."

"It would only slow me down. Look what settling did to him."

Since she had nothing to add to the conversation, Gellia watched their hostess and her teacher and studied them closely, listened to all they said. It surprised her how easily she remembered all that Connylia had taught her. She could tell Cassius was irritated but the countess either ignored that fact or was unaware.

The countess was graceful, yet she seemed to ignore some of the rules of etiquette Gellia knew, so she started to wonder if the countess felt she was aged enough to not follow the rules. Also, Gellia noticed the countess was much easier to read than her teacher. Gellia nibbled on a slice of orange while she watched Cassius' fantastically restrained mannerisms, which she never appreciated before. Of course, in the past she either tried to ignore him or was too busy trying to do as he taught to notice. Indeed, he showed signs of emotion but not nearly as much as what he truly felt. Gellia wondered if anyone else noticed such things or if it were because she spent so much time near him.

For the first time she saw him enjoy the wine he sampled. She was accustomed to him sniffing what he was served and refusing to drink it, but this he seemed to savor. She watched him change postures as the countess spoke and saw how the woman reacted. Cassius seemed aloof as he always was, but Gellia noticed how the corner of his eyes tensed ever so slightly when the countess offended him. It appeared the countess could only see the smirk he wore so well. No, every move he made was deliberate; she finally appreciated and admired it. If that were the way to go about things, then that was the way Gellia would follow. Not that she sat there slovenly but she concentrated for a moment, adjusted her demeanor until it felt appropriate, and carefully reached for her goblet. She was immediately rewarded as Cassius turned to look at her. Gellia didn't smile, although she wanted to. She continued to listen to the countess.

"I suspect that if you were to take a maia she would have to be of the most fantastic, most magical, most intelligent, most perfected bloodlines to ever exist," the countess teased.

Cassius raised his eyebrow as he turned back to the countess. "Certainly no one you know, even if I was looking."

The countess chuckled. "...So what did you bring her this time?"

He set his goblet down on the mosaic table. "Lunan satin."

"Good heavens. You must have offered Gallylya's head to the goddesses to get your hands on that..."

Gellia felt her heart swell with pride with her distraction, and continued to work very diligently at control while her mind started to wander. Things such as: what would happen next? Hopefully they would return to Sen Dunea soon. And, what was his purpose? Would he ever tell her?

The countess still spoke. "...There isn't much happening today but for the royal guard looking for the two of you. My advice is get some sleep while you can. It's not as if you can get any sleep back home."

Gellia carefully dismantled the meal before her with the delicate fork and smiled serenely at the countess.

"Is she usually this quiet?" the countess asked as she watched the girl for a few moments.

"It's a recent development. Usually she's threatening me or threatening to take over the world." Cassius said, smiling. He examined his student.

"Well," the countess replied, "it seems that she is your new best friend—or is she competition? I have many things to accomplish this day so I will bid you farewell for now, and if I don't have the opportunity to send you off, have a good journey and I'll send the girl in a month." The countess rose to her feet and marched away.

"This is a beautiful place," Gellia said.

"I suppose."

"You're as inconstant as weather. Would you have traded something for me in Fuarmaania?"

"The Fuarmaanians would never have anything I want."

"They had me. And supposedly an alliance."

"They never had you, princess. They lost you the day you were born and they knew it. I have the alliance I wanted."

There had to be more, Gellia thought. He seemed as if he was going to say something else but he didn't, he just sat there and looked at her. She knew that Cassius was just obstinate; he thought he might tell her but decided otherwise. Gellia fought back a scowl. The games had started. Cassius smirked at her. He was behaving out of spite. "So I suppose I won't have any answers because I need you more than you need me?"

"Something of that nature."

"I don't believe it. You wouldn't have spent all that effort fetching me from Fuarmaania then rescuing me from the Zephrons and hauling me through a dank river and ruining your hair if you didn't have some use for me." She placed a morsel in her mouth and chewed with minimal jaw movement as she tried to forget that he scrutinized her.

"I've told you before that I have a great many reasons letting you come with me, and my hair is far from ruined." He ran his fingers through the length of it as proof. She noticed it looked much longer than she remembered and it sparkled with delicate silver chains.

Gellia took a sip from her chalice and set it back down without even slightest click as it touched the table. "There's something bigger afoot here, more so than you've led me to believe and that countess knows it. You don't have any choice but to do as she asks because there's nothing you can do to her to make it otherwise."

"You can ruminate about it on your own until I come for you tonight. We have a task set by the King of Sen Dunea." He stood and started to walk away. "Should be rather routine."

Her eyes narrowed as her ire rose. "Your grand scheme certainly is complicated, isn't it?" she said softly. "I don't appreciate being used as a pawn, so I don't know why you continue to do it because I could eventually leave you, even just to return to Dournzariame." When Cassius stopped and turned, she knew she had tread on dangerous ground. He came to sit at the table and stare at her.

"You've spent a lot of effort on me. All my training, time and work to lure me out of Fuarmaania, all the time spent in Sen Dunea to continue my education and strengthen me. Even this time in Dournzariame, and you sent some army as a decoy, then braved a man who I can barely appreciate, but know that he is no one to be taken lightly, in a formidable empire... Yet you hardly use your power. I would assume you can mask it as old mages can, which would seem to be less effort than not using magic at all. They say you're aligned with the emperor, yet you say you won't give me to him. Does anyone know you're a traitor? Or am I the one you're lying to? It is my life. Surely you must know why I have questions."

Cassius was silent and impossible to read. For a few long moments they looked at each other and Gellia felt that there was an unspoken conversation going on between them. Finally Cassius spoke as he tapped his finger on the table. "When I set foot in that pathetic castle with you and that girl ogling me from the library window I knew you were one worth my time. Finally. I'll send for you." He rose again and left.

***

Gellia wandered through the grand manor house to admire the ornate architecture to calm her thoughts. While she wandered she saw few other people and certainly no one that looked like a student. She came to a large room where several portraits hung on the walls. One was of the countess when she was young, there were a few other Zephron ladies depicted and Gellia came to one with two ladies, one of the two was Connylia. Connylia looked so young, so fresh, and she was beautiful beyond words. The woman who stood beside her in the portrait was not quite Zephron. She had straight blond hair, refined features but didn't stand in the same posture as the rest; she also had a mocking gaze Gellia found unsettling.

"My greatest student," the countess said from behind Gellia.

Gellia jumped. "Yes?"

"Connylia was my greatest work and with the help of our specialized teacher," she nodded at the painting, "she became perfection, in Zephronia and Xzepheniixenze."

"Who is the other woman?"

"Baroness Zantedeschia Adamina Vazepheny of Tintagel, the most feared mage of her time." The countess smiled.

"What happened to her?"

"She died in Zenobia." The countess took Gellia's hand and placed it in the crook of her aged elbow and walked her father down the wall to another picture, one much smaller than the others and much simpler. Amongst the others it was nearly unnoticeable. It was of Connylia again and someone else. A man. Gellia held her breath and resisted the urge to touch the strokes of charcoal.

"It was a festival, one we hold every year for the girls, and the boys from the academy. Connylia was here at the time. Adamina convinced her to attend for she and I made arrangements." The countess smiled. "We had several entertainments planned for the children, fortuneteller, a few games and an artist to do sketches. A quaint festival it was." Gellia couldn't take her eyes off the picture. He looked so kind, and he seemed to look right through Gellia, as foolish of a thought as it was.

"So there they are, your many-times-great grandparents, the Emperor of Xzepheniixenze, Creator of the Golden Age, Razhiede Lucian Zapheny and Connylia Duvray."

"He's Zephron," Gellia said. Yes, kind but also detached, perhaps even amused. She felt a sudden pang of deeply rooted sorrow.

"An enchantment so he could remain here unseen," the countess said. "He took a great risk to see her." She patted Gellia's hand. "But is time for you to be to bed. You have a busy life awaiting you."

Gellia stared up at the gilded canopy and mused about how she had done the same thing in Fuarmaania. It seemed like a waste of daylight to be sleeping, but there was no helping it if she wanted rest. The blankets were so cozy compared to the rock on which she last slept. She yawned. There was a knock on the door. Had she been asleep? It was dark outside her window. "Yes?" Gellia mumbled. Indeed, sleep still had its heavy weight on her.

A feminine voice came from the other side of the room. "It's time to go, miss. Your lord's waiting for you."

"Thank you," Gellia replied.

She crawled from the bed and found her traveling clothes had been laid out for her while she slept. They were new, and much sturdier than what she'd been wearing when she left the palace. A servant helped her dress before she said goodbye to her room and left to find Cassius. She found him in the stable yard where Amarynth and Nighthawk stood ready and awaited their riders. Gellia hugged her stallion and petted his neck. Her thoughts turned briefly to Tempest, her old friend.

Cassius smiled. "Let's be on our way, shall we?"
As quickly as they arrived, the two companions left. Gellia wasn't sure if she cared to return to the school. Dournzariame was more appealing, honestly. She was happy to be on the road again, with her trusty steed and her comrade on their way to whatever it was they were up to. She had to admit despite her trepidation, she preferred to be galloping under the stars into the unknown than being imprisoned in her life in Fuarmaania.

All the stars seemed to be out that night as they cantered silently along the lonely road. Fireflies were their only company. They covered more ground than she thought possible in just a few moments. Amarynth and Nighthawk were as swift as she could have dreamed. "Do you think anyone will see us?" Gellia asked.

"Possible, although it is less likely than you might think."

"We're on the road. How can they not find us?"

"Easy. We are Xzepheniixenze; the night protects us. It's part of our magic. Don't give me that look. I don't know what I have to tell you to convince you that you are indeed Xzepheniixenze. Surely you received spiteful treatment in Dournzariame."

"The Zephrons said I am Xzepheniixenze although I don't feel that I am…What's that ahead?"

"Hmm. Just what I thought."

"What?"

"I've been watching them for a while."

"Who are they?"

"Looks like they're from the Academy."

They came to a stop lightly as though they rode horses made of air. They watched from the middle of the road, the knights drew closer. There seemed to be at least a dozen or more, their armor clinking and hiding the Xzepheniixenze whispers. "What do we do? Go into the fields?" Gellia asked.

Cassius responded with his mind voice. *No, they'd see the movement. We're almost better off just standing here and moving around them as they pass.*

We're really that invisible?

Honestly it depends on what talents they have.

How can you be so calm?

Why should I be nervous? There are always plans within plans, princess. Nothing is currently out of my control.

Are you going to use your magic? Gellia asked.

Perhaps.

Can we fight them, I mean with swords?

Hah. I may be decent with a sword but I'm no one to take on a small army. If they're from the academy they wouldn't be easy to best.

I can hear them talking.

Hmm.

What? What? Gellia nearly shook in her saddle. Not from fear, though.

One of them does have the ability to sense us. He hasn't used it, though.

Gellia glanced around. *Where?*

Feel that? He smirked at her.

I don't know. I think so. What do we do?

Cassius sighed and gathered the reins. *Run.* Nighthawk shot off the side of the road and Amarynth dashed after him before Gellia could react. She heard Cassius mutter when she caught up. "…Damn Nighthawk. I could use Julian right now." The grasses around them whipped the horses' legs as they galloped through the field with the Zephrons behind them. "What are we going to do now?" Gellia called. "Gallylya probably knows where we are now."

"Most likely."

"Well?" If Gallylya found them in the open, he would be more likely to attack, that was for certain. Gellia's heart raced.

"Hang on to Amarynth."

Gellia felt the energies swirl around her in an emerald chorus and her body seized. Before them appeared a glowing green doorway. In the split second it took for the magic to form, Gellia tried to rein in Amarynth out of fear. They were falling through a void until the ground was finally under them once more.

A green light flashed behind them and was gone. "Where are we?" Gellia stammered. Amarynth stood as calm as the silent moon while she clung to his back. They faced a tiny light in the distance. They were near a forest, and all alone again. Everything smelled of fresh rain and mildew. "Where are the Zephrons?"

"In Zephronia," Cassius said.

It thundered and started to pour. She clutched Amarynth's mane. Lightning illuminated her companion's face for just a moment so Gellia could see his expression hadn't changed from that of someone slightly bored. She also noticed he must have created a barrier so he wouldn't get drenched; she was envious she hadn't thought of that as well.

He spoke again. "We're now in Fuarmaania."

"How did we get here?" She looked around to find anything familiar. In the distance was the castle.

"I created a magic portal to bring us here."

"And why here? I never wanted to come back here." It felt different now. Gellia felt detached from this place, even more than before. She could see her companion's shape in the dark, it moved towards the castle. "What are you doing?" Their horses' hooves made no noise in the mud.

"We're getting involved in a little adventure. I thought it would be good for you."

"What? Why didn't you tell me before?"

"A lot has happened, perhaps you don't realize how long you were in Zephronia. The Sen Dunean princes were captured when they were on a hunting trip. I told the king that you and I would retrieve them. All you have to do is have horses ready, and if you like you can fetch your little friends. Just don't take too long. I'll send the princes up to the stables and I'll even give you Currain to help."

"The Fuarmaanians might kill me if they see me," Gellia said. Or worse, capture her.

"Kill them first. Or don't let them see you—I don't care. I can work with whatever you decide to do as well as whatever you botch. Let's be off."

It was so familiar, but so strange all at once. There was a light on in the room that had been hers. Compared to the palaces she'd just been in, this was indeed pathetic and small. She could only imagine how Cassius could have felt living here.

As usual, the guards at the gate slept. Gellia and Cassius parted ways just inside the entrance and Gellia stayed for a moment, remembering. She felt so different. She never lived there. What a miserable pile of rubble it was. It looked barely livable, nearly a ruin. The stable yard smelled of old dung and muck. Her true resentment for the place was realized. She'd ridden into the stable yard hundreds of times before, but this time she marveled at the truth of things.

Amarynth's hooves made no sound on the patchy cobblestone. Once she dismounted, he disappeared into the dark. It was very nice not having to worry about the care of a horse.

She looked around for anyone awake. The stable boys were asleep in the hay room and reeked of ale. Quiet footfalls. "Currain?" Gellia whispered into the dark. She wrung out her cloak, the water spattered on the stone floor.

"Happy to see me?" He smiled as he came to her.

"Let's harness Tempest and Cress' horse together to a wagon. I don't think Corrah knows how to ride." How she'd convince them to come with her she didn't know.

"Fine, I'll let you and Tempest reminisce while I find a wagon. Meet you outside." They parted.

Tempest whickered to Gellia as she approached. Silently she ran back and forth with the harness and placed it on the grey. She wasn't sure how long it was since he'd been harnessed, so the situation could turn out to be very interesting, especially when there were no lanterns lit. With rub rags she wrapped the stallion's hooves and led him outside to meet Currain with the other horse.

The rain beat on the roof, drowning out much of the noise. The horses were cooperating by not whinnying. Lightning struck nearby. "Where are those two?" Gellia said while she tried to soothe the nervous horses. "What's taking so long?"

"Aren't you fidgety," Currain said. "You should never rush vengeance."

In a few moments the princes skittered from the servants' door. "Hurry!" Gellia said and climbed into the wagon seat. Lucifer and Mervrick clambered into the back of the wagon and Gellia set the horses off at a trot out the gate. "We have to make a stop," she told them. "You'll have to take the lines."

They cantered around the castle, globs of mud flew everywhere as the rickety wagon rattled over the bumpy ground. Gellia pulled the pair of horses to a stop and tossed the lines to Mervrick. Amarynth appeared and Nighthawk trotted away as Gellia started to climb the drenched, mossy side of the castle to Cresslyn and Alexandria's room, using her magic to aid her. She surprised even herself with how quickly she moved up the slippery stones. "Cress!" she called as she pulled herself in through the window. She almost laughed. Who would have believed she'd be doing this?

"Gellia! Oh my goodness! You've come back!" Cresslyn leapt from their bed and ran to her. "I thought you were dead. You're soaked." Her friend Alexandria was there with her, looking shocked.

"I'm here to rescue you. Alexandria, go fetch Corrah and be quick and quiet about it," Gellia said. The room smelled stale and dirty and damp.

"I've missed you!" Cresslyn said. "And what are you talking about? Rescue us from what? How did you get up here? You're wearing boy's clothes! You look so different! You're getting water all over the floor."

"We have to leave—I'll explain later. Take your blankets." Gellia ran to the bed and ripped the blankets from it. "Tie them together, see? We have to climb out the window." She started to knot the ends together in a manner the princes had shown her.

"What? Have you gone mad? What is this all about? You don't know all that's happened."

"I told you I would explain later."

The door opened and Corrah entered with Alexandria. Oh "I thought you were lost, poor lamb!" Corrah wailed.

"No time for that, Corrah, we have to go!" Gellia spoke in an ever increasing volume. "Quick," she tied the end of their makeshift rope to the bed post. "Out you go. No time for dressing, just go." She leaned out the window. "Hold them fast!" She tossed a few extra blankets over the side. The two horses were jumpy with all the commotion.

"Who are you talking to?" Alexandria asked.

"It doesn't matter." Had they any idea about anything at all? Didn't they realize they were in a hurry? "Go! Out the window." Gellia thought of pushing them out but was sure Corrah would crush the princes as they tried to catch her. She called on her magic again to aid their descent.

**

"Baron, I didn't expect to see you again," the king said. Hugh backed away and felt for his sword that leaned against the nearby wall while the Xzepheniixenze waited. With all the strength he could muster the king swung his sword.

Cassius swatted the blade from the king's shaky hands. The king shrunk as the baron regarded him as someone would a parasite. The king trembled and stared, couldn't blink for fear he would lose his enemy in the shadows. Cassius took a step closer and the king fell into a chair. He placed his muddy boot on the king's collarbone. "I don't normally deal with such excrement as you. But I wanted to have the pleasure of watching you die. You and all this other human filth degrading sacred ground."

"Mercy," the king mouthed. The fear, the confusion shone in his bloodshot eyes.

"You are undeserving of mercy, however I am short on time so mercy you shall have." He snatched the cord holding a curtain and started to tie the gluttonous man to the heavy chair. He took his time with the job, slowly tightened the ropes around the sweaty, trembling king. Hugh gasped and whimpered. "You coward," Cassius rumbled, and fastened the final knot. He walked away and tipped a candelabrum onto the floor. The fire quickly spread through the rushes and up the dusty tapestries.

The king called to his killer, "I thought you said you'd give me mercy," he cried, his voice desperate and shaky. He jerked in the heavy chair, tried to escape.

Cassius chuckled. "Make no mistake, this is merciful." He watched the king squirm in his misery.

***

"My goodness these are the prisoners!" Corrah yelled from the back of the wagon.

Gellia swung onto Amarynth. She remembered a time when she would have needed help from a mounting block. Why these memories came back now she didn't know. "They're my friends."

"Look, the castle's on fire," Cresslyn shouted. The women huddled together in the back of the wagon and watched the growing flames. Screams and shouts joined the sound of the roaring inferno. Gellia could tell it was aided by magic.

"Oh no!" Alexandria cried. "My family will think me dead."

"What will we do?" Corrah wailed. "What will happen to everyone?"

"Let's away," Gellia said as she watched the flames build. "Their fates are none of my concern." She heard the screams from within and felt only apathy. The women with them cried and fretted, which was frustrating. Gellia started to wonder if she'd done the right thing by rescuing them, for it seemed they would rather burn. She hoped they'd cry themselves out soon, for the journey with a wagon would be difficult and they'd need their strength.

The wagon bumped along beside her. She was certain Cassius would catch up with them—it was more important they were on their way. As parts of the castle exploded and she felt Cassius' power, the harness horses jumped and tried to flee. Mervrick kept them in hand while the women continued to blubber. There would be no other survivors from the castle, Gellia knew that for certain. She didn't look back again.

About the Author

GB MacRae grew up with her family and horses in rural New England. She started writing stories from a very young age, and started writing novels in her teens. She has a bachelor's degree in Literature and Culture from a small Central New York college, and loves to research anything and everything.

Her home is near Lake Ontario in a rambling old colonial house with her family and beloved pets. You can find her on Facebook, Pinterest, Twitter, at gbmacrae.com, and occasionally at sci-fi conventions dressed in one of her many costumes. You might even catch her dancing.

Made in the USA
Monee, IL
20 August 2023